What is Wyrdwood?
https://www.angelmccoy.com/wyrdwood-home/

DEDICATION

I *must* dedicate this—my first romance novel—to Debbie Heimer Bergerhouse. When we were in high school, we split the cost of a subscription to Harlequin romance novels. It was one of those things where you get a handful of books every month for your sub fee. I couldn't wait for each delivery. Deb and I would divvy up the books, read them, trade them, and giggle over them. I've known no one who reads as fast as Deb. It was inspiring.

Our shared enthusiasm for books influenced my desire to become a writer. Ever since, I've had "write a romance novel" on my bucket list. Done. Check!

Deb and I became college roommates. She taught me how to sew, and I was a bridesmaid at her wedding. We traveled together to Venice—the most romantic of cities. Since then, our paths have diverged, but she is a fixture in my heart. Not just for the shared love of books, but for all the memories we built together in our formative years. Deb, I've never forgotten how we poured over our piles of magical books together. I wouldn't be who I am today without you.

ALSO FROM WYRDWOOD
by Angel Leigh McCoy

Cupid Missions series
Christmas Cupid

Catsitter Mysteries series
Catsitter's Conundrum
Catsitter's Curse
Catsitter's Collar (coming 2024)

Reluctant Undertaker series
Satyr (coming 2024)

Wyrdwood Welcome Trilogy
Stalking the Moon
Jumping the Moon
Hexing the Moon

Wyrdwood Historical Society series
Nurse Magdaleine
Charlie Darwin, or the Trine of 1809

Wyrdwood Origin Stories
Pipsqueak

Mission Cupid Series

Christmas Cupid

by Angel Leigh McCoy

CHAPTER 1

C'mon, Jazz. I'm going to be late for work!" Jackie Li hurried around the apartment in her waitress uniform and socks.

"I'm comin'," replied Jasper a.k.a. Jazz, Jackie's seventeen-year-old brother. He sprawled on the couch, console controller in hand, playing a video game. He didn't move.

Jackie grabbed her dress off the door then stuffed her fancy boots in the overnight case. She checked her watch, calling, "You've got two minutes until I'm out the door—with or without you. You want a ride to practice, you better get a move on."

"All I gotta do is put on my shoes."

Jackie retrieved her make-up bag from the bathroom. She would need it after work to prep for her date. As she slipped her feet into her work shoes, she double-checked her list and ticked off each item. She did not want to forget anything.

Jazz had not yet turned off the game.

"Jazz, now!" Jackie pulled her coat out of the hall closet. "You can't skip practice again, or they'll kick you out of the orchestra! If they kick you out, how are you going to get a music scholarship? If you don't get a scholarship, you go to community college. You've got to think about your future. It's less than a year away."

"Okay, just a minute! I'm almost through this level!"

Jackie closed her eyes and took a deep breath. It didn't help. "Jazz, I'm leaving. I can't be late again." She picked up the dress bag, the overnight case, and her keys.

Jazz cried, "Hold on!"

"I'm going." Jackie opened the door and stepped into the hall. She went to the elevator and pressed the Down button.

A loud ding made Jackie jump. The elevator arrived.

Jazz came tearing down the hall, clutching his saxophone case and dragging his coat behind him.

"I'm coming! Jeez!" Jazz ran into the elevator, making the old thing bounce with his weight.

The elevator doors gave a groan and closed on his heels,

catching his coat. He gave a mighty tug and pulled it free.

Jazz grumbled, "You can be such a jerk."

Jackie's jaw clenched. She turned to face her brother and stuck a finger in his chest. "Oh yeah? Well, I'm the jerk who cleans up after you. I'm the jerk who's working my ass off to keep a roof over our heads and food on the table. I'm the jerk who drives you to practice so you don't lose your place in the orchestra. The least you can do is get off your butt when this jerk needs to get to work!"

"Yadda, yadda." Jazz mimicked Jackie's voice. "I do everything for you. I gave up everything for you. I'm the only family you've got." He heaved a sigh. "Whatever."

The elevator stopped. Three long seconds passed before the doors opened.

As soon as he could squeeze through, Jazz stepped out into the parking garage and headed for their car.

Jackie stood where she was until the doors slid inward again. She stuck her arm out and forced them back open.

"Well," Jackie muttered to herself, mimicking her brother's voice. "Happy birthday, sis. Hope you have a great day. I love you. Thank you for all you do for me." She hoisted her dress bag higher on her back and strode to the car.

The ride to Jazz's high school was silent. At the last minute, Jackie remembered to say, "Don't forget. I've got a date tonight. Don't wait up for me. I may be late."

"Whatever," Jazz replied. He unhooked his seatbelt. "I need some money. The guys are going out for pizza after practice."

"In my purse."

Jazz dug around for Jackie's wallet. He found it. "All you got is a ten?"

"Take it or leave it. That's all there is."

Jazz took it. He dropped the open wallet back in Jackie's purse then opened the car door and climbed out.

Jackie reached for her wallet to close it and tuck it back in its place. She started to wish him a good day, until he slammed the door shut and ran off.

Jackie's eyes filled with tears. She blinked them back.

"He doesn't mean it," she told herself, watching his back as he walked up to the double doors. In her psychologist voice, she said aloud, "A teenager's rebellion is a natural byproduct of growing independence and the transition into—"

A car behind her honked and made Jackie jump.

"—adulthood." Jackie glared into her rearview before putting on her signal and pulling away from the school.

CHAPTER 2

Jackie arrived five minutes late to work. Everyone noticed. She hurried into the locker room, put away her things, checked her hair, then scooted out into the Daisy Diner. She wove into the breakfast-rush chaos with practiced ease.

At the diner, Jackie was most often known as "Hey, lady!" and "Yo, Miss!" She even answered to "Excuse me!" She could carry a tray with eight full glasses of water, side-step good ol' boy Max Funkalstein's grabby hand and remember the three orders thrown at her as she sidled between tables: catsup for table five, extra napkins on two, and a refill for the attractive businessman seated at the bar.

Jackie took her emptied tray to the space behind the register. She sheltered from the world there, near the kitchen. The clatter of plates and sizzle of frying meat drowned out the worst of the Christmas carols being piped into the dining room.

Bonnie leaned against her. Jackie's best friend and confidante since high school, Bonnie Gundersen was a true ginger, as Neanderthals were forever asking her to prove. It was shocking how men still thought that was a great conversation starter.

When God was handing out legs and *chutzpah,* Bonnie was at the front of the line. Meanwhile, Jackie had been in the toilets, probably popping a zit.

Bonnie leaned past Jackie, reaching for a saltshaker, and pecked a quick kiss onto her cheek. "Happy birthday, girl!"

Jackie beamed at her friend. With those three words, the cloud left behind by her brother blew away. "Thanks!"

"What time's loverboy coming?" Bonnie placed the salt shaker on her tray.

"He knows I'm off at seven." Jackie turned as the door's bell chimed. Two tall people walked into the diner.

"How many dates is this?" Bonnie kept her hair in a bun when working, but a strand of it had come free and was swinging across her cheek. She puffed air at it to make it go away.

Jackie half-registered the sound of a plate sliding across stainless steel, followed by the order-up bell. Bonnie stepped sideways and pulled the plate of pork tenderloin, green beans, and mashed potatoes onto her tray.

Jackie grabbed a couple of menus and and put her welcoming smile on her face. She headed out to greet the newcomers.

"Can we have a corner booth, please?" The man winked at the woman beside him. She hugged his arm.

The secret, Jackie thought. *They have the secret.* She waited as they removed their coats and scooted in, sitting on the same side. They overturned their coffee cups in perfect synchronicity.

Yeah, Jackie thought, *these two are gonna be up all night.* A little thrill ran through her. *Maybe I will too.*

Jackie had been dropping unsubtle hints for days that she'd like her birthday to be special. When Mitch had called to invite her to dinner, she'd been over the moon. He wanted the same thing she did.

Jackie crossed paths with Bonnie. They moved around each other with the grace that comes from years of practice.

Jackie said, "Four." She knew Bonnie would catch that she was answering the question: how many dates is this? She stepped onto the rubber mat that gave her feet a modicum of relief and took two fresh glasses from the stack.

"Four?" Bonnie picked up a dishtowel and wiped up a spill of gravy on the pass-through window. "Does that mean you guys have already... bount chicka bount bount?"

Jackie laughed. "No." She filled glasses with ice and water.

"No?" The incredulity was apparent. "Why? Baby doesn't like the bount?"

Jackie lifted her tray and said, "Oh, baby like the bount, don't you worry about that." She headed out toward the couple. Over her shoulder she said, "Tonight's the night."

"Ooooweee," Bonnie called after her. "Happy birthday!"

Jackie liked Mitch, a lot. The first three dates had been fun, of the casual variety. She'd made him dinner, and they'd watched movies on her couch. He'd never invited her to his place, but that was okay. He said her TV was better than his, and he didn't mind hopping the bus to come over. He didn't have a car, but in the city, you didn't need one—not really.

Jackie strode across the diner to deliver the water glasses to the couple, playing invisible as they canoodled. Mitch didn't do that kind of thing with Jackie. Not yet. Jackie imagined it took time to build intimacy. Honestly, she didn't have much experience with working relationships. She'd dated, sure, and she was no virgin, but that wasn't the same as the togetherness displayed by the couple in booth 7. That was magical.

"Excuse me? Miss? Check, please?"

Jackie broke from her reverie and told the kissers, "I'll give you a few more minutes," then went to get the check for table 2.

"So where's he taking you?" Bonnie asked in passing. She headed out onto the floor without waiting for the answer, carrying a tray of plates, drinks, and condiments.

Jackie punched buttons on the register and printed the bill with efficient focus, using one hand to grab the paper and the other to pull a bill folder from the pile. She hustled out to table "2," dropped the check, and asked if they needed anything else. They had their credit card ready, so she took it straight back to the register.

Bonnie was already there, gingerly pushing buttons with her long-nailed fingers.

Jackie said, "He didn't say where we were going. It's a surprise. I made it clear that I was ready to take it to the next level." She grinned, a burble of excitement rising inside her. It was going to be perfect. She'd even bought a new dress and lingerie.

Sliding the printed bill into a folder, Bonnie said, "Hubs took me to the Captain's Table for my birthday. I hear they have amazing Christmas decorations this year. If Mitch doesn't have anything planned, you could suggest it?"

Conspiratorial, Jackie leaned into Bonnie. "Oh, he's got something planned, all right." And together, they laughed.

"You really like this guy, huh?"

Jackie stopped moving to consider the question. "I do. I can imagine us old together. I sure could do worse. He's got a great job—of the suit-wearing variety. He's cute, right? We would make beautiful babies together."

"I'm so happy for you. You've been single for too long." With the client's receipt and card in one hand, Bonnie nabbed a ketchup bottle off the back counter with the other.

"Okay, Mom. Don't worry. I think he might be the one." Jackie twitched her nose and smiled. "I've got my white picket fence all picked out. I've been waiting for the right guy to come along. That's all."

"Well, I want to double-date with you."

Jackie shrugged. "Next week? After tonight, my life will get a lot more interesting."

"Careful what you put out to the universe, sweets. I can't wait to see how this turns out." Bonnie headed toward the dining room, calling, "Next week would be perfect."

"Have no fear," Jackie replied. "My plans include your kid marrying my kid and making us co-grandparents."

The front doorbell rang as a group of six teenagers—a mix of boys and girls—bustled in, chattering with rambunctious enthusiasm. They took the large booth in the corner—in Jackie's section. She hurried over with menus, then waited as they slid one by one into the booth, like a waddle of penguins taking turns on the ice slide.

They were the same age as Jazz, and Jackie had the sudden realization that she'd never seen her brother in his natural environment. The couch in their living room didn't count. She wondered if he even knew any girls. He'd never had one over.

Something ached inside her heart, a hole in her connection to her brother. There was so much she didn't know about him. *She made a birthday resolution to learn more about Jazz's life.*

"Hello!" said one of the girls, and Jackie realized she'd been standing there in a trance, lost in thoughts about Jazz. She gave them a smile and stepped forward to pass out menus.

"Miss. Excuse me," called another patron, an older woman who hadn't removed either her pink wool coat or her gloves. She gazed up at Jackie with wet, white-blue eyes. "I didn't order chicken. I wanted turkey."

Jackie blinked at her. She distinctly remembered the woman ordering the baked chicken. For the briefest moment, she considered telling the woman that it was turkey—to see if she could get away with it—but she didn't. She picked up the plate and smiled.

"I'm so sorry, ma'am. Let me fix that for you."

The woman nodded with haughty approval and turned her attention to digging in her purse.

Jackie carried the plate into the kitchen. "I need a turkey plate, two cheeseburger plates, nachos with extra jalapeños, a Philly cheese—no jalapeños, a grilled cheese combo, and a Cobb salad with vinaigrette instead of blue cheese, hold the croutons."

"Something wrong with that?" Roy asked, nodding at the chicken plate Jackie was holding.

Roy owned the Daisy Diner, named for his late wife. He wore a hairnet over his short-cut hair and a grease-stained white apron over his black pants and blue shirt. He'd been a fry cook for decades, and he was a master at preparing diner cuisine, performing the movements with barely a thought.

"Just a misunderstanding, boss." Jackie pulled a to-go box from the pile and slid the rejected meal into it.

"Is it that old broad again? She does this every week. I can't believe—"

Jackie lifted a hand to quiet him. "Easy now. You'll give yourself a hernia. She can't help it."

"She's old."

"True." Jackie closed the Styrofoam box. "Back in five."

The diner had a door that opened onto the alley in back, where the dumpsters and broken chairs hung out. Jackie took the box of food and stepped out into the noise and city stink. Car horns blew in the distance, making a syncopated sort of rhythm over the snatches of cellphone conversations heard as people walked by at the end of the alley.

Jackie scanned the alley, seeking a familiar sight. When she saw it, she headed toward it. A pair of worn boots stuck out beyond the last dumpster, their laces undone, toes scuffed with years of travel. As Jackie approached, she made a wide arc so as not to startle the boots' owner, an older man dressed in layer upon layer of raggedy clothes. He was of an indeterminate race, his face browned by years of open-air living, his gray hair matted into dreadlocks. He and his dog shared a refrigerator box, and he had a pile of his belongings at his side. In his hands, he held a book, open to somewhere in the middle.

"Whatcha reading, Mason?" Jackie asked, stopping to speak to him.

"Jonathan Livingston Seagull," Mason replied, looking up. His eyes dropped from Jackie's face to the food box. "It's a commentary on the power of letting go. Speaking of which, that mystery box wouldn't, by any chance, be for me, would it?"

Jackie smiled and handed it over.

Mason set his book aside. "You are a lifesaver, Miss Jackie," he said, the warmth in his voice obvious.

"It's chicken. I hope that's okay."

"You kiddin' me?" Mason beamed. "I was thinkin' pigeon was soundin' good, so this is extra special. Thank you." He opened the box.

Another voice sounded near Jackie, male, foreign enough to sound snobby. The man snarked, "Charity helps no one."

Jackie watched the retreating man in his long black raincoat and old-fashioned Baker-boy cap. She frowned. "You're wrong."

The man stopped and half turned back. "Why should he change? He has his meals delivered to him."

Jackie's hackles rose.

Mason ignored the man, his focus on his meal. He picked some dark meat off the bone and offered it to his dog—an old mutt with soulful eyes and scruffy fur.

Jackie snipped, "Maybe it's not about that. Maybe it's about connection and kindness, about sharing and thinking of others instead of yourself. Maybe it's about not judging but loving. Acknowledging someone's humanity."

The man studied Jackie, his lips tight. Then he gave a curt nod and turned away, walking on as if nothing had happened.

"Great speech," said Mason, licking chicken grease off his fingers.

"I meant every word." Jackie waited until the man had left the alley before wishing Mason a good night and returning to the diner.

She rankled for a full hour after the rude encounter.

The shift passed slowly. Jackie's feet had had enough. A glance at the clock on the wall told her she had only fifteen minutes left. The dinner crowd had thinned, and Jackie's replacement had arrived.

"What are you waiting for?" Bonnie dropped her bus bin full of dirty dishes onto the rack. "He's picking you up here, yeah?

Go get ready!" She swatted Jackie on the rump. "Git!"

"Okay!" Jackie untied her apron as she made her way along the hallway to the employee room. With one ear listening for the front door to chime, Jackie grabbed her dress and overnight case and scuttled into the bathroom to change.

She had purchased that specific dress because it was sexy without being slutty. A soft knitted sweater dress, it fit her like a glove and brushed her skin in all the right ways. Creamy white, it contrasted nicely with her brown skin and ebony hair. She had knee-high boots to wear with it.

Jackie examined herself in the mirror and was pleased. Her figure was what it was, but plenty of men—and women—seemed to like it. If she could change anything about herself, she'd wish for bigger boobs, but she also believed you should make the most of what you've got.

She applied her make-up to accentuate the exotic curve of her eyes, inherited from her father. His side of the family had Chinese roots. From her mother, she'd inherited her curly hair and warm brown skin. That branch of the family tree was from Northern Africa, more or less. Of course, neither line was pure. Whose was anymore?

Someone banged on the door, making Jackie jump. "Hold on a sec." She picked up her lipstick. She'd chosen a Christmas burgundy, rich like merlot, and hoped it looked kissable.

The knock came again.

"Okay, okay!" Jackie stuffed her work clothes in her case. She gave the bathroom a last once-over to be sure she wasn't leaving anything behind then opened the door.

An old man stood there, giving her a disapproving frown. He grumbled as he pushed past her to get inside, "Blah blah blah... women... blah blah blah."

"Sorry." Jackie put her things in her locker, taking only her coat and purse with her. When she emerged back into the restaurant, Bonnie met her, bright-eyed.

"Wow! You look amazing!" Bonnie admired Jackie while balancing a tray of sodas. "Love the dress! Is that the new one?"

Jackie nodded, pleased.

"Hotchimama!" Bonnie proclaimed. "Why don't you have a seat at '4' while you're waiting? You want a cup of coffee?"

"No, thanks. Mitch'll be here any minute now."

Twenty minutes later, Jackie poured herself a coffee. Ten minutes after that, the mug was empty. Whenever the door jingled, Jackie looked up.

Bonnie sat with Jackie when her shift ended. "So, he's late?"

Jackie nodded. "He's probably doing last-minute preps. He'll be here. Did I tell you his dad teaches in the music department at Virginia State?"

"No, really? You think he can help Jazz get a scholarship?"

"That would be amazing. I haven't met Mitch's family yet. This Christmas, he'll invite me."

Bonnie gave Jackie a confused look. "Christmas is only a week away."

"I expect he'll bring it up tonight. I asked for the time off, just in case."

The bell rang again, and Mitch walked in, checking his phone. Mitch wasn't much taller than Jackie, but he worked out, and it showed—especially when he was wearing gym clothes. Wrinkled, sweaty gym clothes.

Jackie slid out of the booth.

"Hey," Mitch said. "Got your messages. All eight." He snorted. "Let's grab something to go. That movie I've been waiting for just hit Netflix. I'm ripe from my workout, but I can shower at your place, yeah?"

The bottom dropped out of Jackie's stomach, and a flush of bristly heat spread up her neck. "What?"

"Wow, you look cute." Mitch ran his gaze over her. "What's the occasion?"

Suddenly, Jackie's thong didn't feel so sexy. She laughed uneasily and tried to smile. "What's the occasion? It's my birthday, Mitch. You said..."

"Oh, crap. Your birthday." Mitch fidgeted. "Hey... happy birthday!" He leaned in for a kiss that landed awkwardly on the side of Jackie's mouth.

"You forgot," Jackie said flatly.

"No!" Mitch shook his head. "I just ran out of time. Um... I even got you something." He pulled an unwrapped DVD out of his pocket. It was a movie about race cars, women, and booze. He'd already opened the packaging. "You're gonna love it. I figured we could watch it... together. After the other one. Make it a movie marathon staycation. Kinda romantic."

To use a racing metaphor, Jackie's anger hit the gas. She went from zero to eighty in under three seconds. Tone harsh, not bothering to hide her fury, Jackie said, "You're kidding me. This is a joke?"

"A joke? Uhhhh." Mitch looked around for help.

"Nevermind." Jackie deflated. "Just go. I can't do this right now."

"Well...uh. Can I get something to eat first? I'm starving." Mitch spotted the tears in Jackie's eyes. "Okay, never mind. Jesus." He turned on his heel and left the diner.

Jackie felt rooted in place. All the princess moments and true-love endings from her imagination were dying around her with hideous coughs and gurgles.

Ridiculous! Jackie thought. *I'm ridiculous.*

Aloud, she murmured, "Why do I do this to myself?"

"Hey," came a soft, friendly voice. A warm hand rested on her shoulder. Bonnie. "Don't blame yourself. C'mon. Let's sit."

Jackie stayed where she was, used DVD in her hand, watching Mitch as he paused outside to check his phone. She wondered if she was okay and decided she definitely wasn't. Disappointment unfurled in the wake of disbelief and self-disgust. Tears swelled over her eyelashes and slid down her cheeks.

"Poor girl," someone said.

"That guy's a dumbass," said another.

"Tell you what," Bonnie said, voice soft at Jackie's shoulder. "I get off in an hour. The hubs is picking me up. Why don't the three of us go for a drink or ten? We'll celebrate your birthday with comfort food and rum. To Hell with stupid Mitch."

That helped, a little, until Jackie's cellphone vibrated on the booth table. Mitch had sent her a text. He was twenty feet away, just outside the diner's front door where she could still see him, and he was texting her. It said, "This isn't working for me. TTYN." *Talk To You Never*.

A tidal wave of fury surged in Jackie. It crested and came crashing down on the café. People screamed—in Jackie's mind. Or perhaps it was her own scream as she tumbled into black waters, vision gone red, and lungs unable to catch a breath. Jackie charged for the door, chin down. Blind determination to give Mitch a piece of her mind drove her forward on the balls of her feet.

Someone said, "Uh oh."

Mitch was already on the move again.

Jackie hit the glass diner door with the full force of her indignation and shoved it open as if *it* had pissed her off too. With her intention focused on Mitch, she never saw it coming.

The door stopped abruptly—too abruptly, with a loud thwack—and then slammed right back into her face. It hit her square in the forehead.

Black waters closed over her. The undercurrent pulled her into the depths of a freezing sea where faces floated and tentacles tugged on her. She went down, down, down.

CHAPTER 3

"Call 911," a strange voice barked amidst a cacophony of noises, chair scrapings, footsteps, dish clatter, mumbling, Christmas carols, and the obnoxious bass drum beating a steady rhythm inside Jackie's head.

"Jackie? Honey?" Bonnie was there.

Jackie tried to speak. "Wha—?" She opened her eyes but regretted it the moment her lids fluttered and let in a strobing flash of light. It pumped up the volume on the bass drum. "Owww..."

Bonnie came in close. "Don't move. You hit your head."

Someone picked up her wrist and felt for a pulse.

"Damn," said another strange voice. "She iced that guy."

"Is he dead?" asked someone else.

"Is she?"

I'm not dead, Jackie thought. *Get off...*

"She's not dead," said the man kneeling beside her.

Told ya.

"She's probably got a concussion. Him too."

Him? Had she somehow assaulted Mitch, after all?

Jackie licked her lips and whispered a reasonable facsimile of "Bonnie?"

"I'm here, sweetie. I'm here."

"Bonnie? Is Mitch dead?"

"No."

"Oh." Jackie couldn't keep the disappointment out of her voice. The waves closed over her again. They enclosed her in the depths of unconsciousness.

Some time later, Jackie's awareness returned and spread out as carefully as a hunting party in the zombie apocalypse. She took in the sounds one at a time and tried to make sense of it all—beeps, hushed voices, and squeaky wheels.

She was lying in a bed—not her own. Her head hurt. No, it didn't just hurt, it pounded. Jackie lifted her fingers to touch her forehead and found an icepack there.

A body stepped up beside the bed. An unfamiliar, female voice with a dry note of authority said, "You hit your head."

"Where am I?"

"Arlington General. The emergency room. You have a minor concussion and a hematoma the size of a golf ball. You feeling nauseated at all?"

Jackie shook her head and made a Herculean effort to open her eyes.

A black-haired woman in a white lab coat leaned over her. "There you are. Hello. I'm Doctor Adisa." Her teeth flashed white against dark skin.

"Hi. I'm Jackie."

"I deduced that." The doctor patted Jackie's forearm. "We're going to release you, but you'll need someone to keep an eye on you for twenty-four hours."

"My brother will be at home."

"How old is he?"

"Seventeen. Almost eighteen."

"He'll do. Your friends are in the waiting room. You want me to send them in?"

"Yes, please."

The doctor pressed a button to raise the head of the bed. When Jackie was more inclined than reclined, she let go. "Relax for a little while longer. I'll go get them."

"Thanks, Doctor."

The doctor pulled aside the curtain and slipped out. She closed it again from the outside.

Jackie took a deep breath and tucked her fingers under the cold pack to explore the bump on her forehead. It was round and tight, tender to the touch. "Damn." She thought back to what had happened. Mitch. She remembered the text, and a flush of renewed anger ignited in her chest, spread up her neck and into her head, where it exacerbated her pounding headache.

Footsteps approached from out of sight. The curtain rustled, and Bonnie stuck her head in. Only her head.

"You decent?" she asked with a grin.

Jackie had to think about it. On self-inspection, she realized she was still wearing the special birthday dress. She sighed. "Yeah."

"Too bad." Bonnie entered then held the curtain aside so her husband, Jim a.k.a. Hubs, could step in too. "Our loss."

"My loss," Jackie replied with a chuckle then winced. "Ooh, don't make me laugh."

Jackie's best friend and second-best-friend-by-marriage came to stand beside the bed.

"You're going to have an aurora borealis on your head," Jim said. "Does it hurt?" He was taller and older than Bonnie by a foot and a decade. That day, he had dressed Norwegian-style, with a wool coat, striped shirt, and tailored pants. It suited him. His light brown hair was short, parted on the side, and fringed across his forehead. He could have been James Bond.

Jackie replied, "Like a bad prom, yes."

"You conked your noggin pretty good there, chica!" Bonnie said, reaching to lift the cold pack and examine the lump. "You should see the other guy."

"The other guy?"

Bonnie nodded, mouth pursing and eyebrows rising. "Oh, yes. The one coming in as you were storming out. The door hit him first, bounced off, and hit you. He hasn't woken up yet."

Jim warned, "Bon-Bon, you may not want to upset her too much."

Jackie's head was reeling. "Who? Mitch?"

Bonnie pulled up a chair as she talked. "Not Mitch. I don't know who he is. Jim and I overheard a doctor talking to a relative of his. He's in intensive care."

"Intensive care?" Jackie couldn't believe what she was hearing. "Is he going to be okay?"

"They don't know. He has a concussion, maybe even a brain bleed."

"What?" Jackie attempted to sit up and failed miserably. She fell back on the pillow, weak and woozy.

"Woah. Don't do that." Bonnie found the bed controls for her. "I've got you. Up or down?"

"Up." The bed pushed Jackie up at an awkward angle, and she wriggled until she was comfortable again.

Jim said, "The police are calling it an accident. They talked to everyone at Bella's."

"I didn't mean to," Jackie said, a cloud of misery descending upon her.

Bonnie rubbed cool fingers against Jackie's cheek. "They know that. Worst thing you have to worry about is if the guy sues you. But I'm sure he won't."

Under his breath, Jim commented, "Unless he dies."

Jackie's heart gave a lurch. "What?"

They both leapt to reassure her. "Don't worry!" and "He's probably not going to die."

Suddenly, Jackie did feel nauseated.

It was after midnight when Bonnie and Jim drove Jackie home. Though they offered to come in, she refused them with the excuse that her brother could watch over her. Truth was, she didn't even plan on waking him. All she wanted was to put on her pajamas and go straight to bed. So that's what she did.

Try as she might, sleep eluded her. She lay there, reliving every moment of the night—fighting with Mitch over and over, each time finding the wittier, sassier things she *should* have said, but didn't. Each time having enough poise to *walk* calmly through the diner door.

After much tossing and turning, she dozed off, falling into a fitful, dream-filled sleep.

She awoke to the sounds of her brother clinking dishes in the kitchen. Jackie got up, showered, dressed, and emerged to greet the new day with a groan.

Jazz had settled into his *usual* spot on the couch and was eating cereal from a giant bowl.

"How was your date?" he asked, eyes on his video game.

"Disastrous." Jackie opened the refrigerator. She stood there, staring but not registering what she was looking at. Memories of the night before filled her mind. She closed the door without taking anything. "How was practice?"

"Okay."

"Just okay?" Jackie leaned against the counter and watched her brother, reminded of the mean things he'd said.

Jazz said, "Mr. Kirk has weird taste in music, but whatever. You know?"

Jackie did know. Back in her day, she'd played piano in the school jazz band.

"Is he making you do 'Take Five'?"

"Of course. I'd rather be in P.E." To Jazz, physical education class was the worst possible Hell. He was the polar opposite of athletic. He'd been a premature baby and had never quite caught up with himself. Their mother's pregnancy had come as a surprise to everyone, and given their mother's age when she had him, they were lucky his only challenge was a lack of athleticism.

When their parents died in a car accident, it had fallen on her to become Jazz's guardian. It was an avalanche—in more ways than one. Jackie had been twenty-one. Jazz had been nine. They'd sold the family home and moved into a two-bedroom apartment—the same one they still lived in. Jazz had turned seventeen on his last birthday, and Jackie didn't want to think about being twenty-nine. Three-hundred-and-sixty-four days stood between her and thirty. *Thirty!*

Jackie said, "I have to go out. I may have killed a guy."

"Excuse me?" Jazz sat up and peered over the back of the couch. "Salmonella?"

"No. Hematoma. I slammed into somebody with the diner door. I need to go back to the hospital and see if he's awake."

"Back to the hospital?"

Jackie showed him her forehead. "Yeah, I hit myself with the door too. I'm fine though. They let me go."

"Holy shit! That looks like it hurts, Em."

Jackie touched her fingertips to the sensitive spot on her

forehead. "Yeah. It's kinda sore. I'm okay."

"You don't look okay, but you didn't hear it from me."

"What?"

"Just sayin'. First rule of Fight Club."

"Shut up! I'm gonna go. Don't forget to lock up—"

"If I go out. Got it."

"And practice your sax, Jasper Li. I'll know if you didn't."

"Okay, *Mom.*"

Jackie smiled. In light of recent events, she cared a bit less that Jazz had forgotten her birthday. She gathered her coat, shoes, and purse, then took the bus to the hospital. The ride was uneventful, unless you count the toothless old lady who looked right at Jackie and spat, "Murderer." Or, at least, that's what Jackie heard. On reflection, she realized it could have been any combination of mush-mouth syllables.

The northern Virginia winter was coming into its own, leaving behind the flaming Halloween colors for a starker gray. Before long, the first snowfall would blanket the city with irritation and inconvenience. A chill wind whipped at Jackie's pants legs as she walked along the sidewalk toward the hospital's front entrance. Its icy fingers were way out of line, groping her even through her heavy coat. Admittedly, she'd had to tear out the coat's lining two years earlier when the seams had become too ragged to repair again. She wrapped her arms around herself and hurried along.

The hospital was alien territory. Jackie had no experience with them. She entered through the main doors and stood there, looking for any indication of where to go. People were criss-crossing the lobby, moving in all directions, no help at all.

"Are you lost?" asked a smiling voice. Masculine. Mellifluous Hindi accent.

"I'm not sure," Jackie said. "Can you help me?"

"Maybe if you hum a few bars?"

Jackie looked up into big brown eyes. "Wow."

The doctor, for he surely was one, tilted his head in amusement. "I'm Dr. Bindhita," he said. "I work here, so I'm fairly confident that I can get you where you need to be."

"They brought a man in last night. I need to find out if he's okay. I think he might be in Intensive Care?"

"I see. Let's go this way." Dr. Bindhita touched Jackie's

shoulder, gentle but firm enough to turn her around and get her moving, as if it were her own idea. Which it wasn't. She had the uncanny urge to lean into him. "What is this man's name?"

Jackie sighed. "I don't know. I hit him with a door. He was coming in. I was going out. Um...it was around ten last night."

"Are you a relative?"

"No."

The doctor stopped walking and shook his head. "Only family is allowed in the Intensive Care Unit. We're required to protect the patient's privacy." He pronounced 'privacy' like 'privvacy.' "I'm sorry. I suggest you leave a message for him at the front desk." He pointed to it.

Jackie blinked. Twice. "But it's my fault he's here. Can't you just tell me how he is?"

"I'm afraid not." He took a backstep away from her. "Have a nice day." He abandoned her in the featureless corridor, left her directionless and lost.

Then, luck struck.

At the far end of the hall, she saw a sign that said, "Intensive Care Unit." As she hurried toward it, she plotted the lies she might tell to get the information she needed.

Beyond a set of glass doors, inside the I.C.U., nurses gathered at a desk area, moving around one another as gracefully as she and Bonnie did in the diner's kitchen—years of practice. They ignored Jackie, busy with their own tasks and troubles. She strolled nonchalantly through the area, peeking into each room she passed. All around her, equipment hummed at a subliminally disturbing level. Monstrous devices with cords like tentacles pumped liquid and air into bodies, and electronic displays monitored how close the sick and injured were to death. The machines came only in white, an ill-conceived effort to make them blend into the background.

"Miss? Are you here to see someone?" A veteran nurse scrutinized Jackie with narrowed eyes.

"Yes," Jackie straightened her spine. "I—"

"She's with me," said a male voice with an unidentifiable European accent, his tone of authority firm. "My sister."

The nurse eyed him and nodded. "Only two visitors in the room at a time, please." Confident they would obey her, she spun away.

The man was tall, gray-haired, dressed in a black suit. Jackie pegged him for a mortician, or a lawyer, or maybe a butler. And she recognized him as the snooty man from the alley.

"Come on in, Jackie. Don't be shy." The man entered one of the rooms. "Your victim is in here."

Jackie paused, unsure. Holding her purse in both hands, she crept into the doorway. "You know who I am?"

A man lay unconscious in the bed, tubes and devices attached to him. He had a head of big curls, blonde, that spread out on the pillow and looked startlingly boyish. His face, however, was rugged, even with a breathing tube stuck in it. He had a large rectangular bandage on his forehead.

"Oh my god," Jackie breathed. "Is he gonna be okay?"

"He's in a coma," the tall man said with matter-of-fact crispness.

"In a coma?"

"Yes. Your fault."

"Oh my god!" Jackie moved to the foot of the bed. "I mean… I'm so sorry. It was an accident."

"Even accidents have consequences, I'm afraid."

"What's his name?"

"What do you care?"

Jackie rolled her eyes over to the looming man without moving her head. "Excuse me?"

"He's just some guy who may never wake up because you attacked him." The man folded his hands together, calm, almost serene.

"I didn't attack him."

"Are you telling me you didn't slam the door into him?"

Jackie deflated. "Well, yeah, I did."

"There you have it. As I said, your fault."

"I didn't know he was there."

"Luck of the draw."

Jackie's stomach gave a sad lurch. "What can I do?"

"What *wouldn't* you do to make this right?"

"I'd do about anything, I suppose," Jackie answered. "Anything legal," she amended, used to her brother trapping her with small print. "And I don't have any money."

"Done." Without further ado, the man left. He walked out. No goodbye. No adios. No ciao. No nothing. Just left, pulling the door shut behind him.

"Done?" Jackie echoed. She frowned and stared after him for a long moment, wondering, *What the hell?*

Then she realized she was alone with a man she had put in a coma. She approached him with caution. "I'm so sorry, sir," she said. She patted his hand and spotted the band on his wrist. It had his name on it: Kupidopoulos, Georgio. *Greek, maybe?*

Jackie bent to examine the bandage on his forehead. No blood. That, she felt, was a good sign. *Who knew hitting someone with a door could do so much harm?*

"Don't you dare die," she said, close to his face. "Don't you dare."

She patted his hand again. It was warm. She wanted to leave, but then he'd be all alone. Where was his family? Friends? Was that man in the suit coming back?

A nurse entered to check the machines.

Jackie asked, "Is he going to be okay?"

"We'll have more information once we've completed all the tests," the nurse replied without looking up.

Jackie's thoughts jumbled into one explosive question: "What am I going to do?" She burst into tears.

The nurse lifted her head. "One day at a time, honey. That's all you can do. Say your prayers, and don't give up hope."

Jackie gave a big sniffle and moaned, "Why is this happening? I don't need anything else to worry about. As if I didn't already have enough on my plate."

The nurse turned to face Jackie. "Sometimes, bad things happen to good people. It's all in God's plan."

Jackie watched the nurse walk out of the room.

"And boom," Jackie said with a sassy nod to Georgio Kupidopoulos. "Nurse drops the mic." She heaved a sigh, shoulders drooping, and wiped at her eyes. Her fatigue caught up with her, and she sat in the armchair beside the bed. It was soft and comfortable. She took off her coat, draped it over herself, and curled her legs up in the chair. She figured she'd watch over Georgio until the man in the suit came back. That was something she could do. And it was going well, until she herself dozed off, lulled by the insidious sounds of the hospital.

◆ ♥ ◆

CHAPTER 4

Jackie's consciousness drifted up from the depths of healing sleep. Her head ached, and her neck muscles were tight and sore. She stretched long under the heavy covers and rubbed her bare feet together. Birds chirped outside, and soft footfalls sounded in the hall outside her room. She snuggled deeper into the warmth of the bed. She wanted to roll over and go back to sleep.

"Good morning," said a man in the room.

Jackie sat bolt upright, eyes opening far too fast for comfort.

It was the tall, gray-haired man from the hospital room, standing in a butler's stance, hands clasped behind his back, excellent posture. Impressive. And a bit terrifying.

The question "Am I dreaming?" kept repeating in her mind. She didn't know the answer.

Before she'd opened her eyes, she'd assumed she was in her own bedroom, but this room made her little bedroom seem shabby. It was large and beautiful. There was no dirty-clothes pile in the corner and no books stacked on every surface.

Luxurious jewel tones mingled via the emerald upholstery of armchairs and ruby brocade drapes on the windows. The bed had four posts and a canopy covered in sapphire blue velvet, the richest of fabrics, matching the bedspread folded at the end of the bed. Someone had built a fire in the fireplace. *The fireplace!*

A minute passed while Jackie took in her surroundings. A down comforter in antique white covered her, and Jackie pulled it up to her chin. She scooted back against the headboard and stared with wide eyes at the man. She remembered him from the hospital.

"What do you want?" Jackie asked, breathless.

The man remained still, except for his eyebrows which rose to widen his eyes. "I'm here to orient you."

"Where am I?"

All business, the man said, "Welcome to the Gray Fox Retreat, Jackie. Your first mission as a new cupid."

"A new what?"

The man's face puckered with distaste. "You put my cupid agent in a coma. Someone has to do the job—and that's you. Love waits for no one. You agreed to it last night."

"I did?"

"You did. Until my C.A. is well again, you will stand in for him. I've arranged everything, including a temporary grant of powers."

"Who are you?"

"I'm Georgio's handler. And now, sadly, I'm yours too. You may call me Mr. Amore."

"Did you drug me?"

"I don't have the patience to ride out a panic attack with you. Call me when you're ready to get down to business. You must balance your karmic debt or there will be hell to pay." The man placed a business card on the edge of the dresser then disappeared.

Jackie stared at the spot where he'd been. He hadn't left. He'd just plain disappeared.

"I'm dreaming. I must be." Jackie pinched herself. Hard. It hurt. "Ow. Not dreaming." She lay back and pulled the covers over her head. In the darkness under the comforter, she waited for a return of reality.

Nothing happened.

Jackie threw back the covers, sat up, and swung her legs over the edge of the bed. She was wearing the same outfit she'd worn to visit Georgio.

At the end of the bed, she found the shoes she'd worn to the hospital. Someone had draped her socks over a chair by the fire. Her coat was hanging in the armoire. She put them all on and felt armored.

Opening the drapes, she learned she was on the second story. Beyond the window, she saw trees, lots of trees in every direction. The house had a patio, a fire pit, and several wrought-iron tables, chairs, and benches. Leaves covered the ground—gold and scarlet. The first snowflakes of the season had begun to fall.

"*It's snowing!*" Jackie said aloud.

As if on cue, a stag strode out of the woods and onto the lawn. It stood there, majestic. Jackie held her breath, awed by its beauty. The stag looked up at her, as if it could see her. She thought maybe it did. Pressing her palm against the cold glass of the window, Jackie watched the creature dip its head to eat the grass. The stag's appearance soothed her. Her shoulders relaxed, and she didn't move again until the animal had returned to the woods.

Once it was gone, she resumed her examination of the bedroom. It appeared to be a hotel room. It had a desk with a notepad, room-service menu, and religious reading material. The inn's information booklet told Jackie that she was in West Virginia—*West Virginia!* She'd never been to West Virginia. It was the polar opposite of her world in Arlington.

In the top dresser drawer, Jackie found her purse. Sitting on the edge of the bed, she dug her cellphone out. She had two texts waiting for her: one from Jazz and one from Bonnie.

Jazz had written: *Need new kicks.*

Bonnie had written a novel, without punctuation:

You okay Me and Hubs worried maybe still sleeping hope you're not dead coming by later w/chicken soup Good for a concussion LOL chicken soup good for everything call me my shift starts at 10 & don't worry about your shift Roy got someone to cover call me

Jackie texted Jazz back: *When do u need them? Be home soon.*

Next, she dialed Bonnie.

"Jackie! There you are. I've been trying to get a hold of you, but your phone keeps going to voicemail. How's the head?"

"It's sore if I poke at it."

"So don't poke it!"

Jackie chuckled. "Why didn't I think of that?"

"You would've, eventually." Bonnie's familiar laugh put Jackie at ease.

She blurted, "I'm in West Virginia."

"What was that? I didn't hear you right."

"I said I'm in West Virginia, at some kind of inn."

"Is this your concussion talking?"

"No. I woke up here."

Bonnie sounded incredulous. "I don't understand."

"Me either. All I know is I'm here. And I don't remember how I got here." Jackie felt her anxiety and fear rising.

"Okay, don't panic." Bonnie sounded calm and in charge.

That was, of course, one of Bonnie's super powers—grace under pressure. "Are you safe?"

"I don't know."

"Can you leave?"

"I don't know."

"Try."

"Okay."

Jackie went to the door. Her hand shook as she reached for the knob. It turned, and the door pulled open. It was heavy but not locked.

"Looks like I can get out." Jackie leaned out.

More doors lined the hall. Framed photos hung on the walls between rooms. Those she could see without leaving the room were photographs of mountain trails and the people who traveled them. It gave the hall a cozy, home-like feel—someone else's home, of course. Someone well-off.

Jackie said, "It's fancy. Lux."

"Huh. And you have no idea how you got there? No memory?"

"None."

"What's the last thing you remember? You better not have gotten drunk with a concussion. You're such a lightweight, even without a traumatic brain injury."

"I was not drinking. I was at the hospital."

"You don't remember us taking you home?" Bonnie sounded alarmed.

"No, I remember that! I went back later. I wanted to see the coma guy—Georgio Kupidopoulos."

"Did you?"

"Yeah. I met his boss. The guy was so ticked off at me for what happened."

"Ticked enough to roofie you and carry you to the middle of nowhere?"

Jackie could imagine Bonnie's eyes squinting. "Maybe? He was here when I woke up."

"Holy jebeezus, Jackie! You need to get out of there. Now! Call the cops."

"He said he had a mission for me."

"A what?"

"I might have agreed to it, without meaning to."

"Agree*d to what?*" Bonnie sounded even more shocked.

"I told him I'd do anything to make things right."

"Jackie. What does he want? My imagination is going wild. I'm thinking drug mule. Human trafficking. Singing telegrams?"

"No, no. Nothing gross like that. I told him. Nothing illegal. He wants me to stand in for Georgio."

"Georgio's the guy you put in a coma?"

"Yeah! I kind of owe him."

"Stand in for him how?"

Jackie ventured, "Be a cupid?"

"What the hell does that mean? Erotic dancer?"

"No. I don't think so. Anyone who would want to watch Georgio dance wouldn't want me. The handler said to call him when I was serious about getting down to business. I have his card."

"The handler?" Bonnie gave a frustrated grunt. "Where are you exactly?"

Jackie looked again at the inn's information booklet. "It's called the Gray Fox Inn, #9 Gray Fox Road. You don't think it's some sort of mean-spirited prank, do you? A kind of revenge for what happened?"

"What's the town?"

"Frisson Springs. F. R. I. S. S. O. N."

"Got it. Thanks. Listen, you have any money on you? Your credit card?"

"Let me check." Jackie dug her wallet out of her purse. "Money, no. Credit card, yeah. It's here."

"So he didn't rob you. That's something. Everything else... intact?"

"He didn't hurt me, if that's what you mean. Took off my shoes and socks before putting me in bed, but I woke up in my clothes." It hit Jackie what might have happened. "God, Bon."

"You're okay," said Bonnie, using her soothing voice. "Stay calm. I see it on the map. The inn has a website, so it's legit. Says it's open all year, so it's not like you're stuck at the Overlook Hotel, right?"

"I hope not."

"We're gonna get you out of there. Let me talk to Hubs, and we'll drive up there."

"Okay. Thanks, Bon."

"I'll call you soon."

After hanging up with Bonnie, Jackie considered her situation. She chewed on her lip, looking around the lavish room. *If it was a prank, it was an expensive one.* Questions churned in her mind. *My first mission, the man had said. In West Virginia. A mission? What does that mean?*

A light knock sounded on the door, and someone pushed a paper brochure in under it.

Jackie went to pick it up. It was a three-fold informational brochure. On the cover, it said, "Love To Last," and "Find your own Christmas miracle and renew your love in a beautiful mountain retreat." The event's start date was a few days away.

Opening the brochure, Jackie looked at a promotional headshot of Dr. Georgio Kupidopoulos. He was touted as the leader of the seminar, an expert in love and communication.

Then, right before Jackie's eyes, the brochure swirled. Jackie blinked, fighting down a wave of vertigo, and when she looked again, her own photo had replaced that of Dr. Kupidopoulos. It was a headshot, a good one, though she didn't remember having had it taken. The text had also changed. "Dr. Jacquelyn Li, expert in couples' counseling, will lead daily workshops and provide exercises to deepen the communication and revive the romance in your relationship."

Jackie threw the brochure to the floor as if it were on fire. Talking to herself, Jackie stumbled toward a chair and sat. "Oh my god. So that's what he meant? How is this happening? It's magic. It's... unbelievable. I've lost my mind. My brain is bleeding. I'm having a psychotic break. Hallucinating." She pinched herself again, doubly hard, and it hurt—doubly much. "Oh god! I gotta get out of here."

The flight side of her fight-or-flight instinct hit her gut, overcoming her fear of leaving the secure room. Jackie threw open the door and lurched into the hallway.

A maid pushing a cart laden with supplies took one look and said, "Ma'am?"

Jackie threw herself at the maid, latching onto her arm. "Please. How do I get out of here?"

The maid stammered and cringed away. She pointed a finger in a direction, and Jackie was on her way again.

She found the main stairs before she found the elevator.

The stairwell resembled a grand cathedral, and Jackie looked over the wrought-iron balcony to the lobby below. Tiny white Christmas lights twinkled all around. The curving stairs were wide and carpeted with red and navy plaid carpet.

Windows stretched from floor to cathedral ceiling on the front wall, revealing another wintery view of the property. A circular driveway cut through well-groomed bushes, and a stretch of lawn had paths, benches, and rose bushes trimmed back and covered for winter.

Clutching the iron balustrade with white knuckles, Jackie stared down into the magical room below—motionless, breathless, speechless.

Instrumental Christmas music drifted up to her. In the lobby, a twelve-foot Christmas tree dominated, decorated with all the trimmings. A giant fireplace occupied one wall, its fire crackling happily. The furniture had a rustic elegance, arranged to invite sitting in groups and relaxing. It was the perfect place to sit and read a book while drinking hot chocolate.

The front doors were hardwood with stained glass windows that cast colorful smears on the polished pine floor. The front desk stood sentinel across from the entrance, but it was unmanned. It occurred to Jackie that she hadn't seen a single soul other than the maid and the handler.

Jackie descended the stairs more slowly, careful. She kept one hand on the elegant railing. Once at the bottom, she peered around before storming up to the vacant front desk.

"Hello?" Jackie called. "Is anyone here?" She searched for a bell and leaned over the counter to see if someone was lying dead on the floor. No one was.

She tried again, "Hello?" When no one answered, she stood there, letting her heart rate return to normal. No one had tried to stop her. No one was threatening her. She took a deep breath then another. *I'm okay,* she told herself.

She helped herself to a piece of the peppermint candy from the dish on the counter then continued her exploration like Goldilocks. A pair of wide double doors stood open to one side of the front desk. Beyond the threshold, Jackie could see a restaurant with a bar. The tables had their chairs turned upside down on them, and most of the lights were off. Jackie wandered that way.

"Hello?" she called again.

"In here!" a voice replied from deeper in the restaurant.

Jackie followed it and found a woman seated in a booth by the window, accounting books and papers laid out in front of her. The woman slid out of the booth when Jackie came into view and held out her hand. Her short hair had a hint of silver mingled with the chestnut brown. Slighter of figure than Jackie, but more robust, she wore a rustic black-and-red flannel shirt and blue jeans, old hiking boots on her feet. Her brown eyes shone with warmth.

"Well, howdy." The woman's West Virginia accent held a country-western lilt. "You must be Dr. Li. I'm Lula Miller. Most people call me Lu. My husband and I own the Gray Fox. I'm the one who spoke with your agent." The woman took Jackie's hand in a vice-like grip. She shook it soundly. Lula's eyes drifted to the bruise on Jackie's forehead, and her next sentence came out with slow distraction. "We are so happy to have you here."

The woman's warmth and charm derailed Jackie's worries. She put her fingers to her bruise and said, "I ran into a door."

"Oh," said Lula. "Okay."

"No, really. I did." Jackie tried to sound sincere. "What is this place?" If she had had to guess, she'd have said it was a rehab facility for the rich and famous. It was the only thing that made sense. Except, that didn't make any sense. Jackie was neither rich nor famous. Nor did she need rehab.

"It's the dining room," Lula replied. She yelled over Jackie's shoulder, "Card! Frankie! Come meet Dr. Li!"

"It's just Jackie," Jackie corrected.

With a clatter, a bear of a man exploded into the room through double swinging doors. Dressed in overalls and an old-fashioned red Henley T-shirt, wiping his hands on a blue gingham towel, he crossed the room in fewer strides than should have been possible. A grin turned his face into a landscape of dimples and rosy cheeks, and his blue eyes locked onto Jackie. He stood a foot taller than either Jackie or Lula, and his belly preceded him by several inches.

He picked up Jackie's hand, though he didn't shake it. He held it in both of his own as if it were a baby bird. His gaze locked onto Jackie's bruised forehead. For a moment, his expression shifted to one of worry, but then he put on a big grin and looked her square in the eyes.

"Dr. Li," he rumbled with that same West Virginia accent. "You can call me Card. Short for Cardinal." He winked, surprising Jackie with his resemblance to Santa. He too had a full beard and bushy hair, though his was more brown than white.

"Call me Jackie, please. I'm not a doctor."

"Oh, I understand," said Card. "In your field, I imagine your title puts some people off. Jackie it is."

A woman in a kitchen apron had followed in Card's wake. She folded her arms on her chest and studied Jackie without smiling. She had long brown hair in need of a good conditioning. The highlights she'd put in the previous summer were growing out and streaking from cheek-level to the frazzled ends. Thick mascara turned her long eyelashes into fringed awnings over hazel-green eyes. Her figure was something to be admired—or envied. Jackie guessed her to be the same age as herself, or close to it.

Lula made the introductions. "Jackie, this is Frankie, our bartender. She helps out around the place."

"What happened to your head?" Frankie asked, shifting her weight.

"Oh, it's nothing," Jackie replied. "I ran into a door. It looks worse than it is."

Frankie nodded slowly. "Uh huh."

Card released Jackie's hand. "You must be starving. We're about to eat breakfast. Why don't I make you some eggs? You like eggs? They're fresh, right out from under the hens."

Jackie's stomach growled at the mere thought of food. "I'm afraid I have to get back home. I..."

The look on their faces halted her words. The smiles faded to be replaced by worry.

"Oh," said Lula. "But you'll be back, yes? I mean, you just got here. Did you come to scout the meeting rooms?"

Jackie shook her head and opened her mouth to reply, but Card was faster. "No need to worry. I can show you around the meeting rooms, if you'd like, before you go." As he talked, the smile returned to his face, but his eyes had lost some of their sparkle.

Lula jumped in before Jackie could. "You should eat something before you go, Jackie. What kind of hosts would we be if we sent you out into the cold without a warm breakfast in your tummy. After that, Card can show you the meeting rooms you'll have at your disposal. We have a sauna and hot tubs too. Did you drive here?"

Jackie shook her head. Unsure, she clicked her teeth together. "No, I..."

Lula gest*ured*. "We can call you a cab when you're ready. I'm so glad you came up for the day. You probably have things you'll need. You give us a list, now, and we'll have them ready for you—when you come back." Lula directed Jackie to a table with the grace of a skilled hostess.

So they weren't trying to keep her from leaving, and that eased Jackie's mind. She supposed she could stay long enough to have breakfast. "All right," she agreed. "Do you have coffee?"

"Always. You sit right down here." Lula pulled out a chair. "We'll be right back."

Jackie sat. The restaurant was even cozier than the lobby. The ceiling was high, but only one story, and dark wood paneling covered the walls. Another lit fireplace stood on an unpainted brick wall, its mantel decorated with evergreen boughs and glass balls that reflected the dancing flames. A baby grand piano stood in the corner, closed and silent, waiting like a wrapped Christmas present. It was easy for Jackie to imagine the tables filled, people laughing and drinking, eating from plates piled high with comfort food. Under any other circumstance, the inn would have suited Jackie's taste to perfection.

Nothing made sense, however. Her mind continued to spin its wheels without gaining much traction. There had to be an explanation that didn't involve magic, disappearing butlers, and cupids. The last thing she remembered was being in Georgio Kupidopoulos' hospital room. Maybe *she* was the one in a coma. Maybe her head injury...

Jackie glanced toward the kitchen doors and found Lula and Card peeking out at her. They pulled back in, ducking out of sight. They seemed so excited for her to be there, but she couldn't stay. She was scheduled to work that evening. If she didn't show, she'd lose her job. She should probably call them and warn them she'd be late. Maybe Bonnie could cover for her until she got there.

Her pounding head was making her thoughts thick and

slippery. She rubbed her uninjured temple, a slew of questions bombarding her mind.

How did I get here?

Am I dead?

Is this my Hell?

She dismissed the last idea, considering how the only open flames in her environment were in the fireplaces. She also gave up on the belief that she was dreaming, though she still felt disconnected from reality.

Magic. There was no other word for it.

Maybe I'm in Heaven?

Or maybe, the world is more *complex than I've been led to believe. What if Cupid exists, and I put him in a coma?* It's not like I don't already believe in astrology, birthday wishes, and Christmas miracles. I believe in guardian angels.

Technically, she thought, *Cupid is a guardian angel.*

Oh my god. I put an angel in a coma!

Jackie had an urgent need for strong coffee and an escape from her own thoughts. She pushed back her chair and wove through the tables to the kitchen. Lula, Card, and Frankie were gathering silverware, cooking eggs, washing dishes, and dancing in place, singing along with the radio. "Frosty the Snowman." The familiar old song tugged at Jackie's heart strings.

The smell of frying eggs and butter coaxed Jackie in.

Lula saw her first. "Come on in, Jackie. Come on in."

Frankie looked up then went silent and stopped dancing.

Card didn't miss a beat. He grinned and kept right on singing, bouncing in time with the music.

"Easy with the salt, Card," Lula scolded him. "You know what the doctor said."

"I know, I know."

Jackie entered the kitchen. "I didn't mean to interrupt. I was hoping you had a pot of coffee already made? I really could use some."

Lula pointed to a big silver carafe on the counter. "Yes, ma'am, we do. Help yourself. The mugs are over there with the sugar, and cream's in the fridge."

"Thank you." Jackie smiled her gratitude and went for it. The coffee poured from the carafe, dark and aromatic. The aroma hit her brain first, clearing cobwebs and fighting confusion.

She stood by the carafe, her lifeline to sanity, holding the mug in both hands. It was hot, so she blew on it and sipped carefully.

Her plan started forming as the promise of caffeine soothed her. First, breakfast. Then, she'd find the hotel's business center and use the computer to figure out the best way home. Maybe locate the nearest bus station? Shouldn't be expensive to get a ticket to Arlington. She didn't want to make Bon and Hubs drive all that way. It was her mess, and she had to straighten it out herself.

Jackie leaned against the stainless steel counter. She sipped her coffee.

"You were smart, coming out early," said Lula. "You're welcome to stay here until the seminar begins, if you want. Room and board on us. I imagine you have lots of preparations to do. I've already asked Sam to help you in any way you need. He can be your assistant. Too bad he's not here this mornin'. Card sent him down to White Sulphur to get supplies. He'll be back this afternoon, though. You can meet him then. He learned all about office equipment and stuff in college."

Jackie nodded, thinking how sweet they were. "I'm afraid I have to get back," she said. "I have responsibilities."

In her mind, she made a thousand excuses for abandoning them. *I didn't agree to do a seminar. I'm no doctor, and I am certainly no expert on love. I'm doing them a favor by leaving. I'll send an apology once I get home. The guests will be happy no matter what, spending Christmas here. They don't need workshops or exercises or...*

"C'mon along," said Card, carrying a plate heaped with a scramble of eggs, ham, green pepper, and onion into the dining room. "Breakfast is served." Lula followed in his wake with a tray of utensils and condiments.

Jackie topped off her coffee then brought up the rear. She glanced at Frankie as she was leaving and found the other woman watching her.

Jackie said, "See you later," and smiled.

Frankie nodded once.

◆ ♥ ◆

CHAPTER 5

In the Gray Fox's business office, on the Internet, Jackie had looked up the number of the local cab company and used the retro-80s push-button phone in the lobby to call them. In the back of her mind, she realized that her actions contradicted the possibility that she was actually lying in a hospital bed, a victim of her own brain injury. Action, even if in her imagination, was better than the alternative. She persisted and hoped she'd wake up soon.

The cab company turned out to be a small local outfit. The man who answered had a thick drawl that caught Jackie off guard. Between that and the screaming kids in the background, Jackie had a hard time hearing him. She could only hope that he'd understood where she was and where she wanted to go.

The driver himself, when he finally showed up, wore a blue and gold WVU pullover hoodie with a ball cap to match. He got out of the cab and met her on the curb.

"Name's Sam. Where ya headed?" he asked, glancing around.

Jackie made a beeline for the back door. "Nearest bus station, please."

"That'd be White Sulfur Springs."

"Yes, that's the one."

"You got any luggage?"

"No." Jackie opened the door and slid onto the seat.

"Alrighty." Sam approached, but she shut her own door before he could assist.

The passing scenery as they drove down one-lane roads was rural and scenic. Thick forest came right up to the shoulder, and Jackie spotted the occasional farm or cabin in the distance. Sam pulled onto a two-lane road and increased his speed. The road had hairpin curves and blind switchbacks. On one side of the road, a cliff rose out of sight. Cascades of water leaked out of the cracks in the cliff-face, frozen and beautiful. On the other side, the cliff dropped away to God knew where.

Sam glanced at Jackie in the rear-view mirror then did a

double-take.

Jackie stared out the window, turning her bruise away.

"This is an old loggin' road," Sam said. "You still see the big log trucks drivin' up and down the mountain here. They're a pain in the ass, but you get used to 'em."

"Oh, good," said Jackie.

Sam asked, "Where you from?"

"Arlington," Jackie replied.

"Ah, a city girl. You have a good stay at the Gray Fox?"

"It's a nice place."

"You can say that again. Those Millers are the best of the best. Biggest hearted people I ever met outside my own family. It's a damn shame, the trouble they're in." He glanced in the rear-view mirror at her.

"Trouble?"

"Financial, but you didn't hear it from me." Sam's eyes shifted back to the road. "They'll have to sell if they don't attract more customers out here. It's good to see city folk—like you—comin' all this way. Lord knows it's worth the trip, but try tellin' that to anybody who hasn't been here before."

Jackie nodded. *Damn*, she thought. *For a coma fantasy, this is intense. I refuse to feel guilty. None of it's real.*

Her white knuckles disagreed.

Sam asked, "You do any fishin' while you were up here?"

"What? No. I'm not much into fishing." Jackie got the impression the driver was playing with her.

"Too bad. We got some of the best fishin' in the whole state. People come from all around for the lake. That water comes right down the mountain, over Rock Falls and into the lake, clean as an angel's ass, and that lake is brimming with bigmouth bass. I try to get out there a couple times a month myself."

"That's nice," Jackie replied, checking her phone. No bars.

"This one time, I was up above Bear Ridge, just above the rapids, where the pool's deep. That's the best spot. You can catch Muskie, Smallmouth Bass, Walleye. Them's good eatin'."

"Uh huh."

Jackie let Sam talk her ear off with his taxi banter, nodding and smiling, but only paying half attention to him. She just wanted to get home.

"Say," Sam eventually said. "Aren't you that love doctor

coming to the Gray Fox?"

Jackie met his gaze in the rear-view. She didn't know how to answer, so she said nothing.

Sam continued, "They told me all about you. Aren't you going in the wrong direction?" His tone remained friendly.

"Just keep your eyes on the road. Mind your own business."

"Yes, ma'am." And he did.

The drive to White Sulphur Springs took around thirty minutes. Once there, Sam pulled up at the entrance, and Jackie swiped her debit card to pay. Sam got out and opened the door for Jackie while she was still putting the card away.

Jackie stepped out and looked up into the man's serious brown eyes. She noticed how long his eyelashes were, and that's when it happened. Reality snapped back and locked into place with an audible *ka-chunk*. The world around her spun as if realigning and when it righted itself, Jackie knew beyond a shadow of a doubt that she wasn't hallucinating. She wasn't in a coma or fever dream. She was in West Virginia.

Jackie swayed as if the ground beneath her feet had become unsteady. She leaned into Sam, latching onto his bicep.

Sam took hold of her arm. "Whoa. You okay?"

The full avalanche of implications crashed down on Jackie in that moment, and she didn't know what to answer. *Am I okay?*

"Why don't you sit back down for a minute?"

Jackie diverted her eyes from Sam's gaze and whispered, "You're real."

"Yes, ma'am. C'mon, sit down."

This is happening. Jackie put out a hand to the car, steadying herself further. "I'm okay." It was a lie, but she said what she always said in response to that question. She was always okay. Always. For Jasper. Because someone had to be. Because it was who *she* had to be.

"Hey," said Sam. "If you're in some kind of trouble, we can help. You don't have to go straight back to whatever you're running from."

"What?"

"Lu and Card are happy to put you up for a while." Sam was staring at her bruise again. "You'll be safe there."

"No. It's not like that." Jackie pulled away from Sam's support. "I'm okay. I just got up too fast. Thanks, Mr. Taxi Man."

"It's Sam."

"Thanks, Sam. Drive safe." Jackie took a deep breath, hugged her purse to her chest, and headed into the bus station. She heard Sam shut the car door behind her.

The station was tiny, with cathedral ceilings, and three pairs of dirty double doors lined up on the far wall. The only other living soul in the place was a woman knitting inside the ticket booth. She wore fingerless gloves and one of those hats with ear flaps. Setting aside her yarn, she said, "Howdy."

"Hello," Jackie replied. "I need a ticket to Arlington, Virginia, please."

"Sure. Should be here in about an hour." The woman rang up the ticket and took Jackie's debit card.

Jackie roamed the station. It was too cold to sit still. She found a rickety old dispensing machine and bought a little kit with a toothbrush and toothpaste, a tiny deodorant, a thin washcloth, and a hotel-sized bar of soap. It felt like Christmas.

After freshening up in the scarred bathroom, she wandered around the waiting room. Every time someone came in from outside, Jackie jumped, thinking it was Lu or Card, or Cupid's butler come to find her.

The bus took its sweet time. When it rolled in with its stinking exhaust and exchange of people, Jackie climbed aboard and sidled down the aisle, looking for an empty seat. She went to the back where she could sit by the window. Tucking her purse in between her body and the wall, she relaxed. She was on her way home. The bus ride would last six and a half hours, but that was okay. That should put her in the city in time for dinner. In the meantime, she watched the tiny tinsel-covered towns scroll by, with their rolling drifts of snow and their Christmas decorations all in place. The bus stopped at every single one, though few people got on or off the bus.

Late in the afternoon, the bus arrived at a dirty backwater town abandoned by the industry that had brought it to life in the first place. Factories made of brick and old watermills sat beside a river that sparkled in the weak winter sunshine.

On the intercom, the driver announced, "We'll be here for thirty minutes. There's toilets inside the station and a café for food and drink. I won't wait for you if you're late getting back, so don't dawdle."

Jackie got off the bus with everyone else, happy for a chance to stretch her legs. She felt anonymous as she moved with the group into the station. Her first stop was the ladies' room where she stood in line for the next available stall and was reminded how much she hated public restrooms. With great care, and using toilet paper as a barrier, she made it out alive.

The café was small and adorably country, with a theme of roosters and banjoes. Even the Christmas music was twangy. There too, Jackie had to stand in line, but she was finally able to order a ham sandwich, potato chips, and a small drink. She sat in the corner by the window, where she could keep an eye on the bus driver. He'd walked to the other side of the parking lot and was talking on his cellphone while smoking.

Jackie's phone rang. She looked at it. "Two bars," she said to herself. "I guess I'm getting closer to civilization."

When she saw who it was—Jazz's school—her heart fluttered uneasily. They never called unless they needed money from her or if Jazz was sick or in trouble.

"Hello? This is Jackie Li."

"Miss Li, this is Principal Alders."

"Is Jazz okay?"

"Impossible to tell." The principal sounded sarcastic. "He didn't show up at school today. I got worried when the secretary told me you hadn't called. You're diligent about such matters—usually—so I thought I should reach out."

Jackie sighed. "I appreciate it, Mr. Alders."

The principal's tone darkened. "Miss Li, if he gets one more unexplained absence, he will lose his chance for the Hardy Music Scholarship."

Jackie's jaw clenched. "Oh. I didn't realize."

"Yes. They don't base their decision solely on a student's talent and scholarship but also on their attendance."

"Oh no."

The principal cleared his throat as if about to deliver something distasteful. "I would be amiss if I didn't warn you that this kind of behavior could have repercussions for his future."

Jackie took a deep breath. "I understand. I'll have a talk with him. Did any of his friends also skip?"

"Very astute of you to ask," Alders said. "Leena Johnson has also gone A.W.O.L."

"I see." Jackie watched the bus driver crush his cigarette under his heel and head back to the bus. "I have to go, but I promise, Jazz will be in class tomorrow. Thank you for calling."

Jackie hung up, discarded her trash, and *gently* pushed through the diner's door. "Safe not sorry," she muttered to herself when she didn't put anyone in a coma.

Crossing the parking lot, arms wrapped around herself against the cold and misery, a glimmer caught her eye. A woman had fallen into step beside her, a sequin-covered cream beret on her head. The woman smiled.

"Trouble with your kid, huh?" she asked, expression friendly. "Sorry, but I couldn't help but overhear."

Jackie nodded. "Yeah. Skipped school."

"I know your pain," the woman said with sympathy. "Got three of my own."

"He's a good kid," Jackie told her. "He's got a chance at a music scholarship, if he'd straighten up. He seems to think he knows better than everyone else what's best for him."

"Rebellious. My oldest was a terror when she got to that stage. There was a time when I thought she and I would never reconcile our differences. You hang in there. It may take years, but they always come around. You're still his mom." The woman smiled, and Jackie returned it with one of her own.

They stepped up onto the bus, and the woman sat with her companion. Jackie moved back to her own seat.

Only four more hours to home, she told herself. Only four more hours and she'd be walking into the little apartment she shared with her brother. Jazz would be home from school, probably playing a video game with his best friend. He'd ask her where she'd been, then they'd laugh at the story of her night. He'd tease her, and she'd swat him. Then, they'd have frozen French fries and chicken strips for dinner. Jackie couldn't wait.

The bus left the rest stop on time. It pulled out on the next leg of its journey, and Jackie settled in. Energy sapped, she put her coat between her head and the window and closed her eyes. The constant hum of the bus lulled her, stilled her mind's usual rush, and drove her straight into Sleepy Town.

♥

Jackie shot upright and opened her eyes, her consciousness torn from sleep by a sudden change in the sounds around her. The hum of the bus had stopped.

Bed. Jewel tones. Fireplace.

CHAPTER 6

I'm back at Gray Fox," Jackie said aloud, in disbelief. She looked at herself. She was completely dressed including shoes and purse lying beside her. "Seriously?" she huffed in frustration.

She swung her legs off the edge of the bed and just sat there in a state of confusion, staring out at the dawn-colored sky. The clock on the bedside table said it was 5 A.M.

"Maybe I *should* call the police." As soon as the words left her mouth, she knew it was a terrible idea. *They'll think I need sedation.*

Jackie stood and paced. "This is ridiculous. I have to get out of here." She pulled out her phone. The bus was too slow. With a few clicks of online research, Jackie learned that the nearest airport was an hour and a half away. She could fly. It was six times more expensive, but it would get her home faster than the bus. Once again, she called the cab company.

Jackie was waiting outside when Sam pulled up. She didn't wait for him to get out but opened the back door and climbed in.

When he saw her, a look of confusion pinched his face. "How did you—" His service manners kicked in, and he cut off his own question. "Still no luggage?" he asked.

"No, no luggage."

"Where to?"

"Roanoke. To the airport."

"That's ninety minutes away. I charge extra for trips longer than an hour."

"Okay. Just get me there. Please."

Sam met Jackie's eyes in the rearview mirror. "Yes, ma'am." He turned the radio to a Christmas station and pulled around the circular driveway.

"What time is it?" Jackie asked.

Sam glanced at his watch and replied, "Eight-fifty-three. What time do you need to be there?"

"My flight boards at ten-thirty."

"Well," Sam drawled. "We'll be cutting it close, but have no fear. I'll get you there on time, safe and sound."

"Thank you." Jackie let the warmth of the cab wash over her. She studied the driver for lack of anything better to do. It was the first time she really looked at him. Out of habit, she noticed his wedding ring then took a clinical approach to evaluating him. *Sturdy,* she thought, *in a farmboy sort of way.* He had straight brown hair, cut short by someone whose primary goal was efficiency, not elegance. Though he was probably unaware of it, his hair was messy in back, as if he hadn't bothered to comb it that morning. He sported five o'clock stubble that didn't detract from his looks, and his mouth had a pleasant cant to it. *I bet,* she thought, *he's a wonderful daddy.*

"How many kids do you have?" Jackie asked.

"None."

"I heard them when I called for the cab. Sounded like a dozen or so."

Sam laughed. "Oh, those kids. There's only three, but they're rascals. You got any?"

"No." Jackie didn't want to get into it. Jazz was her only living family, and they were a team. Jacquelyn and Jasper—Jackie and Jazz—against the world. "I don't have time for marriage."

"How come?"

"I just don't believe in Happily Ever After anymore. Relationships are too much work and not enough return."

Sam's eyebrows shot up.

Jackie back-paddled, "Not yours, though. I'm sure your marriage is wonderful. The exception to the rule."

Sam nodded, watching Jackie squirm in the rearview. "Are you a lesbian then?" he asked.

Shocked by his frankness, Jackie said, "Only about ten percent. Thanks for asking."

Sam laughed, "Good answer."

"Has it ever occurred to you," Jackie suggested, "that it's not a great idea to ask such personal questions in your cab?"

"You started it." He glanced into the rearview mirror at her.

They both fell silent. The car was eating up the asphalt, cruising along the highway at sixty-five miles an hour. Jackie took a deep breath. *Home soon,* she reminded herself.

Sam asked, "So, what do you do for a living?"

Jackie hated that question. She wished she could tell him she was a clinical psychologist with a degree from a prestigious university, but it would be a lie. She replied, "I'm a waiter." Saying it aloud always made her feel small, which then made her ashamed of herself. She added her standard defensive explanation. "It's good honest work. I get plenty of exercise, and there's job security. People won't ever stop eating."

Sam laughed into the mirror, and his eyes crinkled at the corners. "So true."

Jackie let the conversation drop. She leaned her forehead against the cool window and closed her eyes, hoping the driver would take a hint. He did.

After a while, she opened them again to watch the scenery. Urban buildings began appearing, industrial, then residential, then industrial again.

Jackie saw a sign that said, "Welcome to Virginia. Virginia is for lovers." It had a big red heart on it.

The next sign that caught her eye said, "Roanoke-Blacksburg Regional Airport." Three miles to go.

Sitting up straighter, Jackie asked, "What time is it, please?"

Sam checked his watch and replied, "Ten eighteen. Hope you got your running shoes on. The airport isn't big, but they take pride in sending you from one end to the other to catch your flight."

"I'll be okay." Jackie's shoes weren't running shoes, but they weren't heels either. She'd given up wearing those when she'd started waiting tables. She found her boarding pass on her phone, checking her gate number.

Sam pulled up at the Departures door. She paid him with her credit card, wincing at the total. *I wonder,* she thought as she got out of the cab, *if I can charge this to Cupid.*

"Have a safe trip," Sam called.

"Thanks. Have a great life."

"I'll give it my best shot," Sam replied.

Jackie shut the car door. She turned and scooted through the entrance, trotting toward Security.

In line to board, Jackie felt like she'd been traveling for a year. The plane was a small one, carrying only fifty passengers. Jackie made her way to the back, pushing past and squeezing through the other passengers in the aisle. Because she'd booked so late, she was forced to sit in the last empty seat, by the toilets, in the middle seat. On one side, she had a gangly college kid whose music blared out of his earbuds just loud enough to scrape against Jackie's nerves. On the other, sat a round grandma, who took out her knitting the moment she settled in.

The plane took off on time, and Jackie did a tiny celebratory dance in her seat. *Home soon.*

The hard part was over.

Jackie took a cab from the airport to home, willing to pay the price for convenience after everything that had happened. She watched out the window, and a sense of relief washed over her. She could get back to business as normal—even if that business involved giving Jazz hell for skipping school.

When she arrived at their apartment, Jackie's brother was on the couch, playing video games with his best friend, Michael Rasmussen—Razz for short, the other half of Razz and Jazz. They'd met as sophomores, and what used to be "Jackie and Jazz against the world" had become "Razz and Jazz against the world." Jackie tried not to resent the kid. He was a good guy, didn't do drugs, and got excellent grades. Still, Jackie was jealous of how close the boys were, and how much less close she and Jazz had become since they'd met.

They didn't even notice her come in.

The smell of home hit her square in the face, and she almost cried. She paused just inside the door, closed her eyes, and breathed a sigh of relief. Suddenly, everything that had happened became a dream. *This here,* Jackie thought. *This is real life.*

"Your sister's here," said Razz with the barest glance over

his shoulder at her. He was a short, soft kid with hair that was too long—by Jackie's estimation—and jeans that never quite fit him.

"Hey!" called Jazz, without looking away from the game. "How was jail?"

"I wasn't in jail." Jackie moved away from the threshold and into the living room/dining room combo. She relished being home, doing the usual things she did—taking off her coat, hanging it up, dropping her shoes by the door, and stowing her purse in a bureau drawer.

"Whatever. Bonnie called and filled me in." He continued pressing the buttons on his controller, killing bad guys. Multitasking. "When can we go get my new kicks?"

Some days, she went through life surrounded by a pack of angry, ill-trained worry-dogs intent on killing her and consuming her dead body. One yappy dog of worry woke from its nap to nip at Jackie's heels. Its name was *Money*. She hadn't seen it since waking up in West Virginia—not until Jazz had reminded her he needed new shoes.

Another annoying worry dog came along behind that one. It's name was *Jazz's Future*. It growled at her, baring its teeth. Its loyal packmate was *Lost Scholarships*, a nasty beast that danced around her, trying to bite her fingers.

Jackie didn't want to spoil her homecoming by snapping at Jazz, but the cacophony of worry dogs was already giving her a headache.

"Jazz." Jackie ignored his question about the shoes. "I left you a ton of messages on your phone. I was worried."

"Yeah, my phone died."

Jackie moved to stand by the couch. "Why didn't you charge it?"

"I kinda dropped it in the toilet, and now it won't turn on. Can I get one of the new models, since we have to get me a new one anyway?"

Another worry appeared out of nowhere. Its bark was the annoying, repetitive yap of a hyperactive chihuahua. Jackie knew it well. Its name was *I Have To Be The Bad Guy, Again*.

She did a full-body sigh, dropping her head back. The plane and bus fares had tapped her out until her next paycheck. If she hadn't ended up in West Virginia... If she hadn't barged through that diner door at a hundred angry miles an hour... If she hadn't given Mitch a second, third, and fourth chance...

"We don't have the money."

Razz looked up at Jackie in surprise. "He's *gotta* try out for the basketball team," he said, as if that settled the matter.

"Razz! Watch out!" Jazz bumped against his friend and waved his controller at the screen.

"Sorry. I got it. Damn. Where'd that douche come from?"

Jackie sat in the armchair, her armchair. It enfolded her like a hug, and she pulled the soft lap blanket over her legs. "You have dinner yet?"

Jazz nodded toward a fast food bag on the floor by Razz's feet. "Razz brought us a snack. There might be some fries left, if you want 'em."

"That's a miracle," Jackie replied, amused.

"I said, 'might,'" Jazz replied.

Razz took his eyes off the screen to study Jackie for a few seconds before asking, "You out on bail?"

Exasperated, Jackie snapped, "I *wasn't* in jail. It was an accident."

Jazz slammed the A button several times in quick succession, "That what *he* says?"

"I bet he's gonna sue you," Razz tossed out.

"He who?"

Jazz replied, "The guy you killed."

"I didn't kill him. I just... put him in a coma."

"He gonna be okay?" For a moment, Jasper gave her his full attention, peering at her with intent, dark eyes that so reminded her of their mother.

"Jazz," said his friend, trying to get Jazz's attention back on the screen.

Jackie had attracted a new worry dog, and she called this one, "Coma Guy."

"Jazz. C'mon, man."

Jackie thought of Georgio Kupidopoulos lying in his hospital bed. "His name is Georgio," she told them, her vision going vague as her focus turned inward. "He hit his head pretty hard."

"Left, left!" cried Jazz.

"Roger," replied Razz.

It hadn't occurred to Jackie that Georgio or his family might sue her. She wondered if her having left the inn would make them retaliate? Movement in the corner of her mind caught her attention, and the biggest worry dog stalked forward, its eyes glowing red, accusatory.

I haven't done anything wrong, she thought. *It was an accident. This nonsense has to stop. I'm home now. They can't whisk me away again... can they?*

The worry named "Cupid" lolled its tongue out with a big grin.

Jackie blinked and said, "Oh no, you don't."

"What?" asked Jazz.

"Nothing." Jackie pushed aside the lap blanket and stood. "How about I make you guys a proper dinner." Cooking was the best way for Jackie to ditch the pack of worries running through her brain, and food was the most efficient way to get Jazz off the game console. Once he was, she could send Razz on his way and have that talk about truancy and lost scholarships.

Dinner included baked chicken strips and French fries—Jazz's favorites. It took a few summonses, but Jazz and Razz paused their game and came to the table. Typical boys, ever hungry, they dug right in, fingers in the lead and yammering in gamer-speak about "weapon stats" and "spawn points." Jackie put the ketchup, a roll of paper towels, salt and pepper out on the table for them. She served them both glasses of soda.

Under normal circumstances, she'd have eaten with them, but that night, her appetite had fled. So, while the boys ate, Jackie secluded herself in her bedroom.

The mismatched pack of worries settled in around her and just stared.

Jackie called Bonnie. "Hey, it's me. I fell asleep on the bus yesterday... and woke up this morning, in West Virginia, again."

"What do you mean? You're still there?"

"No, I'm home now. Somehow, they took me there without my permission or knowledge—twice. It happened when I visited Coma Guy in the hospital. Then it happened again when I tried to take the bus home. I woke up in that freakin' inn. I have no memory of getting there. So I skipped out again. I just left. I flew this time and now I'm home. I made it."

"Wait, is this some kind of metaphor? PTSD? Groundhog Day? You sound...scattered."

"Bonnie, what if it happens again?"

"What are you afraid will happen?"

"I'm afraid I'll fall asleep and wake up back at Gray Fox. You have to spend the night here with me."

Bonnie didn't even hesitate. "Yeah, sure. I'll hit the store and bring chocolate. We can kick Jazz to his room and watch a couple rom-coms. Unless he likes that sort of thing too?"

"He might. Thanks, Bon. You're the best."

"See you soon. Smooch!"

Everything was returning to normal. She'd have to work a few extra shifts to make up for the money she lost—okay, a whole buttload of extra shifts—but that was no big deal. She was used to doing that whenever Jazz needed new clothes, books, or sports equipment. If she saw Georgio's handler, she'd ask him for some reimbursement. Although she'd be just as happy if he never appeared again.

Jackie smiled and relaxed. She took a hot shower to wash off the taxi, bus, and airport stank. Once her skin could breathe again, Jackie yawned big.

By the time she returned to the dining table, Razz and Jazz were focused on their game, *Warchomp*. So much for an after-dinner conversation. It would have to wait until the next day. With the sound of death and destruction in the background, Jackie sat to make a list of everything she wanted to do the next morning before work:

1. Talk to Jazz about skipping school.
2. Write a Yelp review for the Gray Fox. *She owed them that, at least.*
3. Stop by the hospital to see how Georgio was doing.
4. Call the lawyer, a.k.a. the cupid handler, and tell him to stay the hell away. Threaten with a restraining order if necessary.

As promised, Bonnie arrived with chocolate and wine. Her appearance scared the boys into Jazz's room to watch videos on their laptops, and the women had the living room all to themselves. They took up positions on either end of the couch.

"Wanna play *Warchomp* with me?" Jackie asked, joking.

Bonnie laughed. "I'd just kick your ass." She handed Jackie a glass of Merlot. "We've got the serious wine tonight."

"Perfect." Jackie raised her glass in salute. "You always know what I need, Bon."

They both sipped, and then Bonnie said, "By the way, don't worry about your shifts. Your lawyer came by yesterday afternoon and explained—"

Jackie held up a hand to stop her. "My lawyer? I don't have a lawyer."

Confusion settled on Bonnie's features. "Some grumpy dude with a weird accent?"

Grumpy dude with a weird accent, huh? That had to have been Georgio's handler.

Even though Jackie was home, she couldn't seem to escape her situation.

Bonnie continued, "Fancy suit. I bet he's expensive, but don't worry. We set out a tin for donations to help you pay for him."

"A tin?"

"Yeah, it's no trouble. Everybody loves you and wants to help you get through this."

"Oh my god. What did this... lawyer say?"

"He said you couldn't work for a couple weeks, that's all. Roy's already hired a short-term waiter to cover while you're gone. I worked a shift with her today, and there's no way he'll keep her if he can get you back, so you don't have to worry about your job."

"What else did he say?"

"He couldn't give details, but there might be a suit for recompense in the works, if you don't show enough remorse."

"What?" Jackie's heart raced.

Bonnie leaned forward and put her hand on Jackie's knee. "Honey, is that why you went to West Virginia?"

"No! I didn't come here on my own. He brought me here. Twice. Honest, Bon. I'm not making this up."

"I wouldn't blame you if you were. You deserve a few days at a retreat. I'd be totally freaking out right now if I were you. I mean, thank god Roy's got insurance. Let's just hope that guy doesn't die. You don't think he'll die, do you?"

Jackie watched another worry join the rest of the pack. Its

name was Dead Cupid. Her chest had a fat knot in it. She deflated. "I hope not."

"You can counter sue. I mean, you were injured too. It's partially his fault. Then, you could take the money and go back to college, finish your Psych degree. How awesome would that be?"

"I'm not going to sue him. It was my fault, Bon. And besides, I'd use the money to pay for Jazz's tuition first. He's gifted."

"And you're not?"

"Not like him and his cello."

"Hey! Chin up, little chica." Bonnie put an arm around Jackie's shoulders. "Your bro will get rich and take of you for a change, right? That wouldn't be so bad either."

Bonnie gave her a squeeze and added, "I looked up manslaughter on the Web, and apparently they can't charge you with murder unless you were doing something criminal when the death you caused happened. So, you're safe there. Of course, that doesn't protect you from a civil suit."

Jackie groaned. "Well, I can have *them* charged with kidnapping."

"Okay," Bonnie mused. "As my therapist likes to say, let's unpack that. You seriously have no idea how you got to West Virginia? You sure you were there?"

"Sure as taxes," Jackie replied. "

"Why? Why would they kidnap you and drop you at a fancy retreat in another state, then not lock you in?"

"They want me to be a cupid."

"A what?"

"You know, a cupid. They get people to fall in love."

"Oh, a matchmaker? My aunt Ruth on my mom's side is renowned for that. She's got a gift. It's like magic. You could use one of those to help you find the right man."

A flash of annoyance heated her cheeks. "I don't need a matchmaker, *Mom*." She changed the subject back. "Georgio is scheduled to do a marriage-counseling seminar at the Gray Fox Inn in West Virginia, and they wanted me to run it instead."

Bonnie leaned to one side and picked her bag up off the floor. She pulled out a laptop and set it on her lap. "Tell you what. Let's do some research. What did you say that guy's name is?"

"Here, let me put it in. It's long."

Jackie input "Georgio Kupidopoulos." She turned so they could both see the screen.

The first entry on the list turned out to be the Gray Fox Inn's website. It had an informational page about the seminar. For a brief second or two, it showed Georgio's name and picture... until it didn't. Jackie stared at her own face, her own name in big, bold, black letters. "Dr. Jacquelyn Li."

Bonnie and Jackie gasped in near-unison.

"Oh my god!" Jackie shut the laptop as if it held a snake and shoved it at Bonnie. "That's what the brochure did. You saw that, right?"

Bonnie tried to make sense of it. "They must have updated the page."

Jackie stood and paced. She stopped in the middle of the living room and shouted up at the ceiling, "I'm not doing it! You hear me? I refuse!"

As the evening progressed and the wine bottle's contents receded, Jackie's thoughts turned to Mitch.

"He dumped me, Bonnie," she said, voice full of misery. "On my birthday. By text. What is wrong with me?"

"There's nothing wrong with you. Mitch is a jerk. You can do better."

"I'm twenty-nine. Next year, I'll be freakin' thirty! All my friends from high school and college are married now. Some of them have kids. Why am I wasting my life? I've got a crappy job..."

"Hey!" Bonnie cried, mock-offended. When Jackie opened her mouth to apologize, Bonnie shook her head, "No, you're right. It is a crappy job."

Jackie picked at a loose thread on the upholstery. "I missed the party boat. I'm standing on a dock in the dark waving as my friends toast me with champagne glasses from the starboard deck."

Bonnie sighed. "Twenty-nine is nothing."

"Says the woman who's still twenty-eight."

"Not for long."

Jackie swirled the wine in her glass. "You'd tell me if there was something wrong with me, wouldn't you, Bon?"

"Honey, there is nothing wrong with you. You're awesome. If there was anything you could work on, it would be..."

"Yeah?" Jackie perked up a bit. "What?"

"You need more confidence. Trust yourself and take some risks."

Jackie recoiled. "I can't afford to take risks."

"Okay," Bonnie conceded, "but you can worry less. Take better care of yourself."

Jackie laughed. "I'm too busy taking care of everything else. I don't even remember the last time I spent an hour in a bubble bath with a sexy romance novel. God, I miss those days. Everything was so easy in college. They prepared the food for you, gave you a place to live, and all you had to do for it was study. I was fantastic at studying. These days, I'm flying by the seat of my pants, always in crisis mode."

Bonnie patted Jackie's knee. "You're doing a great job. It's okay to slack off from time to time."

"I don't know."

Bonnie leaned forward. "Repeat after me. I'm an adult."

Jackie: "I'm an adult."

Bonnie: "I'm a strong woman."

Jackie: "I'm a strong woman."

Bonnie: "I take care of myself, and I don't need a man or anyone else to take care of me."

Jackie hesitated before mimicking the words, "I take care of myself. I don't need a man or anybody else to take care of me."

With a squeeze to Jackie's knee, Bonnie lifted her wine glass for a toast. "To strong women."

Jackie clinked her glass against Bonnie's and repeated, "To strong women."

CHAPTER 7

The next morning, Jackie awoke refreshed... surrounded by jewel tones, velvety curtains, and a crackling fireplace.

"OH MY GOD!" Jackie cried. "You have got to be kidding me!" She threw back the covers to discover she was still wearing her pajamas, the ones she'd put on for her sleepover with Bonnie: flannel pants with Santa faces all over them. One of the Santas winked at her. It shocked her. Then, she remembered that half the Santas were winking, the other half not.

At the end of the bed, she found a pair of spa slippers wrapped in plastic. She slipped them on and scoured the room for her purse and clothes. Her running monologue took on greater alarm with each passing moment.

"Dammit! They're not here. My credit card. My I.D. My PHONE!" Other expletives came to mind, and she indulged in a few of them as she threw open the door to her room and stormed out.

She stomped down the hall toward the curving staircase.

"No way," she grumbled aloud, hands clenched in fists. "I refuse! Do you hear me, cupid guy? I refuse! I'll *get home* if I have to walk there!"

One of Jackie's slippers fell off. She put it back on, hopping on one foot, and switched to a shuffling run that kept her feet in them, talking to herself the whole way. "Third time's a charm, right? Right?" Jackie's voice carried across the lobby, but she didn't notice. "You can't keep me here against my will!"

Jackie hurried down the stairs. Her rant sped up with each step, words coming faster and faster. "I sling burgers and sodas. I'm not qualified to fix marriages. I don't know anything about love. Hell, I can't even keep a boyfriend. Worse, they break up with me on my birthday... by text! I'm a misery magnet. I am cursed!" She arrived at the ground floor and stopped cold.

Sam, the cab driver, was standing there, watching her with his head cocked to one side, like a confused dog. He opened his mouth to say something, but before he could, Jackie lifted her index finger to shush him.

"Yes," she said. "I'm back. No, I'm not happy about it." She looked down at herself. "And yes, I'm wearing Santa pajamas. Just don't go anywhere. I may need a ride."

Sam watched as she crossed her arms over her chest and hurried toward the business office. Her slippers slapped on the polished wooden floor. Sam's boot heels tapped in counterpoint as he followed her—until, at the office door, Jackie did an about-face.

She demanded, "Are you following me?"

Sam halted. "Kinda. Are you all right?"

Jackie stared at him with enormous eyes. In her mind, she ranted. *No, I'm not all right. A supernatural asshole is forcing me to be here against my will, even though I kind of agreed to it, but now I don't want it. I'm not who they think I am. I can't do this!*

Aloud, she said, "I'm *fine*." She was dangerously close to tears. Jackie's plans had crashed and burned, and she had no idea what to do next. She could try to leave again, but that was getting expensive, and she didn't even *have* her credit card anymore.

Falling asleep was the problem, and she couldn't stay awake forever. She was stuck. The realization hit her like a bucket of ice water.

"The only way out is through." Jackie deflated, all the fight flowing out of her. She leaned against the business center's door jamb. "I'm tired," she said. "Tired... and cold." She realized she was shivering.

"Follow me," said Sam. "I know just what you need." He took a few steps then looked back, head tipping in invitation. "It'll make you feel better." His smile warmed Jackie a bit.

"Don't you have a home to go home to?" Jackie asked weakly, falling into step behind him. She had no will of her own, or so it felt. Might as well trust this nice man with the pleasant face and nice... *Married man.* Jackie pulled her thoughts up short. "Where are we going?"

"To the most comfortable spot in this whole place." Sam led her into the restaurant, to a set of couches tucked to one side. The nook occupied a hidden space behind a grandiose fireplace designed to be viewed from either side. The fire drew Jackie, and she huddled next to it, stretching her hands out into the warmth. On either side of her, bay windows looked out on the patio and tree line. Jackie felt a pulse of childish delight when she realized it was snowing again. Then she remembered she didn't want to be there.

Jackie sighed.

Sam told her, "They don't use the heater down here on the first floor until all the guests arrive for the holiday retreat. It saves energy." He stepped in close to her, hand on her shoulder, and he whispered next to her ear, "If I leave you alone for a few minutes, can I trust you not to throw yourself off a balcony or run barefoot into the forest?"

Jackie's upper lip curled, and she peered at him sideways. "That's not funny."

"Didn't mean it to be. Stay here. I'll be right back. There's a lap throw on the couch over there, if you want it."

Jackie wanted it. She wrapped it around herself and sat in the couch's corner, her feet tucked up under her where they might one day get warm again. She stared into the fire, letting its dance hypnotize her. Its syncopated crackling and popping would have, under other circumstances, soothed her nerves.

I'm stuck, she admitted to herself. *Stuck, stuck, stuck, stuck.* She was deluding herself by thinking she could get home, fall asleep, and not wake up back here. She'd be foolish to try it again.

For the first time, she entertained the idea of playing the role of Cupid. The people attending the seminar were expecting her to fix their relationships. *Crap!* Another wave of panic mixed with anxiety washed over Jackie.

I can't do this. I can't run a counseling seminar. He can't make me do that.

She covered her head with the blanket. Aloud, she muttered, "What am I gonna do? What the Hell am I gonna do?"

"Have some soup?" Sam had returned. "It's Lula's famous chicken noodle. Cures everything."

Jackie peeked out at him. "Really?" It smelled great. "Chicken soup for breakfast?"

Sam nodded big. "Chicken soup for anytime." He set the tray on the coffee table and took one of the two big bowls with him to the fan-backed armchair, companion to the couch. "Crackers there, if you like 'em."

"Thanks," Jackie said, more grateful than she could express. Her stomach was eating itself. She was so hungry. She picked up the bowl and a spoon and took the first bite. Warmth spread through her, from her belly outward. It was delicious. Easily the best chicken soup she'd ever had. The noodles were fat and wide, egg noodles. The chicken chunks were cut by hand, some bigger, some smaller. Vegetables crowded in among the noodles: carrot, celery, something green and leafy, and bits of onion.

They ate in silence, and by the time Jackie had finished, she was rational again, though still exhausted—the way she felt after an eight-hour shift at the diner. Mind drained. Body sore. She straightened the blanket on her, pulling it up to her chin.

"So," said Sam, failing to hide a little smile. "How come you're runnin' around in your pajamas? If you need laundry services, I can arrange that for you. Not that there's anything wrong with wearing your pajamas in public." His smile grew. "Those Santas are pretty merry."

"I don't need laundry services. I've got nothing to launder." Jackie cleared her throat. She didn't dare tell Sam about Cupid. He'd never believe her. So, she lied, "I missed my flight, but my luggage didn't. So... this is all I have."

Sam frowned. "What about the clothes you were wearing? Your shoes?"

That was a good—no, *great*—question. Jackie tried hard to find an answer. Finally, she said, "Someone spilled...paint on them. In the airport. I had to throw them away." *Ah, the webs we weave...*

Surprised, Sam just said, "Oh. And you chose Santa pajamas to replace them?"

"Don't ask."

The silence stretched between them, until Jackie added, "It's been a rough couple of days."

"I can tell. Is there someone you can call?"

"Everybody I know is in Alexandria."

"That's where you're from?" He looked at his watch.

"You late for an appointment?"

"No, sorry. I'm supposed to be meeting the doctor who's running our couple's retreat this weekend. Lula asked me to help with administrative stuff or whatever. You're lucky you're going to miss it. Sounds like an over-hyped psychologist will be pimping romance to a bunch of sappy, sad-sack married couples trying to rekindle their spark." His cynicism couldn't have been clearer.

"You sound like me," Jackie said.

"I never said I disagreed with you about relationships." Sam stood as Jackie opened her mouth to respond, and he interrupted her. "There's an old lost-and-found box behind the counter. Come on, I'll show you."

He headed for the lobby, and Jackie hurried to keep up with him.

Sam slid a cardboard box out from under the desk. Someone had written "Lost and Found" on the side in permanent marker.

Jackie dug through the box and found an oversized green sweater. It had one of Santa's elves knitted on the front and hung an inch past her hands and almost to her knees, but it was thick, and it didn't smell bad.

Almost simultaneously, they both said, "Matches your pajamas," and "Matches my pajamas."

Jackie also found pink fuzzy slipper-boots that covered her ankles and made her look like a wookie from the calves down—a hooker wookie from the 70s. Size-wise, at least, they fit her just right.

Between the soup, the fire, and the warm clothes, Jackie found her mood improving. She posed for inspection.

Sam didn't even bother to hide his laughter.

"Are you laughing at me?" Jackie asked, equally amused.

"You remind me of my Aunt Gert." His laughter burbled up and out.

Jackie stared menacingly at him, hands on her hips. "I'll have you know, Mr. Taxi Man," she said, getting into the spirit, "that these slippers give me super powers." Jackie raised and clawed her hands like a magician. "Embrace your doom, cabbie! Your time has come!"

Sam snorted, laughing without inhibition. Jackie joined him, and their eyes met again. Damn if she didn't like Sam the Taxi Man. He was funny, smart, and he had one of those subtle drawls that made everyone feel welcome, especially her.

When the eye contact went long, Jackie pulled herself away and changed topics. "Um, I need to make some outside calls. Wonder if I could use the phone in my room for that?"

Sam shrugged. "I don't see why not. They can always put the charges on your bill. You don't have your cell phone either?"

Jackie rolled her eyes. "No. It was... I..." Jackie realized she couldn't say she'd left it at home. *Webs of lies...* She said, "It was stolen. In the airport."

"Damn," said Sam. "You have had a rough couple days. Look, I can take you shopping, if you want. So you can get the things you'll need until you get home."

"Maybe," Jackie replied, thinking of her lovely credit cards sitting happily in her purse, in the drawer, in the bureau, at home. "How about I call you if I need a ride?"

"Sure. Any time." Sam's face lit up with a grin.

Jackie thought how lucky his wife was. *All the good men are taken*, her mind added.

"I'm gonna go check my email first. Thank you." Jackie turned toward the business center, took a few steps, then paused. She was carrying the throw from the couch. She did an about-face and held it out to Sam. "Thanks. I, um... thanks." She twisted away, then back again. "And for the soup too. Thanks." Under her breath, she scolded herself. "What a spazz. Jeez."

"You're welcome." Sam studied her with a twinkle in his eyes. Once again, they captured Jackie. He had extremely nice eyes. Expressive. *For a married man*, Jackie told herself. *For a married man.* She hurried across the lobby, her fuzzy slipper-boots swishing across the marble.

Jackie didn't stop until she was in the sanctuary of the business center.

CHAPTER 8

Jackie entered the inn's guest business office and flopped down in the desk chair. She blew out a huff of air and stared at the ceiling. Aloud, she said, "When will they let me go? When Kupidopoulos wakes up? What if he never does? Could I be stuck...forever?" She sat up. "I need to find out."

Bing! Jackie's plan hit the ground running. She logged into her email, checking for anything from Jazz's school—nothing, thank goodness. She did, however, have one from Bonnie.

You disappeared like gone where are you you pranking me?!! call me
Bonnie

A question mark plus two exclamation points. She must be upset.

Jackie replied to the email:

I'm okay. I woke up back in West Virginia, in my pajamas. I give up. There's no way to escape this by just running. I'm going to talk to... (There, Jackie hesitated, considering what to call the cupid handler) ...the lawyer. See if he can fix this. I'll call when I know something.

Did you mean what you said about driving up here? If so, would you mind stopping by my place on the way? I need my purse. It's in the desk in the living room. And my laptop too. It's on the kitchen counter. And my phone and charger off my bed-side table. Can you come? It's a four-hour drive. You could make it here and back in one day. Or, there's empty rooms here. I'm sure we could find you one to spend the night in. Hell, I have a king-sized bed. You could stay with me. Oh, also bring me a coat? Tell Jazz I'm okay and will be back soon.

Thanks!
Jackie
BTW, tell Jazz no parties in the apartment!

Objective #1, completed.

Jackie left the business center, tip-toed and skittered back to her room. She successfully avoided other human beings. As she entered, she found the bedroom still cozy and warm, with a fire burning in the fireplace. It sent a wave of contentedness running through her, incongruous with how she was feeling otherwise.

Next objective: *Talk to handler to negotiate a way out.* The handler had given her his business card, and it was still lying there on the desk. It said his name was "Mr. Ignacio Q. Amore, Esquire." He had told her to call when she was ready to take things seriously. She was as serious as she was going to get.

Jackie lifted the receiver on the room phone and dialed. She found her hands were shaking and hung up. *What if? What if?* A pack of worries descended upon her. They made her heart race and her brain go slippery.

"Stop!" Jackie cried aloud. "One objective at a time. I can do this." She had to prepare what she was going to say when she called him. A list of questions, that's what she needed. The questions bled from her mind, through the *Gray Fox Inn* pen, onto the *Gray Fox Inn* paper. With each one she wrote down, her mind cleared a little more.

Ready, having turned the chaos into organization, Jackie went to the phone and dialed. It rang and rang. Jackie was starting to think he wouldn't pick up, when he did.

"Hello, Jacquelyn. I imagine you have questions for me?" It was him. The gray-haired man in the suit with the hum-drum British accent. Mr. Amore.

"You bet your ass I do!" Jackie replied. "I'm out here in Boo-Foo, West Virginia, with no clothes, no cellphone, no laptop, no money, no nothing! I'm getting sick and tired of being transported... or teleported... or Valdemorted or whatever it is you're doing to me. And boy, do I have questions."

"Look," Amore said with more condescension than patience. "Now that you comprehend your situation's limitations, I'm prepared to assist you in what limited capacity I can. That does not, however, include spending hours on the phone, holding your proverbial hand while you bemoan your circumstance. I understand that you have questions."

"I have so many! Twenty-nine of them, to be exact."

"Turn around. On the bedside table, you'll find a book. It details everything about being a cupid. I suggest you read it in its entirety—that means from cover to cover." Amore wasn't just cool and collected, he was downright haughty.

"I know what that means." Jackie's hackles went up. "Mr. Amore, I do not want to do this.

"It's Amor-ay. It means 'love' in the old language."

"What'd I say?"

"Uh-more." The man mimicked a warped American accent.

Jackie cringed. "Oh. Sorry. Listen, Mr. Amore. Surely, there's some other arrangement we can make?"

"There is no other possibility. You must become a cupid. Lives depend on it."

"But..."

"Read the book."

"How long will I have to...be a cupid?"

"That depends."

"On what?"

"How successful you are. Let me check my schedule. Ah yes. Your predecessor's mission was to bless three couples by midnight on Christmas Day. That's the 25th."

"I know when Christmas Day is."

"That is now *your* mission. Complete it, and you will be absolved of responsibility. Don't complete it, and you'll try-try again until you get it right. You are required to make amends."

Jackie frowned. "Required? By who?"

"It's not who," said the lawyer. "It's whom." *Click.*

"Hello? Hello? You still there?" *Jackie stared at the receiver.* "You hung up on me?" She slammed it down in fierce retaliation. Then, with a heavy sigh, she sat back and let her arms hang limp at her sides. A thought occurred to her. Aloud, she said to herself, "I bet it's three of the couples coming for the retreat."

Her attention came to rest on a bright pink envelope tucked into the book from Amore. Jackie glanced around the room, but nothing else appeared out of place.

The envelope had her name on it, in an elegant anachronous script. Jackie opened it, and a debit card fell out. It belonged to a company called Love, Inc. There was a note.

Ms. Li,
Please find enclosed a debit card for your use. It will
assist you in solving some of the challenges you're
facing. You are allowed a per diem of $222, to be
used as you see fit. The deposits occur daily at 6:00
A.M. Eastern Time Zone.
Sincerely,
I.M. Amore, esquire

It was too late to go shopping that evening, but in the morning, she'd be up and at 'em quicker than Sam could say "Yes, ma'am."

Jackie called the front desk.

A woman answered, "Yes, Dr. Li. How may I help you?" It was Frankie. Jackie recognized the dry, unamused tone.

"Hi, Frankie. Do you know if Sam is still around? I'd like to go shopping in the morning, if he's available."

"I'll let him know."

"Great, thank you." Jackie was about to hang up when her stomach gave a loud gurgle. "Oh wait!"

"Yes?"

"Would it be possible to get room service?"

Frankie sighed audibly. "Sure, what do you want?"

"A burger? And a salad? That would be perfect."

"Rare, medium, or burned?"

"Medium."

"Dressing?"

"Italian."

"It'll be fifteen minutes."

"All right, thank—"

Frankie hung up.

"—you." Jackie harrumphed. "Grumpy much, Frankie?"

With food en route, Jackie was feeling down-right up-beat. She sat on the bed and turned on the television to wait.

Five minutes later, the phone rang. Jackie muted the cooking show and hopped up to answer it. "Hello?"

Frankie said, "It's for you," and then there was a click, and Bonnie's voice came through the line. "...more soda? Oh, it's iced tea? Got it."

"Bonnie?"

"Oh, hey, sugar. So, I talked to the hubs, and we'll come tomorrow, okay? We'll drive out together. I'm not about to pass up a vacation at a country inn. You sure you can get us a room? I don't think you'd like having both of us in your bed, even if it *is* a king. Unless, maybe you *need* a puppy pile?"

Jackie laughed, and then so did Bonnie. Jackie said, "I'll ask if they can give you a room. I'll tell them you're my assistant. When can you get here?"

"We'll leave first thing tomorrow morning, so noonish? Oneish? You want to text me the address?"

"I'll email it to you. Can you stop by my place?"

"You betcha. I'll grab your things."

"Thank you! And let Jazz know I'll be gone for a few days. I'll be back for Christmas, though. I'm not giving up."

"On it, boss!" Bonnie sounded excited.

A knock came on Jackie's door. "Bon, I gotta go. My room service is here."

"Room service! Livin' in the lap of luxury. See you tomorrow!"

"Thanks, Bon." They hung up at the same time. It was oddly satisfying.

To Jackie's surprise, Lu was waiting outside the door. The innkeeper broke into a big smile and announced, "Room service!"

"Thank you," Jackie said, following her to the desk where she set the tray.

Lu lifted the cover off the plate. "Hamburger, medium. All the condiments. And a salad. Frankie put the dressing on the side for you. And I cut you a piece of pumpkin pie, just 'cuz."

"This looks delicious." Jackie's stomach growled in agreement. "All I've had to eat today was that amazing chicken soup."

Lu tilted her head cock-eyed and squinted at Jackie. "You ain't one of those girls who's always on a diet, are you?"

Jackie shook her head vehemently. "No. I have a seventeen-year-old brother who makes sure I eat plenty of junk food."

Lu laughed. "That's good. Well, I'll leave you to it. Call down if you need anything else."

"Um, Lu?" Jackie asked. "I'd like to ask a favor, if you don't mind. I need help with a few things, and..."

"Oh!" said Lu. "You haven't met Sam yet! He's been busy with taxi clients, so he hasn't been around much. He can help you with whatever you need."

"I'm sure he can. But, I have my regular assistant coming tomorrow to bring me some things I need. My laptop and other stuff. Could she have a room for the night? For her and her husband?"

Lu had appeared concerned, maybe even confused, but when the request was out in the open, she smiled and seemed relieved. "Absolutely! We have plenty of empty rooms. They can stay as long as you want them to. Even with the couples coming, we won't have a full house. How about I put them in the room next door? For convenience."

"You are so kind," said Jackie. "I can't tell you how much I appreciate it."

"It is no trouble at all. You're the one doing us a favor.

Don't you hesitate to ask if there's anything else you need." She touched Jackie's arm, and Jackie warmed even more to the other woman.

Jackie ate her hamburger and salad. She decided to save the pie for a midnight snack and tucked it in her mini-fridge. As she passed the full-length mirror, she caught a look at herself—oversized elf sweater, Santa pajama pants, and bed-messy hair. "Such a pretty princess," she told herself with a smile and twirled around.

A knock on the door surprised Jackie mid-spin.

"Housekeeping," said a small, timid voice.

Jackie went to the door, undid the bolt, and opened it. On the other side stood a woman who looked to be in her late thirties, early forties, wearing a uniform of white pants, white shirt, and a bright-red full-body apron that said, "Happy Holidays from the Gray Fox Inn." She had brown hair, cut in an asymmetrical bob, and her face had hard edges—more handsome than pretty, and certainly not soft.

"Good evening," she said with a hint of a smile and a gentle drawl. "My name's Mary. Is there anything you need?"

"Nice to meet you. I'm Jackie. I don't think I need anything, but thank you."

Mary asked, "Would you like me to stoke your fire?"

Jackie blinked. "Excuse me?"

The woman stifled a bigger smile and blushed a bit. At the same time, Jackie realized she meant the fireplace.

"Oh," Jackie said. "Yes, please, come in." Jackie sat down to wait for Mary to be done.

Mary crossed to the fireplace.

Jackie asked, "Mary?"

"Yes, ma'am?" Mary stopped and faced Jackie.

"How many guests are staying in the hotel?"

Mary looked surprised. "Right now? Just you. We've only got bedrooms made up for the couples' retreat. I'll be preparing another one for your assistant and her husband. We close up the third floor in winter. We don't get much business this time of year. Most folks are at home with their families."

Jackie considered that. It said something about the couples coming for the seminar—choosing to spend Christmas away from their fa*milies.*

Mary moved aside the fire screen, took up the poker, and crouched down, poking at the embers.

Jackie settled on the bed. "How many people work here?"

Mary used the shovel and bucket to move ash out from around the embers, "Well, let's see. There's Lu and Card, they're the owners. There's me. I keep the place clean. And there's Frankie. She does some cookin' and tends the bar when folks are here. And then there's Sam, who helps out a bunch. He only comes around when he's needed, though. He's a handyman and drives the car, does odd jobs around the place. Picks up groceries, stuff like that."

"Just the four of you?"

"Yup. We get busy when guests come, but not too bad. I'm just sad we don't have as many guests as we used to. This couple's thing was Lu's idea. We need something like that to get folks in the door. I'm glad you're here. Otherwise, I might've been laid off for the holidays."

"Laid off?"

"Sure. Without guests, the Gray Fox can't afford to pay me. I don't blame 'em. I'm just saying... I'm glad you're here."

"Are you married?"

Mary smiled. "Yes, ma'am. I got three kids. Me and my man been together for ten years next month."

"Congratulations."

"Thank you. What about you? You married?"

"Nope. Never met a guy who could put up with me."

Mary laughed. "There's a lot of mangy dogs out there. Don't let that discourage you. Pays to be picky."

Jackie shrugged. "I used to believe that, but I've given up looking. It's too much work and too little reward."

Mary put another log on the fire then leaned forward and blew air across it. The fire came to life and crackled, taking hold. Replacing the fireplace screen, Mary said, "Well, then, maybe love will find you."

Famous last words, Jackie thought.

◆ ♥ ◆

CHAPTER 9

The next morning, a knock sounded on Jackie's door. When Jackie opened it, the hall was empty except for a pile of neatly folded clothes—sweat pants, a sweatshirt, and a thick pair of socks. On top, sat a folded note.

The note was from Sam. "Come on down when you're ready. Breakfast is on the griddle. Later, I'll take you into town so you can do some shopping."

When Jackie went downstairs, Sam was alone in the dining room. He wore jeans, a dusky blue t-shirt, and hiking boots. His hair had a wind-blown, or hand-mussy, style—which wasn't really a style at all. Just damn cute.

"Thank you for the clothes," Jackie said by way of greeting. She posed to show off her new couture sweatsuit.

"My pleasure. Have a seat," he said. "I made enough for an army." He turned to go.

"You're not eating?" Jackie asked.

Sam cast an amused glance over his shoulder. "I ate an hour ago. I need to clean up in the kitchen or Frankie will box my ears. Bon appetit."

Breakfast was pancakes, sausage, and scrambled eggs, with fresh-made coffee, orange juice, and the best maple syrup Jackie had ever tasted.

Sam disappeared into the kitchen while Jackie ate. Once she was done, she picked up her place setting and carried it to the back.

Jackie pushed through the swinging doors and found Sam sweeping the floor. "You're here by yourself? Where is everyone?" Jackie took her dishes to the sink to wash them.

"Yeah, they all went down to the Christmas farmer's market. Last one of the season before the snow hits hard. Lu wanted me to meet that couples' counselor who's staying here. I'm supposed to help her with her presentation equipment. From what I hear, though, she never comes out of her room."

Jackie froze. What should she say? Different options presented themselves to her.

"*You mean little ol' me?*" *Said with a batting of the eyelashes.*

"*Well, hello. I'm Dr. Jacquelyn Li. Pleased to meet you.*" *Said with a handshake.*

"*Actually, that's me. It's all been a huge mistake.*" *Said with bashful embarrassment.*

"*I heard she died.*" *Said with a pout.*

Jackie didn't want him to know her as anyone other than Jackie the weird waiter from Arlington. If she told him she was Dr. Jacquelyn Li, she would have to face the fast-approaching event. She wasn't ready to do that.

When the silence dragged on too long, Jackie said simply, "I'm ready to go whenever you are."

"You sure you want me tagging along?" Sam asked. "Lu wouldn't mind if you took one of the inn's cars. I can show you on a map where to go."

"Oh." Jackie glanced over her shoulder at him. "Is it inconvenient for you to take me?"

"No. I just thought you might want a little freedom."

Jackie squinched up her mouth then admitted, "I don't have my driver's license with me."

"I beg your pardon?" Sam looked at her like she'd grown a horn in the middle of her forehead. It was a look she'd seen often on Jazz's face.

"I...didn't think I'd need it?"

"Okay." He didn't understand.

"I don't need it very often. Sorry. I take the bus and train in the city."

"Oh."

"I promise I'll be fast. I only need a few things. Buying deodorant would be a win-win for everyone, if you know what I mean. Can you drive me? Do you mind?"

"I don't mind at all, city girl," Sam replied, chuckling. "Your chariot awaits."

Jackie dried her hands on a towel then followed Sam toward the lobby.

"You got a coat yet?" Sam asked.

"I've got an elf sweater."

Sam stopped in his tracks. "Oh, hell no. No way I'm gonna

be seen in public with that damn thing. Not to mention those fuzzy slippers. Wait here. I'll be right back."

"You're high maintenance," Jackie called after him.

When Sam returned, he was carrying a bright orange parka and combat boots that had seen better days. "These'll at least keep the snow off you."

Both the parka and boots were too big. Jackie shoved the sleeves up the best she could, and laced the boots tight.

Jackie looked down at herself and said, "I'm not sure which is worse: the sweater or this coat."

Sam grinned. "Well, no hunter's going to mistake you for a deer." He didn't wait around to be thanked but headed out to the car, letting Jackie clomp along behind.

Jackie sat up front—instead of in the back like a customer.

"What kind of shopping you want first?" asked Sam, putting on his seat belt. "Fancy lady clothes? Grocery store?" He gave Jackie a sly sideways look. "Pharmacy?"

"I do not need medication," Jackie snapped, well aware of what he was thinking. "Can we go somewhere cheap that has everything?"

"Yup." Sam put the car in gear, and they were off. "Tell me again what happened to your luggage?"

"The airport lost it."

"You didn't have luggage with you at the airport."

Shit, Jackie thought, *wishing she was better at lying*. Aloud, she said, "Earlier. I mean the bus."

"No, ma'am. You didn't have luggage then either."

Jackie gave Sam an annoyed look. "I mean before that. When I got here."

"Oh! So you arrived without luggage."

"Yeah."

"Where'd the Santa pajamas come from?"

"Maybe I'm one of Santa's elves!" Jackie turned in her seat to stare at him.

Sam nodded slowly, several times. "You know, if you're in some kind of trouble... Runnin' from the law, or..."

"Don't be ridiculous," Jackie said. "I'm okay. Honest. Just having a rough holiday. It'll all be over soon."

"Anything I can help with?" Sam turned his face toward her, his expression concerned and so sweet, so handsome. That urge to kiss him resurfaced, and Jackie felt a tickle deep in her belly. The right front tire hit gravel with a startling growl. Sam jerked his attention to the road and eased back onto the asphalt. "Sorry." He sat up a little straighter.

Jackie said, "Just keep your eyes on the road, okay? I'm fine." She thought, *I'm fine, but I'll never forget the look on your face just now.* She sighed, settled back, and watched the countryside go by. *Married man. Married man.*

After a while, Sam asked, "So, you're a waitress, huh?"

"Yeah. Not on purpose, though." Jackie changed the subject. "What about you? How'd you come to be working at the inn?"

"Hold on," Sam said. "What do you mean by that? Not on purpose?"

Jackie thought about it, looking out the window at the countryside blanketed with snow. She didn't want to lie to him, so she told him a portion of the truth. "When I was in college, I was working toward a medical degree, to be a clinical psychiatrist. I had it all plotted out. Then, my parents were killed in a car accident."

Sam didn't say anything, but Jackie could feel his gaze toward her.

"Eyes on the road," she said, pointing out through the windshield without looking at him.

"Yes, ma'am."

They passed an old red barn in a field with two horses running in the snow, and Jackie was briefly distracted by the beauty of it. When the scene was behind them, she said, "I have a brother. He's twelve years younger than me. His name's Jasper, but everybody calls him Jazz. There wasn't anybody to raise him, so I quit school and went back home to take care of him."

"You gave up your dream for him?"

Jackie shrugged. "Not just for him. For Mom and Dad. For myself. It was more important that he be okay. You know?"

Sam nodded. "Yeah. I have a sister." He turned on his blinker and pulled into the parking lot of a giant budget department store. "Here we are."

"So, now you," Jackie said. "What brought you to the inn?"

As Sam maneuvered into a parking spot, he chose his words carefully. "I have a lot of memories there. I grew up in these parts, and when I was in college, I used to visit their daughter for the holidays. I guess you could say I never got along well with my own folks, and Lu and Card were like surrogate parents to me."

"You went to college?"

"You sound surprised."

Jackie caught his gaze. "No, it's just... I don't know."

"I'm smarter than I look. I went to W.V.U., majored in environmental engineering."

"Impressive."

"Eh," Sam smiled as he put the car in park and turned it off. "It'd be a lot more impressive if I was working in some D.C. firm, making six figures." He unhooked his seatbelt.

Jackie got out and stood with her eyes closed, breathing in the cold air. "I love how it smells here," she said. "It's so fresh."

"I reckon you're used to breathing that nasty city smog, aren't you?"

"I guess so. I never noticed it before now."

"My granny once said that all you need to live a long, healthy life is good food, good water, good air, and goooood lovin'."

Jackie laughed. "How long did she live?" They walked side-by-side toward the front entrance.

"Well, she's 92 and still feisty as a miner on payday."

Jackie's grin spread of its own accord, and she looked up to find his expression proud and amused.

The Santa ringing a bell at the entrance to the store gave Jackie a wink, and Sam pulled out his wallet to drop a couple dollars in the red bucket.

"Merry Christmas," said Mr. Claus.

Jackie and Sam replied, "Merry Christmas."

Inside the department store, the music was chipper and full of Christmas cheer. A cacophony of sounds enveloped them: people talking, registers beeping, and carts clattering.

Jackie paused for a moment to take it all in. It wasn't all that different from the one at home, and for a moment she felt a wave of locational disorientation. The store was a slice out of time and space, as if it existed in all places at once. It even smelled like the one at home.

Sam grabbed a cart, backing it out, and swinging it around to her. "You okay?" he asked.

"Yeah, sure. Let's get this show on the road." She pointed

toward the Women's Clothing department. "You don't have to come with me, if you don't want. We can meet up later."

"Are you kidding? I haven't had this much fun in ages. It'll be like adventuring into a foreign land. Just don't ask me to hold your purse."

Jackie grimaced at him, but said, "Deal."

The Women's department was fully stocked and had several good sales going. Jackie filled the cart with a variety of pants and blouses that she planned to try on. Sam did wander off when he spotted the electronics section, and Jackie seized the opportunity to look at Ladies' Lingerie. She needed panties and bras. Not much bra, fortunately. A couple lycra sports bras would do the trick. But the panties... Jackie settled on a bag of granny panties that were on sale. Good enough in a pinch. *Hell,* Jackie thought, *good enough for the rest of my life, since I'll never date again.*

She was looking at them when Sam came up behind her and loomed over the cart. He started picking through her finds.

"Have you lost your mind?" he asked, not sounding the least bit like he was kidding.

Jackie stuffed the bag of panties into her coat so he wouldn't see them.

"The jury's still out," she said casually, arm draped across her stomach to keep the panties from falling out. "Why?" She wasn't sure what to do with her other hand, so she put it on her hip.

"These are all thin, girly things."

"Womanly. And what's wrong with that?"

Sam picked up a silky nightgown that Jackie had thrown in the cart on a whim. He held it high. "No, no, no," he said and disappeared with it, cutting through the racks and out of sight.

Jackie watched him go with a huff of irritation. He had a lot of nerve running off with her nightgown.

"Ma'am," said a sharp voice behind Jackie.

Jackie turned to find an elderly woman with a silver flat-top frowning at her. Her nametag said, "Eloise."

"Me?"

"Yes, ma'am. Do I need to call security?"

Jackie didn't understand. "I'm sorry. What?"

The woman looked pointedly at Jackie's stomach, and a bell went off in Jackie's head. "Oh!" She pulled out the panties and put them in her cart. "I wasn't stealing them. Honest. I just didn't want...him to see them."

Eloise's sour expression made it clear she didn't believe Jackie. She made the two-fingers-to-the-eyes *I'm watching you* sign, then turned on her heel, and went back to the clothes she was reracking.

"Honest!" Jackie called after her. She tucked the panties in under the other clothes. "If I were going to steal something, it wouldn't be old-lady panties on sale!"

Sam said, "It's not nice to make fun of your elders." He'd returned.

"I'm not!" Jackie's cheeks heated up. "What did you do with my nightgown?"

"I exchanged it for this." He held up a red-and-green plaid flannel nightgown, of the granny variety.

Jackie sneered. "Flannel?"

All casual, Sam replied, "Sure. Didn't you say you were married to yourself? Might as well be warm and cozy, if sexy isn't your thing."

Shocked, Jackie cried, "I never said sexy wasn't my thing. I can be very sexy."

"Oh?" Sam's eyes went round and innocent.

"What do you mean by that?"

"Nothing. All these lightweight clothes are fine for the city, but we're in West Virginia, in a remote inn, in the mountains, at Christmastime. You buy those, and you'll end up freezin' your... tats off."

"Excuse me?"

"Your tattoos. Freeze 'em right off." Sam was doing a terrible job of hiding his amused smile.

"How do you know I have a tattoo?" Jackie did have two, a butterfly on her hip—a college whim—and a chain of daisies around her ankle.

"I saw your ankle. I just assumed you had a second one somewhere. Not many people stop at one."

"You assume a lot of things."

Sam shrugged and tossed the flannel pajamas in the cart. "You can keep all these city clothes if you want, but if you do, that reindeer sweater is gonna become your best friend. Plus there's always the chance we'll get snowed in."

"Snowed in?" Jackie hadn't thought of that. She suddenly saw the wisdom in his critique. "Okay," she agreed. "I'll get warm clothes."

Jackie put back the clothes she'd chosen, hyper-aware of Eloise shadowing her around the Women's department. She picked out two pairs of jeans, a pack of knee socks, a purple two-piece long underwear set—thermal—and a couple turtlenecks. Her one big-ticket item was a pair of snow boots. That almost blew her allowance. Jackie spent the rest on bare-necessity toiletries.

She calculated the total *very carefully*, knowing from personal experience how embarrassing it is to have your credit card denied at the register. She just hoped Amore had done what he'd promised.

Standing in line with her at the register, Sam asked, "You sure that's all you want to get?"

"Yeah. I've got a friend on the way. She's bringing my coat and some other things. She'll be here later today."

Sam helped move items from the cart to the conveyor belt.

Jackie watched as Eloise elbowed the bagger away and took his position, inspecting the items that came down the conveyor.

Sam asked, "She driving out from D.C., this friend of yours?"

"She is. I called her last night." Jackie did her best to hide the panties and bras from Sam, sliding them in under the turtlenecks.

"How long is she staying?"

"Only one night."

"So I guess that means you won't need me anymore as your driver?"

"You're not off the hook just yet. She's bringing my license, but after seeing the wild roads here, I'm not sure I want to drive on them."

"And you? How long are you staying?"

"Longer than that." Jackie still hoped to get away before Christmas Day.

"Guess you're stuck with me then."

Eloise lifted one of the bras into mid-air, turning it this way and that as if Jackie may have hidden something in it.

Jackie nearly choked. She waved the flannel pajamas at Sam to get his attention, "These better live up to the hype, mister."

Sam laughed, "Oh, they will."

"Mr. Campbell!" came a loud, high-pitched voice.

Someone pushed against the back of Jackie's knee and squeezed by her. Another one followed, and before she knew it, she and Sam were surrounded by a rag-tag band of children.

"Hey, guys!" said Sam, patting each one on the head or shoulder, depending on their sizes. "What are you doing here?"

"Chrithmuth shopping," said a girl who was missing her two front teeth. She looked bundled up for Antarctica, all covered but her sweet face. Chaotic black curls escaped the edges of her knitted cap.

"I see." Sam smiled warmly down at the child.

"Sir," asked Jackie, teasing, "are these children bothering you?" The kids all turned big eyes and open mouths up at her, then broke out in a cacophony of explanations.

"He knows us."

"We know him."

"He's our friend."

"We're not botherin'."

Sam watched them, eyes shining.

Jackie burst out laughing. "All right then," she said. "Carry on." She continued unloading the cart as the kids told Sam about their shopping spree. Apparently, they each had $10 to spend on their Secret Santa gift, and that was a big deal.

"Guys, guys," said Sam, interrupting them. "This is my friend..." In that moment, Sam realized he didn't know her name. Jackie saw the realization in his eyes.

"Jackie," she supplied. "Great to meet you." She broke eye contact with Sam and waved at all the children.

"Jackie," Sam repeated.

Again, the kids turned big eyes to her. It didn't last long, and three of the four turned back to Sam, tugging on his coat for attention. The eldest, a girl of about thirteen, held out her hand to shake Jackie's. "I'm Matina." She was dark-skinned, her face round, and eyes the most beautiful brown.

Jackie smiled and shook. "Glad to meet you. How do you know Sam?"

"He helps out around the children's home sometimes." Matina indicated the other three and herself. "That's where we all live."

As if he'd been half listening to their conversation, Sam interjected, "They'll be coming to the inn for caroling on Christmas Day." He met the girl's eyes. "Right?"

"Yes, sir! We been practicing." Matina grinned. "I hope Miss Lula is making those sugar cookies again this year."

"You can bet on it," Sam replied.

A tall man with a child hanging onto each hand came up to us. "So this is where y'all got off to," he said to the children before giving Sam a big smile and freeing a hand to shake with him. "Sam."

"Robert. You've got your hands full."

"Nothing I can't manage." Robert was pushing fifty, his face wrinkled in a hound-dog sort of way, crinkles at the corners of his eyes and mouth where he'd smiled enough over the years to earn them.

"This is Jackie," said Sam. "She's staying at the Gray Fox."

"What do you think of the inn?" Robert studied my face for the answer.

"I love it. It's so beautiful there. And the owners are so nice."

"Takin' good care of ya, are they?"

"Oh yes. Very much so." Jackie noticed that the checkout woman had finished running her things across the scanner. "Excuse me," she said, turning away.

To Jackie's great relief, the total came in under the limit. She ran her Love, Inc., credit card through the machine.

Eloise slipped away, satisfied that Jackie hadn't stolen anything. The next time Jackie looked up, she was just gone.

Jackie smiled at the young woman behind the register, "Your bagger is very...diligent."

"Oh, that's just Eloise. She lost her husband last year, and she ain't got nobody else. The store's kind of her whole life. She didn't do anything to offend ya, did she?"

"No," Jackie replied. "She was fine."

"She gets complaints sometimes, but the manager can't bring himself to fire her."

"Oh. Well, he must have a kind heart."

Sam and Robert had stepped to one side to have a quiet conversation, and the kids had migrated with them, chattering among themselves and looking at the items on nearby shelves. They eventually broke off, with waves and good-byes for Sam.

Jackie waved back too.

Sam returned to her side.

"Children's home?" Jackie asked, taking her receipt from the cashier.

"It's a group home for kids who don't have family to care for them," Sam explained. "Card and Lu are benefactors. The whole community helps them out. I do handyman work for them when they need it. They live in an old farmhouse that's seen better days."

"And Robert?"

"He and his wife Sandy run the place. They're good people."

They walked to where the bags waited in a cart, placed neatly there by Eloise. Jackie picked up one and Sam took the other.

Sam said, "You'll meet Sandy on Christmas Day. It's a Gray Fox tradition that the children come caroling."

"I can't wait," Jackie said, feeling warmed by the very idea. Despite that, the cold hit Jackie with breathtaking force when they left the store. Shivering, Jackie hurried to the car. As Sam was pulling out, Jackie glanced back at the store and saw silver-haired Eloise standing at the front window, glaring out at her. The woman made the two-fingers-to-the-eyes sign again. *I'm watching you.* She held Jackie's gaze until they moved out of the line of sight.

CHAPTER 10

Jackie and Sam entered the lobby with the spoils from their shopping spree and stood on the mat, stomping the snow off their boots. Jackie unzipped the giant orange coat and slipped it off. Underneath, she was wearing the green elf sweater.

"Thanks for the loan," Jackie told Sam. "I'm going to take a shower and put on clothes that fit me."

"About time," Sam said, joking. "I was starting to think you were getting attached to that old sweater. My opinion of you was suffering."

Jackie hugged herself. "Don't dis' the sweater, mister. It's warm."

Card came in from the restaurant. "Ah, Dr. Li, there you are! I see you've met Sam, your assistant."

Sam turned his head this way and that, searching for Dr. Li. "She's here?"

Card looked confused. "Why, yeah. Right here."

Jackie lowered her hands and stood up straight. "I'm Dr.... I'm... I'm Jacquelyn Li. Jackie. Please, call me Jackie."

Sam frowned. *"You're* the couples' counselor? You said you were a waitress."

"I am." Jackie cringed. "When I'm not being a couples' counselor." She shrugged. "Awkward. Hi."

"YOU'RE the couples' counselor?" Sam repeated, incredulous enough that Jackie's knee-jerk defenses kicked in.

"What? Is that really so hard to believe?"

"Well," Sam stammered. "I mean... I've heard that all psychologists are a little squirrelly. No offense. Not that you're squirrelly. I mean, since I met you, you've been kinda... You know. Just didn't see this coming. Like, at all."

Card interjected, "Sam! What's gotten into you? Be nice to our guest."

Jackie could only stare at the floor. *Squirrelly. I'm not squirrelly. Except I am.* To Card, she said, "It's okay. He's just teasing me, aren't you?"

Sam said nothing, worry clouding his expression.

"Excuse me. I need to go to my room." Jackie picked up her bags and headed for the grand staircase.

Voice low, but not so much that it didn't carry, Card asked Sam, "Isn't that the sweater your Aunt Gert got you?"

"Mm hm," Sam replied, and at just that moment, Lu cried out in the restaurant, "Card!"

Jackie paused and looked back.

After only a beat, Card was off at a trot, hurrying toward his wife. There was no denying the panic in her voice.

Jackie met Sam's alarmed gaze then watched as he ran after Card. She debated. It wasn't her business, but... maybe she could be of help? She dropped her bags and followed the men at a slower pace. She arrived on the threshold between the lobby and the restaurant in time to see Lu fly into Card's arms, her cheeks wet with tears.

"We're too late, Card. They're gonna take the Fox."

"Woah there, Lu. What are you talkin' about?" Card's voice was a low, gentle balm. "Tell me what's happened."

Sam stood near them, but not too close, his back to Jackie. Frankie appeared in the doorway to the kitchen. Jackie remained where she was, unsure about advancing further.

Lu pushed a piece of paper at Card. "The bank..." She was crying again, and Jackie felt her heart ache for the woman.

Card took the paper and scanned it. He held it out to Sam then hugged Lu even tighter. She almost disappeared within the embrace of the big man. "Don't worry," he said. "We're gonna be okay. The seminar's gonna earn us enough to keep the bank happy. Those couples will need booze and massages. Dr. Li is our angel. With her here, we won't lose anything. I promise, honey. I promise. Settle down now. It's Christmas. Miracles abound."

"Promise?" asked Lu, sniffling and sounding small.

"I promise," Card replied.

Sam cast a dark look over his shoulder at Jackie.

Jackie felt a shift in her world.

CHAPTER 11

Jackie stood still in the center of the lobby, and the world revolved around her, spinning her mind and disorienting her heart. One question repeated over and over. *How can I leave now?*

She stepped back and headed for the stairs, pausing by her shopping bags. To her surprise, tears swam in her eyes, and she had to swipe them away to see. She was further surprised to find her arm caught in a firm hold.

Sam leaned in, his teeth clenched. "You better not let them down." His eyes flashed with protective fury.

In his eyes, Jackie saw love—love for family—and she promised, "I'll do my best."

"You better." Sam appraised her, and Jackie saw something in his face, something that hadn't been there before, that made her uneasy. "I don't know what kind of game you're playing. Maybe you're just nuts. But you better pull yourself together and make this seminar a success, or..."

"Or what?" Jackie asked, voice quiet and unchallenging.

"Or I'll report you for fraud," Sam said with commitment, his face tight with emotion. He released her arm and strode out the front door. It slammed behind him.

Jackie froze, shaking. It hit her how he must see her. The thought made her stomach uneasy.

Jackie showered in the hot water for a long time, thinking about... well... everything. The inn, Georgio, Card, Lu, Frankie, Jazz, and Sam. *How did I get here? Why is this happening?*

Afterward, she put on the robe provided by the inn—a white, thick, and cozy terry hug that was a few sizes too big for her and covered her legs to well-past her knees. She sat on the bed in the warmth radiating from the fireplace and picked up the cupid's handbook from the bedside table.

I have to do this.

The book wasn't big, but it wasn't small either. It looked like a standard romance novel. The cover had a buff man and buxom woman embracing, in love, or maybe just in lust. The title read, "Cupid Manual for the 21st Century." Jackie flipped it open to the table of contents. There were only four chapters.

1. Recognizing Love
2. Rules of Engagement
3. Blessing True Love
4. Troubleshooting

Jackie sat back and started reading.

What is true love? True love is the deepest and strongest connection any two people can have to one another. True love is a bond that, once blessed by a cupid, supersedes even the bond of marriage.

It is the duty of the cupid to identify true love and...

Two hours later, Jackie awoke from a deep sleep, groggy like a hibernating bear. She stretched in the bed. Rolling over, she spotted the cupid manual, and that sinking feeling returned to her belly.

"True love," she said aloud. She'd believe in it, once upon a time. At twenty-nine, though, it seemed a ridiculous concept. She'd seen too much dark and troubled water pass under that bridge. Jackie propped herself against the pillows and picked the book back up. She read the first three chapters, taking notes on a notepad as she went along. She skipped the last chapter on troubleshooting. Mr. Amore had said she should read it in its entirety, but so what? She'd read the last chapter when she ran into trouble.

She closed the manual, lifted her chin, and said aloud, "That's not so complicated. Identify the couple with true love. Touch them both at the same time while they're looking in each others' eyes. Say, 'Blessed be thy love,' and voilà, done. Times three couples."

She allowed herself to hope. Maybe *this isn't so bad after all. Maybe it will all work out. The inn will be saved, and by Christmas, I'll be back in Alexandria. Maybe, just maybe, I can fake this enough to get by.*

Fake it 'til you make it, the voice in her head said.

Jackie started a two-cup pot of coffee brewing—compliments of the inn—and sat down at the desk. Pulling a pen and notepad out of a drawer, both labeled "Gray Fox Inn," she started to arrange her thoughts for real.

When were the guests arriving? Jackie checked the brochure, shocked once again to see her own face smiling back at her. The schedule said they'd arrive on the 22nd—the day after next. She breathed a sigh of relief. *Okay, I have some time to get my shit together.*

The seminars and events began early in the morning on the 23rd. *Even better.*

Jackie tried to plan the seminar. She created charts with dates and hours but couldn't fill in the details.

I should start with a speech of some sort, shouldn't I? she thought. Then, she said aloud, "Welcome to the Gray Fox Inn, ladies and gentlemen." She hated the sound of her own voice. It felt fake.

She paced. She sat. She stood. She stared out the window.

I have no choice, she thought again. Amore, the Universe, Fate, God, Whoever... had cornered her. She returned to her notes. *My two years studying Clinical Psych must have stuck with me. I can do this. Fake it 'til you make it, right? It can't be that much harder than herding customers at the diner.* The little pep talk she gave herself bolstered her in the short term.

Bonnie and her husband Jim were late. Despite every intention of getting out of bed and hitting the road early, they didn't get moving until after noon and didn't arrive until twilight.

Jackie was waiting in the lobby, watching their headlights come up the driveway when they pulled in, having called ahead to let Jackie know they were close. She watched Bonnie leap out of the car almost before it had stopped and hurried out to meet them.

"Jacksie!" Bonnie cried. "Have you seen these trees? The snow? These mountains? Holy Hanukkah, it's beautiful here." She spread her arms wide and turned in place. "I'm coming every year, from now on!"

When out of her restaurant uniform, Bonnie had the kind of fashion sense most people called "quirky." She mixed patterns in bright colors and liked bold accents such as flowing scarves and funky tights. Her ginger hair hung to just below her shoulders, but her bangs barely reached her eyebrows. She wore bright lipsticks and cat-eye glasses, and she had a flair that Jackie didn't.

Jackie was more class and comfort than sass and style. Dressed in her new jeans and turtleneck, Jackie felt right at home. So what if she was still wearing the fuzzy slippers. They were growing on her.

Bonnie's spin stopped, and she rushed Jackie, taking hold of her shoulders and looking her right in the eyes. With extreme seriousness, she stage-whispered, "We brought tampons. Just in case."

"Oh," Jackie laughed. "Thanks! Good thinking!" She hugged her friend. "I'm so glad you're here."

Jim, the Hubs, emerged from the car at a more leisurely pace. This counterpoint of demeanor complemented Bonnie, smoothed her rough edges and kept her feet on the ground. Jackie loved how they loved each other, and she had never seen them fight.

"Hey, Jackie," Jim said, coming around the car. A gust of wind tousled his blond, devil-may-care hair. "How many guinea pigs gave their lives to make those boots of yours?"

"Hey, Jim," Jackie replied, laughing. "Thanks for coming."

"Lady in distress," Jim said with a grin. "It's my calling." He opened the trunk and started pulling out suitcases, one of which was Jackie's.

"I want to hear everything," Bonnie said, bending into the front seat to grab two purses.

"I already told you everything." Jackie took her purse from her friend.

Bonnie bounced a little. "Well, I want to hear it again. I mean, jeez! It's not every day your best friend becomes Cupid."

"I'm not *the* Cupid. I'm *a* cupid." Jackie shook her head and laughed, aware of how ridiculous it sounded. "Over dinner, okay?" She slung her purse over her shoulder and moved to the back of the car to pick up her suitcase. "Let's get you settled in, first. I'll get someone from the inn to register you."

Jim shooed Jackie away. He picked the suitcase up. He carried it in one hand and Bonnie's in the other. He slung his own bag across his back by the strap. Jim was nothing if not brawny.

Jackie led them into the lobby. She was excited to show off the place, as if it somehow belonged to her. Lu and Card were there, waiting with welcoming smiles. Jackie made introductions, and the business of getting checked in was underway. Card insisted that Jim and Bonnie were not to pay for anything, that they were guests of the house through their association with Dr. Jackie Li, their savior.

Jim raised an eyebrow at the "Dr." prefix, but before he could ask about it, Bonnie gave him a little kick. He understood the meaning of that and said nothing.

◆ ♥ ◆

CHAPTER 12

Lu and Card put the Gundersens in the room next door to Jackie.

Jackie returned to her own bedroom while Bonnie and Jim got settled in. She hung up the clothes they'd brought, hugging the stack of familiar clean underwear—not granny undies. She layered a button-down shirt over the new turtleneck and finished the outfit off by wrapping her neck in the scarf Bonnie had packed for her, a thick pashmina that she rarely wore when at home. It would be perfect for the inn and even had Christmas colors in it—reds, greens, navy blue, and white.

Digging in her purse, she found her phone and its charger. The battery had a smidge of juice left. She found the Rasmussens in her contact list and dialed.

"Hello?" Mrs. Rasmussen, Razz's mom, answered with a suspicious note in her voice.

"Hi, Carole," said Jackie. "It's Jackie, Jazz's sister."

"Jackie!" Carole's tone changed, warmth rushing in. "How are you?"

"I'm in a bind, actually."

"What's going on? Do you need help?" Carole was ten years older than Jackie, but she could be a life-long friend—if Jackie had the time to make it happen. They moved in different groups but had an easy rapport when their paths did intersect.

"I'm stuck in West Virginia for...work. It's looking like I might not be back in time for Christmas. I was wondering. Would you mind letting Jazz spend Christmas with your family? I'm so sorry to do this, but I don't want him to be alone for the holiday, and—"

Carole interrupted with enthusiasm. "He's more than welcome, any time! Shit, he's already part of the family. Razz'll be over the moon that he won't have to make small talk with his aunts, uncles, cousins, and grandparents." She laughed.

"Thank you," Jackie said, relief in her voice. "I hate being away, but I have no choice. I owe you guys a pie for this."

"You don't have to worry. He and Razz have each other's backs, and at his age, the nostalgia of Christmas isn't what it used to be—if you know what I mean. He'll be happy to have a big plate of turkey and mashed potatoes and all the video games he can play."

Jackie thanked her again then excused herself. She couldn't ignore the discomfort of not being with her brother on Christmas, but he'd be safe, well fed, and having fun. Truth was, he would have spent a portion of the day over there anyway, even if she were home.

After Jackie hung up with Carole Rasmussen, she speed-dialed Jazz. It went to voicemail.

"Jazz here. I'm a busy man. Leave a message or don't. I'll call you back... or I won't." Jazz chuckled, the sound cut off as the recording ended.

"It's your sister. Give me a call. I'm back in West Virginia at the Gray Fox Inn. I'll text you the address and phone number. I may be here for a few more days, maybe even through Christmas. I've arranged for you to go to the Rasmussen's on Christmas Day. Mrs. Rasmussen says you're more than welcome. I'm sorry. I know I haven't missed a Christmas with you since...well, ever. We'll have a special Christmas dinner just for us when I get back, and we can exchange gifts then. Okay? Call me if you need anything, and please, please, please, do NOT trash the place while I'm gone. I'm trusting you, Jazz. If I come back to a mess, I'll—" The line went dead. "Dammit." Jackie let out a deep sigh.

Jazz will be okay, Jackie told herself. A nasty worry-mutt responded with, *But what if he's not? What would Mom and Dad say about leaving him alone on Christmas? Christmas, of all times. It's letting them down.*

Aloud, Jackie said, "I have no choice. I'll make it up to him."

Jackie went downstairs to the restaurant to get a table for dinner.

Lu had the perfect spot set for them, right by the fireplace. She was waiting, placing cloth napkins, when Jackie arrived. "Howdy. I figured you and your friends would be about ready for a bite to eat. Have a seat. Can I get you something to drink?"

"A glass of wine, please?"

"We've got that. For supper, we have brook trout or pork tenderloin. I reckon both those take white wine. Is that all right?"

"Perfect." Jackie pulled out a chair.

A squeal from the lobby signaled Bonnie and Jim's arrival. The view from the top of the stairs was squee-inducing, Jackie knew from experience. They came into the restaurant, laughing.

Jackie waved them over.

"This place is to die for," Bonnie said. "Me and Hubs want to live here all year."

Jim agreed. "Time slows down here. I'm already so much more relaxed than I ever am in D.C."

"It's pretty special, isn't it?" Jackie said. "I like it a whole lot better now that I have my clothes and posse here with me."

Jim and Bonnie took seats at the table. Bonnie asked, "How'd you end up here without any clothes?"

Like any good server, Lu appeared as if by magic. She set a basket of bread and three wine glasses on the table.

Jackie shook her head and changed the subject. "The first day I was here, I saw this gorgeous buck come out of the forest outside my window. It was snowing. I've never seen anything like that."

"That'd be Ol' Bill," said Lu with a grin. "He's been around here for ages. Cole and I put berries out for him in the winter. We like to think of him as our guardian spirit."

Jim asked, "Why do you call him Bill?"

Lu smiled, remembering. "Our daughter named him when she was little. She just knew it was his name, and who were we to argue?"

"See?" Bonnie said. "That's what I'm talking about. So charming!"

"Can I pour you some wine?" Lu offered, filling each glass. "We have brook trout, baked with rosemary and lemon, and pan-fried pork tenderloin on the menu tonight. Do you know what sounds good, or do you need more time?"

Nobody needed more time. Both Jackie and Bonnie chose the trout.

"You'll like it," said Lu. "Card caught 'em himself this morning. They're fresh as they get."

Jackie and Bonnie made eyes at each other and oohed.

Jim chose the tenderloin. They served it with homemade biscuits and gravy. That won him over.

Lu headed back to the kitchen.

Jim watched her go. "Are you sure it's okay that we're here? I don't want to impose. They're not letting us pay for anything."

"It's okay," Jackie replied, keeping her voice low. "This couples' weekend is important to them. Their business is in trouble."

Jim frowned and let sarcasm taint his words, "Oh, that makes me feel better."

"Don't worry," Jackie told him. "You're going to earn your keep tonight. I need to come up with a plan for this seminar, and you guys are going to help me."

"We get to be cupids too!" Bonnie injected excitement back into the conversation.

Jim smiled when he looked at his wife. He couldn't worry too much with her around.

Bonnie—who never forgets anything—turned the conversation back to where Jackie had derailed it. "You were telling us how you ended up here with no clothes, no purse, and no I.D."

Jackie leaned forward and lowered her voice. "It sounds like fiction, I know. But it happened just like I told you. I fell asleep somewhere else and just woke up here. It happened three times. First time, I was at the hospital with Georgio Kupidopoulos— the man I put in a coma. I fell asleep in the chair. Second time, I was on a bus headed back to D.C. Fell asleep on my seat. And the third time, I made it all the way home. You came over, but when I woke up next morning, I was back here, still in my Santa pajamas."

"How do you explain it?" Jim frowned as he reached for a piece of bread from the basket. "You sure you didn't dream all that?"

Bonnie huffed. "Magic happens. And Jackie stepped in a big ol' pile of it." She turned back to Jackie. "I believe you, honey, because even if I didn't, I'd want to pretend it was true."

"Okay," said Jim, skeptical but willing to entertain the idea. "So, Bonnie told me you slammed the diner door in this Kupidopoulos guy's face, and you're here to take his place?"

"That's it in a nutshell. I need to bless three couples with true love."

Jim's eyebrows went up.

"Start with us!" Bonnie leaned toward Jim and offered her face for a kiss. He obliged.

Jackie watched, her heartbeat obvious in her chest. She noticed something about them. Something she'd never noticed before. Not quite a glow, but a warmth and a clarity. She knew beyond a shadow of a doubt that their love was true.

"All right," she said, pushing back her chair. Jackie stood and walked to stand behind them. "Look into each other's eyes and think—I don't know—lovey thoughts."

Jim and Bonnie did just that, smiles spreading on their faces.

Jackie put her hands on their shoulders and said, "Blessed be thy love."

She didn't know what she'd been expecting. Tinkling bells? Confetti? Fireworks would have been nice. None of those things happened.

Bonnie asked, "Are we supposed to feel any different?"

Jackie shrugged and returned to her chair. "I don't know. The book didn't say what it would feel or look like. I just know I need to do that three times before Christmas. You're one. Two to go!" She picked up her glass and raised it for a toast. "To true love."

"Wait, there's a book?" Jim asked, more interested.

"Yeah, a cupid's manual. The butler gave it to me."

Lu and Frankie came out of the kitchen with trays of food. In addition to the main dishes, they brought big bowls of cheddar mashed potatoes, green beans, and "Christmas corn." Jackie gasped. Christmas Corn was a dish her mother had made when she was little. It had always been her favorite. Her mother had made it with corn sliced off the cob, green and red peppers chopped small, bits of onion, and raisins, all fried in ghi to give it a nutty hint.

Frankie avoided meeting Jackie's gaze and examined Bonnie and Jim with the subtlety of wait-staff.

Jackie said, "Lu, this smells amazing."

Jim chimed in, "And it looks even better. I'm starving."

Lu was pleased and spent a moment fussing around with serving spoons and bowl placement. "Enjoy," she said. "But save room for dessert. We have pecan pie, just out of the oven."

Bonnie moaned. "I love pecan pie."

"Then, darlin', you're in the right place," Lu replied.

The food overshadowed the conversation for a while, leaving room for only moans and short comments about how delicious everything was.

Then Sam came into view from the lobby. He pulled Jackie's attention to him like a magnet. His cheeks were ruddy from the cold. He removed his heavy coat as he crossed the restaurant, pausing to hang it on the back of a chair at another table. He stopped beside Jackie.

"Evenin', Doctor Li," he said, tone flat.

"Jackie," she reminded him. "Let me introduce..."

"Yeah," Sam looked from Bonnie to Jim. "This must be your friend-assistant. And her husband?"

"Bonnie, Jim, this is Sam. He's the only taxi driver within twenty miles."

"At your service." Sam offered his hand to Bonnie.

"The local charm just keeps on coming," Bonnie said, shaking it.

Jim half-stood and shook hands as well.

Bonnie suggested, "Why don't you join us? Lord knows we have more than enough food." She indicated the fourth chair.

"Oh, I'm just here for Lu's pecan pie. A little bird told me she'd made a couple."

"Please?" said Bonnie. "We don't bite."

"I could use some of those mashed potatoes," said Sam, smiling. He grabbed a plate and silverware bundle off the sideboard then took the empty chair at the table.

Jim resumed eating, and Bonnie sat back with her wine. Jackie met Bonnie's gaze and saw the jump of her eyebrows. The expression spoke volumes.

Sam unfolded his napkin and spread it across his lap.

"So, Sam," Bonnie said. "What do you think of our good doctor?"

Sam's gaze caught on Jackie, stayed there long enough that she felt heat painting her cheeks, and finally, he said, "I'm looking forward to seeing her work her magic."

Jim stopped eating.

Bonnie repeated, "Her magic?"

Jackie jumped in, "Metaphor. He's speaking metaphorically."

With his casual West Virginia drawl, Sam said, "I think there's a good chance she's going to steal..." He paused just long enough to make Jackie tense, then continued, "...everyone's hearts." Though his tone was light, the pause wasn't.

Bonnie leaned in. "When are the couples arriving?"

Jackie focused on her plate. She hated the turn her friendship with Sam had taken.

Sam said, "Day after tomorrow, late afternoon. We have four coming in. Christmas is a slow time for remote inns like this one."

"Four?" Jackie asked. She did the math. Four couples. Three true loves. Well, two, if Bonnie and Jim Gundersen counted as one. That meant she'd fail with at least one of the couples, maybe two. The thought made her frown.

"Yeah, four." Sam studied her for a moment, his own expression serious. "Didn't you get the information packet we sent?"

Jackie shook her head.

"Damn, I should've followed up with you. That's my fault. I'll print it out for you after dinner."

Lu brought out servings of pecan pie for everyone, including Sam. "This is my great-grandmother's recipe," she said. "The secret ingredient is a touch of cloves. Now you can't tell anyone that. It stays in the family."

Frankie came out of the kitchen, wiping her hands on a towel and scowling at the table. Jackie watched her for a moment, noting how displeased she appeared. After a pause, she came over and stood by Sam.

"Sam, you want a beer with that?"

Sam smiled up at her. "No, thanks. I can get my own. Matter of fact, I think I need a glass of milk to make this the perfect dessert." He pushed back his chair. "Anyone else?"

Jackie was thinking the same thing.

"No," said Frankie, resting her hand on Sam's shoulder. "I'll get it for you." She turned to go, and Sam sank back into his seat.

"Me too, please," Jackie called. She pointed at Bonnie, then Jim, but both shook their heads in refusal.

Frankie glanced back, and Jackie could have sworn she saw venom in Frankie's eyes. *She's jealous,* Jackie thought. *Or protective. Maybe she's friends with Sam's wife? Well, she's got nothing to fear from me. I don't want any man, much less a married one.* She turned her focus to the warm slice of pecan pie wafting sweet goodness up to her nose.

"Going skiing tomorrow morning," Sam was saying. "I heard they got fresh powder up on the mountain."

"Skiing?" exclaimed Bonnie. "I haven't been skiing since I was in high school."

"You're welcome to come along. You can rent skis or boards, helmets, and bibs at the lodge. But I have to warn you, I leave early. I need to be back a little after noon. I'd only planned to go for a couple of hours."

"That sounds perfect!" And that was how Bonnie got Jackie and Jim into situations they'd never have gotten into themselves.

Jackie's belly twisted into guilty knots at the thought of going to a ski resort. She wasn't there to have a good time. It felt like cheating, like too much self-indulgence. Without any breath to spare, she said, "I should stay here and..."

Bonnie latched onto Jackie's arm with both hands. "Stop, Jackie. You have to live your life. Right, Sam?"

Sam's face went stoic. "If Jackie has work to do, then..."

Bonnie wasn't budging. "We've got all afternoon to plan and prepare, honey."

Sam was leaning over his pie, but his eyes were on Jackie. "It's up to you," he said. "Are you ready for the couple's counseling?"

Subtle, Jackie thought. In her head, she checked off all the reasons she shouldn't go. She felt guilty for having fun when Jazz was stuck at home alone. She wasn't prepared for the seminar. Also, she knew that the memory of her parents' deaths lurked in the back of her mind. Would it come rushing forward if she found herself at a ski resort?

"There's plenty of time," Bonnie said. "Please..."

Sam asked, "When was the last time you went skiing?"

Jackie took a deep breath. Truth was, she used to be a great skier.

She thought back to the feeling of gliding, swooping, and swerving down the hill, the cold wind making her cheeks, nose, and ears pink, the fresh air filling her lungs, and the warm sweatiness of her body inside the ski suit. She remembered how tired her muscles and mind were at the end of the day, and how lovely it had felt to sit by the fire and drink a hot toddy with her college friends before wandering off to bed—only to start all over the next day.

She remembered relaxing in a cabin with five of her best friends. She remembered how the phone had sounded when it rang. And she remembered what the officer on the line had said to her, "Miss Li, it's Officer Dylan from the Alexandria police. Do you have a friend or family member there with you?" She remembered how her heartbeat had scattered, how the fear had swelled up in her throat, cutting off her breath.

At one time, she had loved skiing, but she hadn't been up the mountain since the day her parents had died. After that day, she'd had neither the funds nor the time. At the mere thought of being on the slopes, her jaw tightened, and she fought to relax.

"Eight years ago."

Bonnie gave a knowing nod. "Since your parents died?"

Jackie cringed. She hated the sympathy people showed you when they learned you were an orphan. Even after eight years, she didn't want it brought up and definitely didn't want to talk about it. "I have too much to do. You guys go on without me."

Sam studied her with dark, serious eyes.

Bonnie used her puppy-dog eyes. "That's what you always say. Pleeeeease. It won't be the same without you."

"I'll think about it," Jackie said, none too enthusiastically. "If we get some work done tonight. Which means, we should head up to my room and get started."

Bonnie cheered and bounced in her chair.

Jackie resolved to put on a strong front, as she always did— on the outside.

CHAPTER 13

Jackie's planning for the 'love seminar'—as Bonnie called it—went much better than predicted. Inviting Bonnie and Jim had been the best idea Jackie'd had.

As promised, Sam delivered a packet of materials that included information on the couples. Each printed page bore a fancy design at the top and her name: "Dr. Jackie Li, Counselor." Jackie presumed they had once said, "Dr. Georgio Kupidopoulos." She sighed.

Bonnie lounged on Jackie's bed. "Tell us about the first couple."

Jim slouched in the overstuffed armchair by the window, hands on his full belly, eyes half-shut, and a smile on his face.

Jackie read aloud, "Ada and Arthur Kaluza. Married for 14 years."

Bonnie nodded sagely.

"They filled out a survey. Let's see. Looks like Arthur wants more sex, and Ada wants more romance."

"Typical," Bonnie said. "They're gonna be easy. Fix the lack of romance, and Arthur gets all the sex he can handle."

Jackie wrote on her notepad, '*Tips to increase romance.*'

Bonnie waved her hand in the air. "Next!"

"Gita and Tiffany Gupta-Smith. They've been together since high school, married for five years. Hm..."

"Go on."

"Gita wants a baby, but Tiffany isn't ready for that."

"More complex, this one." Bonnie lay back and stared up at the ceiling. "Babies are big issues for couples. For some people, parenthood is ingrained in their DNA. They would do anything to have kids. Not something Jim and I ever felt. Right, Honey Hubs?" She lifted her head to find that Jim was sound asleep in the chair.

Jackie watched the love spread over her friend's face and felt it warm her as well. She said, "Tiffany didn't say she never wants children, just that she's not ready. So, I think we need to get them talking about why that is."

"Bingo! Communication is the best lubricant," Bonnie said. "Who's next?"

"Nicholas Wolfe and Natalie Pasternak. Their profiles are just a list of links. It doesn't say why they're here."

"Let's take a peek." Bonnie rolled over, adjusting her laptop so they both could see. "Looks like they both have video blogs." She browsed to Natalie's site and clicked play on her most recent video.

Natalie sat at a drawing table, dressed in black pants and a black tank top, multiple silver necklaces around her neck. She greeted them with a smile. "Today is all about Snicker Snack, the little fairy whose job it is to trim things." As she talked, she started to draw. "My life has grown a bit too complicated, and I'm finding I need Snicker Snack to help me simplify it. I may need his help to trim some things out. Time is limited, and my art has to come first. Snicker Snack knows all about this kind of trouble. So, I'm invoking him. He will show me what I should eliminate, who I should leave behind, and how I can regain control of my world."

The creature on her drawing table emerged from the paper with each stroke of her pen, a darkly fantastic being with intense eyes and a pair of elaborate Victorian sewing scissors so large relative to the fairy's diminutive size. The creature had to hold them in both hands.

"Wow," said Bonnie. "She's good."

A tear slid down Natalie's face and landed on the drawing, splattering and scattering a bit of the ink. *What—or who—was Natalie considering cutting out of her life?*

"Crap," Jackie huffed. "These are real people." She pushed the profiles away. "Bon, what am I doing here? I can't help anyone with their marriage. What do I know about marriage? I'm just going to mess them up even more."

From within her halo of ginger hair, Bonnie studied Jackie for a moment before sitting up. She leaned forward as if she were about to say the most important words Jackie would ever hear.

She said, "No way."

"But I…"

"Neh!" Bonnie raised a finger to stall Jackie's objection. "You know more than you think you do, lady. Remember all those hours you spent studying Psychology? Interning in Dr. Heebee Jeebee's office?"

"Dr. Hebener."

"Right. That guy. When you quit school, you didn't dump all that knowledge off at the curb. It's still in there. Jeez, Jackie, you still read *Psychology Today* for fun. You got this."

"But…"

"Neh! You got this." Bonnie sat back. "Besides, the couples will do most of the work, right? You just provide the atmosphere and prompts. You're facilitating, not fixing them. If they can't do the work, it wouldn't matter if you had three PhDs. If being married to this bozo has taught me anything, it's that marriage is work. It's totally worth it, but it's hard freakin' work. If you smelled this guy's socks after a day on the job, you'd divorce him for me."

"I heard that," Jim slurred without opening his eyes. His next breath came out with snort.

Jackie considered this. "So what's your secret? How do you make it work?"

"Oh, if I had a cupcake for every time someone asked me that, I'd die a happy woman. It's pretty simple. You have to be real. That means honest and sincere. Not just with your partner but with yourself. Too many people live in a made-up world with made-up feelings, and the real person gets buried under expectations and fears. We're going to crack these people open like walnuts and see what meaty goodness is hiding within their shells."

Jackie said with wonder, "I love you."

Bonnie grinned.

The next morning, Jackie descended the grand staircase into the lobby, ready to renege on the ski trip. She planned to say she had too much work to do. *Yeah,* she thought, knowing she was lying to herself. *That'll do it. I'll stand firm. If that doesn't work, I have back-up excuses.*

Sam was in the dining room, setting out plates and silverware for breakfast. "Mornin'," he said. "Breakfast will be ready in a few minutes. How'd your planning session go last night? Is there anything you need?"

Jackie approached the table. "I have a list of supplies I'll need, notepads, pens, things like that."

"I'll go get them for you tomorrow morning."

"Thanks. I just came down to—"

"Hey, I've got something for you." Sam turned away.

Jackie noticed a suit bag draped over another table. "You what?"

Sam unzipped the bag. Inside was a ski suit, feminine, turquoise and hot pink. Warm...and cute.

"Sam, I'm not—"

"Lu said I could lend it to you. It belonged to her daughter." Sam's expression turned sad as he ran his fingers over the coat's fabric. The tenderness and sadness in his face were palpable.

Before she could stop it, her thought escaped aloud: "You love her."

Sam nodded. "I did. With everything I was." He dragged his eyes from the ski suit, turning his face to one side and gazing up at the ceiling.

Jackie asked, "Where is she now?"

When Sam didn't answer, Lu's voice softly entered the empty space. The innkeeper had come up behind them. She said, "Crystal died almost five years ago. Cervical cancer."

Jackie murmured, "I'm so sorry."

Lu nodded her thanks. "I've kept her ski suit in the closet ever since, and it's foolish of me. Someone should wear it, ski in it. Laugh and have fun in it. Crystal would want that."

Jackie stared at Lu, at a loss for words.

Lu smiled, her eyes crinkling at the corners, her dimples showing. "Who better than you, Jackie? You're doing us a big favor. The least we can do is make sure you don't freeze to death while you're here."

Jackie had rehearsed so many excuses for not going. None were sufficient in the face of this kind, heart-heavy gesture.

I have too much work to do.

These couples are relying on me.

I can't afford to get sick right now.

I'm not here to ski. I'm here to save marriages.

In the glow of the Christmas lights, in that cozy and magical place, none of them held the power of truth.

Jackie gave in. "Thank you. I'll take good care of it. I...appreciate your hospitality."

Lu pulled Jackie into her arms. She whispered, "You remind me of her. You've got a big heart."

After a second of surprise, Jackie hugged her back.

The aroma of bacon, eggs, and fresh-baked biscuits enveloped them, and Lu released the hug. Everyone turned to see Frankie coming from the kitchen with a tray of delights. As usual, the woman's tight-lipped expression remained unbreakable, but no one paid it more than a passing thought.

As if on cue, Bonnie and Jim arrived. The four of them sat together and dug into a good ol' fashioned country breakfast. It was glorious, and Jackie found she had the appetite of a lumberjack. She wasn't the only one. They all tucked in with enthusiasm, much to Lu's delight.

After demolishing a plate of eggs, bacon, hash-browns, and biscuits with real butter and homemade gooseberry jelly, Jackie sat back and tried again to call Jazz. He'd have beeen getting ready for school, so her chances of catching him were good. When he didn't pick up, she listened to his message and left a curt, "Me again. Call me." She checked for an alert that he'd texted, but he hadn't.

"Bonnie? You saw Jazz yesterday, right? Was he okay?"

Bonnie looked up, her fork hovering with a chunk of egg skewered on it. "Yeah. He was fine."

"What was he doing?"

"Luxuriating in independence. Stop worrying." Bonnie gave Jim a look that said *I told you so,* and then she added, "He's sixteen, not six. And he's one of the smart ones. It's good for him to be out from under Sis's watchful eye for a few days."

"That's what I'm afraid of."

"Afraid he'll like it?"

"No! That he'll..."

"What?"

A pack of worries popped into Jackie's head to wag their tails at her. Get himself killed? Arrested? Take drugs? Talk to strangers? Skip school? Make a girl pregnant? Blow his chance at a scholarship? Cross the street without looking both ways? Put unwashed garbage in the recycling bin?

Jackie shook her head. "I don't know."

Bonnie laughed and reached over to put her hand on Jackie's arm. "You worry too much, Jacks. He's a good kid. Trust him. Give yourself permission to have some fun. Real life will be there, waiting for us, when we get back."

She's right, Jackie thought, giving her friend a smile. However, there was a big BUT trudging along behind that thought. *But what if...*

Jackie picked up her coffee in both hands and sat back, hiding behind her mug as the worry dogs stalked her.

Driving to Snowshoe Mountain didn't take long, but the hairpin turns slowed their progress. The car crawled upward one switchback at a time, with Sam driving and Jackie, Jim, and Bonnie tucked into the back seat. Frankie had claimed shotgun before anyone else could. Even Sam had appeared surprised when she'd showed up with a pair of skis, but Sam had strapped them to the roof along with his own, bundled everyone into the car, and off they'd gone.

Bonnie was in Wonderland and commented every five minutes about how beautiful West Virginia was. More snow had fallen overnight, but the morning sky was clear and blue. She pointed out scenic farms, horses in fields, and the tumbles of ice on cliffs where the water seeping from them had frozen.

"Makes me wish I was a photographer," Bonnie told them.

"It's never too late," Sam called from the front.

It was a good day—the kind of day spent with friends. Adventure loomed ahead.

Even Frankie chattered and smiled more than Jackie had ever seen her do. Jackie found herself fascinated by the other woman's change of demeanor, how her face lit up when she smiled, and how her eyes sparkled when she looked at Sam.

An unidentifiable bother niggled Jackie. She chalked it up to distaste that Frankie was enamored with a married man—or so it seemed.

Frankie watched Sam with a happy expression. "We should do this more often."

Out of reflex, Jackie glanced at Sam's left hand. His wedding ring was gone. He smiled back at Frankie and laughed at something she'd said only loud enough for him to hear.

Jackie understood. Maybe she was meant to cupid-bless Sam and Frankie? She closed her eyes, took a deep breath, and let it out slowly. *Sam and Frankie? What about the wife? The kids? What about...?*

Her stomach lurched, and Jackie turned her gaze back to the road ahead. *I'm not here to judge,* she told herself. *Breathe. Keep your eyes on the road.* The last thing she wanted was to get car sick.

Once they'd arrived at the ski resort, Jackie emerged from the car into a bustling snow-draped town. The wind tugged at Jackie's hair and nipped at her cheeks. She paused for a cleansing breath, glad to be out of the car. The resort resembled a bustling Alpine village combined with a fancy D.C. apartment complex. Every inch was geared toward servicing tourists. All around them, people gathered, carrying their skis and snowboards, talking, laughing, and taunting one another.

The resort sat atop a mountain. The view was spectacular with the sun glinting off the snow-capped mountains.

Jim joked, "It's all downhill from here."

Every one laughed. Jackie's came out with an edge to it, nervous and forced. In her experience, anxiety had two modes: either hard and fast, or sneaky and slow. That morning, Jackie's anxiety stalked her with slow malice, remaining just out of sight, taking its time—time during which everyone rented skis, bought lift tickets, and talked excitedly about the various slope choices. They carried their equipment out to where the ski lift was picking up and dropping off riders.

As they approached the ski lift, Jackie lagged behind. The words, "I can't," slipped from her lips, and she halted in place. No one noticed, and the others continued toward the lift.

Sam was the first to turn around. "Everything okay?"

I can't, Jackie's mind repeated. *What if he's not okay? What if I miss a call from his school? From the police? What if...*

"I'm going to wait for you guys in the lodge," Jackie said. "I'm sorry, but I..." Her anxiety finished for her, *...can't. I just can't.* "You go on. Have fun! I'll be waiting with hot toddies when you're done." Jackie tried to smile, but it was flat and tight.

Sam frowned.

Bonnie closed her eyes and took the stance of a long-suffering friend.

Jim just watched Jackie with a worried wrinkle on his brow.

Frankie shrugged. "C'mon," she said directly to Sam. "Let's get while the gettin's good." She tugged on his arm, and he went, his gaze remaining locked on Jackie until the last minute.

With a pleading look, Bonnie tried to get Jackie to change her mind. It was futile. She knew it.

"Go on!" Jackie encouraged. "I'm fine. Really. Once I hear from Jazz, I'll catch up with you." She waggled her cellphone at them. "I'm sure he's going to call any minute now."

"Don't drink all the rum before we get back," Jim called over his shoulder. He pulled Bonnie along with him.

They went on without her. Jackie trudged back to the lodge and found an empty bench outside it. She leaned her skis and poles against the lodge's log wall and looked at her cellphone. She sat on the bench, in the eye of the storm. People having fun swirled around her.

A memory surfaced, and she had an overwhelming sense of déjà vu.

One other time, she'd sat on a bench in the bitter cold, whipped by the wind, as the sun set on her world. She had clutched her cellphone then, too. Nose running. Tears freezing on her lashes. Tourists draining from the scene and trudging back to their cozy bungalows and cabins where they would drink wine and talk about what a wonderful day it had been, preparing to go home to their families.

Jackie's parents had been late to pick her up. It was Christmastime. Jackie was going home for the holiday after her ski trip. Her parents had insisted on picking her up at the ski resort instead of at college.

"It's a shorter drive," they'd said. Her dad had yelled from across the room, "Tell her we'll be there in time for dinner. I'll spring for fondue at the lodge for her and her friends."

Mom had said, "We'll be at the lodge around six, honey. Don't be late."

"I won't," Jackie had replied. And she hadn't been.

The call had come at seven-fifteen—from the state police. "Is this Jacquelyn Li?"

"Yes."

"I'm sorry to inform you there's been an accident."

An avalanche of feelings had buried the details of what he'd said. They'd sent a car for her. She'd ridden in the back, small, frozen, and unblinking, all the way to the hospital. Upon her arrival, an anonymous doctor had informed her that both her dad and her mom had died. The doctor had sat with her, holding her hand. She didn't remember the doctor's name nor even what she'd said. All she remembered was the feeling of a strong hand holding her limp one.

Sitting on the bench outside the lodge, Jackie imagined

again how her parents must have bundled themselves into the family car. They must have been talking, laughing, and fighting over which radio station to listen to. Jackie imagined how her dad would have grumbled about the cold without meaning it, and how her mom would have commiserated with him, her tone half love and half sarcasm.

Jackie had learned later that a drunk driver had crossed into their lane.

Her imagination filled in the blanks.

"Hey," came a gentle voice. "You okay?" A hand pressed heavy and warm into her shoulder, and Jackie jerked away, startled.

She looked up and registered that it was Sam. A tear ran down her cheek.

CHAPTER 14

Sam joined her inside her emotional whirlwind, sitting down beside her.

Jackie asked, "What are you doing here?"

"I wanted to make sure you were okay."

"Yeah, I'm fine. Honest."

"You're crying because you're fine?"

Jackie heaved a sigh.

Sam said, "You can talk to me, you know?"

"Christmas is when my parents were killed." Jackie blurted—to shut him up, or so she told herself.

The silence that followed was heavy and thick. Jackie spoke to push it aside. "No one warns you that the people you love could disappear from your life. I got the call... I was skiing with friends."

"So that's why you didn't want to come."

"I'm fine," Jackie insisted. "I'm going to sit this one out, if that's okay with you."

Sam's hand rested on hers. "I'm sorry."

"Thanks."

"And that's why you're so worried about your brother?"

Once Sam had said it aloud, Jackie realized the truth in it. She'd never been away from her brother at Christmastime, on the anniversary. It felt like abandoning him in his time of need.

"Yeah, I guess so." Jackie withdrew her hand from under Sam's and focused on her phone. "I've left him a dozen messages and texts. He's usually good about getting back to me."

"I'll wait with you."

"No." Jackie stood abruptly.

"Oh. Okay." Sam appeared taken aback by her vehemence.

Jackie didn't want to be the one to spoil the outing. She didn't want to have lost her parents. She didn't want to feel like that anymore. So, she did what she'd done with Jazz a thousand and one times over the years. With her hand balled into a fist so tight her nails bit into her palm, she said, "I'm fine. I'm just not in the mood to ski, okay?" Before he could answer, she pushed through the doors and into the warm lodge, into the smell of wood smoke and leather. The noise from outside drained away.

Sam followed more slowly.

Jackie spotted an empty table in the farthest corner and headed for it. As she sat down, Sam caught up with her and leaned his skis against the wall beside hers. He sat down opposite her and studied her.

"I'll wait with you," he repeated, tone firm. "Let's order something to drink. Coffee?"

Jackie gritted her teeth and stared at him. She didn't want sympathy. She'd never wanted that. It made her feel weak.

"You know, when I was sixteen," Sam said, "I was pretty rebellious. Nothing illegal. Not too illegal anyway. I was a typical teenage boy living in a boring small town. My folks gave me lots of trust. I made mistakes, sure, and sometimes they had to help me clean up my messes, but that was all part of growing up."

Jackie sighed. She looked down at her hands. She understood what he was telling her, but she'd experienced how quickly a loved one can be taken away. In a breath. In a blink. In a heartbeat.

"Tell you what," Sam said. "Why don't you make one run down the slope? What will it hurt?" He smiled, and the corners of his eyes crinkled up with merriness. "C'mon. We can go together. I'm sure your brother is fine. He's probably having the time of his life."

The worry dogs growled.

"Sam!" called Frankie, striding across the lounge toward them. "You coming?" She looked like a badass, filling out her ski suit in all the right ways, her cheeks flushed, goggles sitting above her forehead.

As Jackie watched Frankie approach, it hit her in the gut how much she differed from the woman. Frankie was cocksure, ready for the adventures of life. Jackie, not so much. Jackie had spent eight years since her parents' deaths in survival mode. In caretaker mode. She loved Jazz with all her heart and would do it all again without hesitation. But, when she compared herself to Frankie, she saw—truly saw—what that twist of fate had done to her, to her life, and to her dreams.

"Go on," Jackie said. "We can all meet for lunch once you're done. I'll be here. I want some time alone."

Frankie wasn't taking "No" for an answer. She tugged Sam up out of his seat.

"Give the lady some space," said Frankie.

"You sure?" Sam asked, eyes on Jackie.

Jackie nodded. She watched them go, saw Sam look back at her multiple times en route to the door, and put her best faux smile on for him. She even gave him a little wave. *See? I'm fine.*

The door to the mountain, to the sky, opened and Frankie and Sam passed through them. When the door closed again, it was like a shroud falling on the world. Jackie sat there, staring at it, her vision swimming with tears. She hadn't cried for her parents in years. But then, neither had she stood on top of the world, where all her inner turmoil was exposed.

Jackie hid away for an hour, drinking coffee and pretending to read a book from the shelf by the fireplace between glances at her cellphone.

"Making the most of the *per diem*, I see," said a judgmental, British-accented voice.

Much to her surprise, Ignacio Amore loomed over her, dressed in a thick wool coat—gray—that covered him to his knees, a bright red scarf, and a herringbone ivy cap. He pulled out a chair at her table and sat, removing his leather gloves.

Jackie sputtered, "I... What?"

"Don't trouble yourself with explanations for why you're here instead of at the inn. I don't care. This is a courtesy call. Did you read the manual?"

Jackie nodded, relieved that she had. "Yes. I read it."

"Do you have any questions?"

Do I? Jackie considered it. She floundered, trying to think of any. Truth was that she hadn't thought about being a cupid since she'd woken up that morning.

Amore removed his gloves and hat, then set them aside. He looked at Jackie with casual indifference.

Jackie shook her head.

"No questions?" Amore asked again.

Jackie shook her head again.

"Then, I have to wonder why you're tucked up in the darkest corner of this establishment, all by yourself." He spoke as if he were discussing the weather. "How do you expect to cupid, if you're being stupid?"

Jackie blinked. "Excuse me?"

"You can't hide from this, Jacquelyn. Either you do your job, or I will be forced to file a rather unflattering report with my boss. That would be bad for all of us, so I suggest you get off your arse. How will you learn to recognize true love, if you don't practice?"

Jackie shifted in her chair. "I don't know how to recognize true love."

Amore's upper lip curled as he mimicked her with an extra whine, "I don't know how to recognize true love." He leaned forward on the table, gaze intense. "Is that true?"

"Yes?"

Amore nodded and nodded some more, studying Jackie, leaving her to squirm in the uncomfortable silence.

Jackie said, "Yes. It's true. I don't..."

"Stop." Amore raised his palm to her. "Have you even tried?"

"Tried to what?"

"To recognize true love when it's right in front of you." Amore turned to hook his arm over the back of the chair and look around the room. "What do you see here, Jacquelyn?"

Jackie closed her eyes, took a deep breath, and wished he'd leave her alone. When he cleared his throat, she knew the wish had failed. Opening her eyes, she looked around the room—for the first time since she'd arrived. The conversations going on had been a hum of background noise that hadn't broken through to her consciousness until just that moment. She saw friends, couples, and families, sitting, standing, moving. In an instant, her world expanded beyond the bubble she'd made for herself.

Amore asked again, "What do you see?"

"People."

"Do any of them stand out to you?"

Jackie scanned the room. It had a warm glow that emanated from lamps with golden glass and the fire dancing in the fireplace. Spoons clinked in mugs, and the shuffle of fabric provided an undercurrent as people moved. The variety of colored hats was festive.

Shaking her head, Jackie had no idea what Amore wanted her to see.

"Look closely. There's true love in this room. Can you find it?"

There were several obvious couples in the room, some alone, some with bigger groups. Holding hands. Arm in arm. Sitting close to one another. But none stood out to Jackie. "I don't...," she said. "Where?"

"It'd be cheating if I told you. Keep looking."

Jackie's frustration was rising, with him, with herself. "I can't," she said, and the moment the words were out of her mouth, she spotted them. Behind the bar. Two men laughed together, weaving in and out of each other's paths as they made drinks. The glow was there. The same one she'd seen with Bonnie and Jim.

Amore said, "Yes." He put his hat on his head and picked up his gloves.

Jackie watched the couple, seeing their ease with one another, the way they predicted each other's movements, not unlike how she and Bonnie were after so many years at the diner—but more.

Amore stood. "True love, my dulcet Jacquelyn, is a tangible aura."

"Can I work my cupid woo-woo on them?"

Amore coughed, and Jackie would have sworn he was attempting to cover a laugh. "No," he said, stoic as ever. "They've already been blessed." He turned to leave. "It's time for you to stop living in fear, Jacquelyn Li. There's more to life than martyrdom."

Jackie said, "I have a question."

Amore paused and looked back at her. "Yes?"

"Why me?"

Amore's eyebrows shot up in surprise. "I've asked myself that many times since I met you."

"So, why? There must be lots of others who are more qualified than me."

Nodding in agreement, Amore said, "Truer words were never spoken, and yet... reality is what it is."

With a frown of frustration, Jackie watched Amore stride out of the restaurant, leaving no chance for any more questions. She turned her gaze back to the happy couple. All her self-imposed troubles suddenly felt small and petty. The dogs of worry had scattered, either in fear of Amore, or in the wake of her realization.

Reality is what it is, Jackie thought. Her mind chewed on her situation, and a niggling voice in her head was calling her out. It challenged her to get off her ass and out into the crisp weather. It berated her with words like "coward" and "weak." It told her Jazz was fine and that she wasn't being protective. She was being *a ninny.*

After that, every couple in the lodge, their laughter, their voices ringing with excitement and happiness, reminded her of what she was missing, what she wanted for her life. When she eventually returned to Alexandria, she'd have to get back to the daily grind of work and taking care of Jazz. But for now... For now, she was a cupid, caught in a fantasy unlike anything she'd imagined for herself. And while she knew—well, she hoped—it wouldn't last beyond Christmas, she could embrace the weirdness for a while. The one thing she knew beyond a doubt was that, if her parents had been there with her, they would not have wanted her to hide away by herself.

Jackie pushed back her chair, stood, stretched, and finally headed for the fresh air.

◆♥◆

CHAPTER 15

Jackie put on her skis and stood in line for the ski lift. Once the decision had been made, she felt her excitement rising. The cold air made her nose run, and her cheeks tightened. She felt alive. She felt like her old self, the self who hadn't lost her parents, who hadn't had to become a parent, who hadn't had to give up college or a steady paycheck.

She spotted Sam before he saw her. He was shooshing down the last leg of the run. She recognized him by the color of his suit and the angles of his body. He wore no hat, and his hair was wind-tossed, sticking up over the band of his goggles. He was strong and agile, moving down the hill with ease, slaloming around slower skiers. The grin on his face told her everything about how much he was loving it.

The moment he saw her, his grin spread even wider, which made her smile in response. He changed direction and skied up to her, stopping with control at her side. He pushed his goggles onto his forehead.

Sam said, "Hey there. You change your mind about skiing?"

"I found a little... clarity, shall we say." Jackie moved forward as the line progressed toward the lift. "You look like you're having fun."

"A little," Sam replied with a wink that made Jackie's stomach do a flurp. She turned to one side, hoping to hide the blush of pleasure she felt burn in her cheeks.

Jackie asked, "Have you seen Bonnie and Jim?"

"Our paths have crossed. They seem like they're having a good time. They were on the lift, going up to the intermediate slope just as I was coming down. Did you want to wait here for them?"

"No." What Jackie wanted was to ski. Her excitement was igniting her urge to use her body and to feel the wind.

It was her turn to get onto the lift, and Sam moved in to join her. The seat slid up behind them and they settled onto it. Sam pulled down the safety bar, and then they were being lifted up and way. All around, the beauty of the mountain and the valley provided a magnificent view.

Jackie asked, "You come here often?"

So easy was Sam's laughter that Jackie had to join in. She hadn't realized how her question would sound.

"Just about every week in the winter. It clears out the cobwebs." Sam draped his arm along the back of the bench, behind Jackie's shoulders.

Jackie liked how that felt. *Married man,* she reminded herself. Aloud, she asked, "What about your wife and kids? Do they come with you sometimes?"

"No wife. No kids."

Dumbfounded, Jackie turned to stare at him. "You wear a ring. I heard your kids on the phone."

Sam met her gaze for a long moment then burst into laughter. "Those are my sister's kids. I share a house with her and her kids. She's a single mom, and I help out. You'll meet them at Christmas dinner."

"Your sister?" Jackie felt a profound sense of relief. "But you wear a ring."

"I drive a taxi. If I don't, I get hit on by strangers."

"Really?" Jackie could see why, with that face and body of his.

"You'd be surprised how many lonely women—and men— there are in the world. All ages. I just like to have an excuse so I don't hurt their feelings when I turn 'em down."

Teasing, Jackie sang quietly, "Just a gigolo..."

Sam laughed aloud, the sound warm and unhindered. His eyes twinkled as he looked at her, and Jackie knew hers were just as bright.

I like him, she thought. *Maybe, when all this cupid nonsense is done...* She didn't have a chance to finish the thought.

"Get ready," Sam said, directing Jackie's eyes off himself and forward to where the lift platform was coming up. They prepared to disembark.

The platform slid up under their skis, and Jackie slid forward, leaving the bench. The slope appeared ahead of them, and Jackie moved her poles into position.

"After you," said Sam, waving a hand with gentlemanly grace.

Jackie responded with a half-nod, half-curtsy, then pulled her goggles down over her eyes. "See you at the bottom." She checked around her for other skiers then put all her attention on pushing off.

Initially, the incline was smooth. In college, she'd skied the black-diamond slopes, so she felt confident on the intermediate one. Her heartbeat accelerated, and she felt the rush of adrenaline that always accompanied her runs. The mountain rose up to meet her skis, and she controlled her speed with turns. The snow was perfect. The sky stretched overhead, blue, cloudless, cold, and clear. The slope spread before her, lined on either side with trees.

Entering the flow of skiers and snowboarders, she concentrated on bending her knees, on balance, on attempting to predict the terrain. She jumped over a small bulge and was passed by a bunch of teenagers racing one another. The cold air filled her lungs and brought her mind to high alertness.

Then, her phone rang. It buzzed in her coat pocket.

Jazz!

Jackie slowed down and pulled off one glove. "Wait, wait!" she said aloud, as if Jazz could hear her. "Don't hang up. I'm coming!" She plowed to a halt and unzipped her pocket. She had the phone in hand and saw that it was a telemarketer—not Jazz—when a body crashed into her, wrapped an arm around her waist, and practically threw her forward into the snow. Cast off-balance, she fell forward, arms and legs flailing. The other person's momentum came down with her to land on top of her.

"Hey!" someone shouted. A waterfall of voices responded: "Hazard!" "Watch out!" "Get to the side!" "Coming through!" "Shit!"

A poof of powder covered her face, and Jackie sputtered, wiping at it with her gloved hand. She squirmed out from under her attacker and rolled so she could see him.

It was Sam lying beside her. He had snowflakes on his long lashes.

"Why'd you do that?" Jackie asked.

"I just saved your ass. Why'd you stop?"

"I got a call. I thought it might be my brother."

"You..." Sam rolled off Jackie and sat up. One of his skis was gone. "You could've been killed. Or seriously injured. You can't stop in the middle of the slope like that."

"Sorry." Jackie looked down the slope to where several people were flipping her the bird and shouting obscenities back at her. She looked up-slope. Sam had tackled her off to the side enough that they weren't in immediate danger, but they needed to move.

Jackie's skis were still attached to her boots. She wiggled into position to get to her feet and found her phone lying in the snow where she'd dropped it. She tucked it in her pocket then turned her attention to Sam, surprised to find he wasn't also on his feet.

With care, Sam was rolling the ankle of the foot that had lost its ski.

Jackie ski-walked to stand uphill of him, where any skiers coming down the mountain would see her. "You okay?"

Sam's mouth flattened into a line. "I think I sprained my ankle."

"What?" Jackie crouched down.

"Get me my ski, will you?" Sam indicated the one that had fallen off, lying several feet away from him.

Jackie did as he requested. He re-attached the ski to his boot.

Sam squared his skis off perpendicular to the slope then, using his poles, tried to push up to his feet. He nearly succeeded. He cried out in pain and collapsed back to the ground.

Jackie rushed to help him but wasn't properly balanced and nearly ended up falling again herself.

"Definitely sprained," said Sam.

Misery in every word, Jackie said, "I'm so sorry!"

Another skier—Frankie—skidded to a stop beside Jackie, spewing powder up her leg.

Frankie cried, "Are you hurt?" She approached Sam more carefully.

"Ankle," said Sam. "Won't hold my weight."

Frankie turned on Jackie, her face twisted with anger. "What were you doing? Texting?"

Jackie's only reply was to make a remorseful face.

"Oh my god." Frankie dropped to one knee beside Sam. "You had to bring the city folk up the mountain, didn't you?" She got one arm under his shoulder and began to lift. "Let's get you up."

Jackie ski-clomped around to Sam's other side, feeling like a clod. "How can I help?"

"Just stay out of the way," Frankie said.

And so, Jackie followed them down the slope, an inch at a time until they were at the bottom. The lodge there had a first-aid station, and Jackie stayed with them as they moved toward it. They paused on the porch, and Frankie helped Sam take off his skis.

Jackie hovered, useless.

The interior of the first-aid station smelled like cleaning supplies. It could have been a city clinic, except the only other people in the station were a teenager and his mother. He had his arm in a sling and looked pale as a ghost.

Frankie helped Sam into a chair.

A woman in navy blue scrubs came out of the back room and approached Sam.

"Hi," she said. "I'm a nurse practitioner. You can call me Tina. Where does it hurt?" She had dimples that deepened in her cheeks when she smiled.

Jackie's phone rang.

All eyes turned to her.

Frankie said, "You better take that," and her sarcasm was biting.

Digging the phone from her pocket, Jackie checked the caller I.D. It was Jazz.

"Sorry," she said and quickly answered. "Jazz!" As she talked, she headed toward the door and out into the cold. "Where have you been?"

"Hey, sis." Jazz didn't sound the least bit concerned—about anything. "My phone died. I just got your ten thousand messages."

"Dammit, Jazz! I was worried." Jackie paced on the porch.

Incredulity put an edge on Jazz's reply: "Why?"

"I didn't know if you were dead, or in jail, or what. You have to answer when I call."

"Okay, *Mom*, settle down. I'm sixteen, not six."

Jackie took a deep, calming breath, and bit her tongue on the scolding words that were threatening to roll out of her.

A group of skiers walked by laughing.

Jazz asked, "Where are you?"

"I'm still in West Virginia," Jackie told him. "I have to be here until after Christmas. I'm sorry."

"Eh, no big. I'll just hang with Razz. He thinks he's getting a new console."

Another group walked by, talking animatedly about the slopes.

Jazz added, "Sounds like you're having fun."

"No," Jackie replied. "I am definitely *not* having fun."

"Well, why not?"

"Because...I don't want to be here. I should be there with you. It's almost Christmas."

"Oh, for chrissakes, Jacks. Pull the stick out of your ass for just once."

"Excuse me?"

"You heard me." Jazz moved the phone away from his mouth to speak to someone in the room with him, "Yeah, yeah. One sec. My sister's having a meltdown."

"I am not having a meltdown!" Jackie raised her voice, drawing the attention of those around her. She turned her back on them, facing the window of the clinic, only to find Frankie staring out at her with a critical look on her face.

Jackie repeated, more quietly, "I'm not having a meltdown." She moved the phone to her other ear, turning away from Frankie.

Jazz said, "I have to go. Me and Razz are in a tournament tonight."

"So." Jackie didn't want to say goodbye. She felt like she should say something more. The conversation so far had been dissatisfying. "Everything's okay then? How's school? You've been getting enough to eat?"

Jazz heaved a sigh big enough to blow out even Jackie's numerous birthday candles. "Yes—on holiday break—and yes. Stop worrying. I can take care of myself. Go have fun, Jacks. I'll see you when you get back. Bye!"

Jackie opened her mouth to say more, but Jazz hung up before she could get it out.

"Okay," she said, staring down at her phone. "I guess you're all right." She looked up and met Frankie's eyes again. For a moment, she was tempted to hold the phone back to her ear and pretend to talk, just so she wouldn't have to face Frankie's disapproval, but she didn't. She straightened her spine and went back into the warmth of the clinic.

"...need an X-ray," the nurse practitioner was saying. "I'll splint it for you, but you're going to need to go to the hospital. It's swelling up good. My guess is—bare minimum—you sprained the heck out of it. Worst-case scenario, it's broken."

Jackie felt the blood drain from her face.

CHAPTER 16

The trip to the hospital delayed lunch into early afternoon. By then, the group had returned to the inn, and Lu set out sandwich makings for everyone. This proved a solemn affair for everyone except Bonnie and Jim who talked excitedly about their skiing adventures, promising they'd be back every year.

Jackie could barely even eat. She picked at her roast beef sandwich, pretending to smile and nodding with the flow of the conversation.

Sam was high on pain killers, seated in an overstuffed armchair with his foot propped up on an ottoman. Frankie waited on him, hand and foot, and refused anyone else's help.

Jackie watched as Frankie put together a sandwich for Sam, and it occurred to her, not for the first time, that the two might have feelings for one another. For reasons she didn't yet understand, this made her even more miserable. Her urge was to get out, to leave and spend some time alone, but she didn't want to lock herself away in her room with Bonnie and Jim there.

The ringing of the desk bell in the lobby drew everyone's attention. A figure dressed all in black stood in full view through the dining room entranceway. He wore a long coat and had long, black hair, shaved close on one side and draping down over his eye on the other side. In his hand, he held his cellphone up, apparently filming and talking as he did so. He had on fingerless gloves and leather pants, and his boots were heavy and thick-soled.

Jackie couldn't hear what he was saying, but she noted the way he posed for his own camera, lifting his chin for just the right angle, and flashing his eyes to underscore something he said. He waved his free hand in the air with exaggerated grace, fingers slowly curling like a magician's. Jackie recognized the eye make-up and gothic styling. She'd had friends in high school and college who had liked to visit the goth clubs in town, dressed to the nines in black and red, lace and leather.

Under her breath, Jackie said, "Nicholas Wolfe." For surely it was him, husband to Natalie Pasternak, here to have Jackie save their marriage. Jackie's throat clenched and her belly did a flop. The couples were arriving.

"Oh, it's beautiful!" came a female voice. "Art, look at the Christmas tree!"

Art's response was inaudible.

"Art and Ada Kaluza," Jackie said, guessing.

Bonnie perked up. "We gonna go meet them?"

Jackie felt a spike of anxiety. "Let's let them get checked in first."

Three couples congregated at the front desk. Natalie Pasternack was there, dressed similarly to her husband in all black, the coat fitted to her and Victorian in style. She wore knee-high boots and black leggings. Her make-up was dark and dramatic. She turned in place, her smart phone attached to a high-tech, handheld rig with a microphone and view screen. She smiled into the lens when she brought the camera back onto herself.

Gita and Ruth Gupta-Smith waited for their turn to check-in, standing slightly apart with their luggage beside them. They talked quietly to one another, pointing out things in the lobby that caught their eyes. Gita had the dark skin and hair of a woman with Asian Indian heritage. Her wife, Ruth, had similar dark hair, albeit longer, but her light skin suggested she was of European descent. They resembled one another in dress and stance, much the way old married couples tended to do. They both wore ski jackets and blue jeans, with thick scarves around their necks.

"Card!" shouted Lu as she sped out to greet them with Frankie on her heels.

"You sure?" asked Bonnie, sounding surprised.

"Yeah. I think maybe I'll go do some shopping. I need to get some things for tomorrow's sessions."

Bonnie sat forward. "Really? Like what?"

"Stuff. Crafty stuff and stuff. You know." Jackie just wanted to get out, go away from the inn, from the chaos of couples, from Sam, and from Frankie's accusatory side-eye glares. "Wanna drive me?" The idea was so enticing, Jackie managed a cajoling smile.

Jim shook his head. "Sounds like a job for you two. After that lunch, I need a nap. The car keys are in our room, though."

Bonnie nodded. "A shopping adventure!"

Jackie pushed back her chair, eager to be gone. "Let's do it." She waited for Bonnie to rise then strode out and through the lobby, giving the group gathered at the front desk a wide berth. She hit the stairs at a trot and was up them before Bonnie or Jim had stepped on the first stair.

As she walked into the store, Jackie kept an eye out for Eloise.

Bonnie had her cellphone out and was typing in notes of what they'd need. "You're going to have them make gratitude lists, yeah? We should get some notebooks and pens for everyone."

"Definitely. And art paper and supplies, markers, crayons, maybe some felt and yarn or something—for when they make Christmas cards." Jackie had been surprised at how many ideas they'd come up with for activities.

Bonnie continued the thread, "And we should see if they have roses, for date night."

"Ooh, good idea." Jackie smiled, feeling her energy rising. "Maybe boxes of chocolates too. Might help put them in the right frame of mind."

"Might put *you* in a better frame of mind, too. Let's get extra."

"Agreed."

They roamed the art supply and Christmas decoration aisles looking for anything crafty. They found cheap wrapping paper in bulk, ribbons, mistletoe, and fake holly. Bonnie insisted they peruse the toy aisle as well. All in all, by the time they were done, Jackie had spent almost all of her cupid daily allowance, and Bonnie had a couple bags of presents for everyone.

They made their way to the checkout aisles and got in line.

"Back again, hm?" said a crackly voice from behind Jackie.

Eloise had found her. She wore a blue vest, hanging open, over a red T-shirt that said, "Happy Ho Ho Ho."

Jackie smiled. "Yes. We needed some supplies. How are you today, Eloise?"

"Where's Sam?" Eloise looked around. "Not with you this time?"

"No." Jackie indicated Bonnie. "This is my friend Bonnie. She's helping me."

Bonnie gave a smile and a little wave. She began to place items on the conveyor belt. "Hi. How do you two know each other?"

Eloise nodded to Bonnie but ignored the question and turned her attention back to Jackie. She had an agenda. "Y'know, that man is a good'un. He's wooing my Frankie. They're thick as thieves, those two. I wouldn't be surprised if there wasn't wedding bells in their future."

"Your... Wait. You're Frankie's mom?"

Eloise gave another firm nod. "How long you plannin' on stayin' at the Gray Fox for?"

Jackie frowned, looking up at the tall, tough woman. Knowing her relation to Frankie, she could clearly see the resemblance. "Only until after Christmas."

"Good. I bet the city's missin' ya, ain't it? Frankie says you're some famous psychologist."

Jackie recoiled. "No. I'm not famous, and I'm not a psychologist. I'm..." She didn't know what she was.

"An inspirational speaker and marriage coach," Bonnie supplied.

Jackie gave her friend a quick smile of gratitude.

Eloise said, "Frankie an' Sam grew up together. They're like two peas in a pod. I reckon it's true love, yeah, I do." She squinted one eye at Jackie, scrutinizing her.

Jackie didn't know what to say. An uncomfortable silence prickled between them.

Again, Bonnie to the rescue. She said, "Jackie, it's our turn to check out."

Jackie glanced at the clerk. "I better..."

Eloise had already started walking away.

"Nice to see you again," Jackie called.

"Wow," said Bonnie, leaning in to add under her breath. "Imagine having her as a mother-in-law."

Jackie laughed. "Right?"

The Gray Fox Inn had a large room for meetings and conferences that Lu had said Jackie could use for her seminars. It was surprisingly well-teched-out with wireless Internet and a large-screen television hanging on the wall for presentations. It could seat a dozen comfortably around its large table.

Jackie and Bonnie spent the afternoon decorating the room with holiday spirit, stringing Christmas lights and garland, and setting out notepads, pens, and other supplies that her participants would need.

"This looks great!" Card appeared in the doorway to the room, hands on his ample hips, an even more ample smile on his face. "Nice job, ladies."

Jackie was on a chair, hanging the mistletoe over the doorway.

"Thanks," said Jackie. "I wanted to put the guests as much at ease as possible."

"Well done." The man skirted around Jackie's chair and stepped into the room, going toward a closet door in the far corner. "I just need to grab something out of here, if you don't mind."

"No, you're not bothering us." Jackie pushed the pin up into the ceiling and let the mistletoe dangle. Satisfied with her work, she stepped down from the chair—and right into Sam, who had just appeared beside the chair.

Knocked off balance, she tipped into him. He, on crutches, didn't have the stability to counterbalance her, and they both leaned against the doorframe. Jackie pressed into Sam's chest. His arm went around her. Her breath caught in her throat.

He was strong and sturdy, even when his equilibrium was in question. Between his crutch and the door frame, he managed to stabilize them both.

"Oh my gosh," Jackie said, feeling the heat of his chest against her palms. She could smell his cologne, an evergreen aroma that she usually didn't notice—but this close... It took her breath away.

Jackie felt a fire ignite deep in her belly. She looked up into Sam's eyes, her face lifted to him, and they held like that for what seemed an eternity. It was truly only a second, maybe two.

Bonnie's face appeared in Jackie's peripheral vision, grinning. Bonnie pointed up at the mistletoe and said, "Might as well be the first. It's a Christmas rule!"

When Jackie realized what she was suggesting, heat flooded her cheeks. She looked up at Sam to see mischief and amusement in the crinkle of his eyes and the tilt of his mouth. "Might as well," he said.

Before Jackie knew what was happening, Sam had captured her mouth, pressing his lips to hers. Jackie forgot to close her eyes, until the sensation sent electricity to her core and awoke something deep in her.

It was a simple and respectable kiss, Jackie would tell herself later. No tongue. No moving. Just lips touching for the first time. And when it was over, Jackie felt herself wobble again. Sam's arm tightened around her.

Jackie pushed off against Sam's chest and stood on her own two feet again. She cleared her throat.

Sam leaned on his crutch, watching her.

"Um," Jackie said, turning away, embarrassed. "How's your ankle?"

"Better."

"Good. I'm sorry about that." Jackie picked up the chair and carried it back toward the table.

"You can stop apologizing. After that kiss, I can't be mad at you."

Jackie caught Bonnie's expression as she passed by. Her friend had a knowing smirk on her face, and Jackie blatantly ignored it. She said, diverting the topic, "So... Bonnie and I are getting things ready for tomorrow."

"Yeah," Sam replied, "I see that."

A rustling-shuffling-banging noise came from the closet at the back of the room and all eyes turned to see Card backing out with a box in his arms. On the side, in black marker, it said,

"Santa Suit."

"You going to play Santa?" Bonnie asked, excitement in her voice.

"Do every year," said Card. "For the kids at a local children's home."

"The ones who are coming to carol on Christmas Eve?" Jackie asked, moving to stand beside him.

"Yup, that'd be the ones. Lord knows they got little enough magic in their lives." Card shook his head and tucked his thumb in his suspenders. "We do what we can to brighten their holiday."

"That is so kind of you," said Bonnie.

"It's nothin'. Me an' Lu have just as much fun as they do." Card laughed deep and very Santa-like. "Lu's got gift bags made for each of 'em, so they don't go away empty-handed."

If Jackie hadn't already fallen in love with Card and Lu, she would have at that moment.

Card said, "C'mon, Sam. Let's you and me leave these ladies to their work. Tonight's the welcome dinner for our guests, so we got some preppin' to do."

"Yes, sir," replied Sam, voice warm. He led the way back out into the hallway, with Card following, box in his arms.

CHAPTER 17

Jackie chose wide-legged navy dress pants and a salmon-colored sweater for the welcome dinner. Her hair was behaving surprisingly well, despite the static electricity that had been plaguing her all afternoon. She put on a touch of mascara and light-colored lip gloss, but otherwise didn't bother with make-up. She'd given herself permission to skip wearing make-up when she'd started waitressing. She hated the hassle more than she liked what it did for her face. And, as Bonnie said, "Make-up was invented to make us more attractive to the opposite sex, kind of like how female baboons have rouged asses to let males know they're ready to mate." After that, Jackie had never looked at rouge or lipstick quite the same way.

Nervous energy tickled Jackie's stomach as she descended the stairs and crossed the lobby toward the restaurant. She paused just outside, hearing voices coming from the dining room. She'd wanted to be the first down, but apparently some of the couples had already arrived. Card's laughter rose above the others, and quiet piano music—"We Wish You a Merry Christmas"—provided the backdrop.

Jackie paused just outside the double doors, took a deep breath, and said to herself, "I've got this." She put a smile on her face and stepped boldly forward into the dining room.

A quick scan of the room revealed that Lu and Card had pushed tables together to make one long one for the group. Nick was seated alone near one end, cellphone in hand, thumbing something into it. He wore all black, even his hair dark against his pale skin. His wife, Natalie, had changed into a blouse with Victorian ruffles at the sleeves and neck. She stood by the tall windows with their navy velvet drapes. She was posing to take a picture of herself with the arm of her selfie stick extended.

Ada was sitting at the other end of the table from Nick, talking animatedly with Gita and Ruth. Her husband, Art, had propped himself up at the bar with a martini at hand. He kept looking at his cellphone, oblivious to the rest of the room.

To Jackie's surprise, someone she'd never seen before was seated at the piano. He was dressed in a cream-colored turtleneck that brought out the warm brown of his skin and hair. He rocked as he played, watching everyone as his fingers worked their magic. He caught Jackie's gaze, smiled, and nodded politely. Jackie returned it.

Frankie was behind the bar, wiping the counter with a rag. She wore a classic bartending shirt: black button-down. Her eyes kept drifting to the fireplace where Sam was propped up in his armchair, injured leg lifted onto the ottoman. He had added a corduroy jacket to his jeans and dress shirt. His injured foot had its therapeutic boot on, thick and heavy-looking. He was being nursed by a high-ball glass with clear liquid in it.

Lu and Card waved Jackie over to where they stood at the end of the bar.

"Hi," Jackie said.

Lu stepped forward to meet her and took hold of her wrist. "We heard from Jenkins, the fourth couple, this afternoon. Seems they're not coming."

"Why not?"

Lu shook her head. "They didn't give a reason. Jus' cancelled. That's okay. You can work with only three, right?"

"I suppose so," replied Jackie, though she was doing the cupid math. She had to bless three couples before Christmas was over, and her chances of success had just diminished by a significant percentage. She looked out at the room, at the three remaining couples, and sighed.

Lu said under her breath, "You've got your work cut out for you."

Jackie couldn't agree more, but she put her smile back on and said, "I like a challenge."

"Glad to hear it," Lu said, voice low but excited. "So's you know, Frankie's going to start pouring the wine soon, so if you wanted to speechify or do a toast, you'll be able to. Dinner's comin' in about ten minutes."

Jackie smiled, "Thanks."

Card asked, a conspiratorial note in his voice, "So what's the plan?"

Jackie wondered the same thing to herself. *What was the plan?* Despite all her preparation, list-making, and thinking about it, she still felt unprepared. Something hadn't clicked. Aloud, she said, "Tonight is about getting to know each other. Social more than anything. I'll be mingling and encouraging our guests to do the same. I think I need to observe them a bit and get to know them better."

"Well," said Card, "you holler if you need anythin'. We're here to help."

Jackie watched Frankie go around the table offering to pour a glass of wine, first to the cluster of three ladies, then to the solo man at the other end of the table. The time had come to let out the clutch.

As she crossed the room, she became acutely aware of Sam's eyes on her and was reminded of the kiss. She didn't let their eyes meet for more than a half second, looking quickly away again as the blush returned to her face. She lifted her chin and kept moving, focusing on her destination. *It's only normal,* she told herself, *to feel a little crush on Sam*. He was, after all, attractive—extremely so—and nice, funny, helpful, thoughtful, intelligent, *single*... Jackie took a deep breath. *And wooing Frankie.*

As if to underscore her thought, Frankie left the table and walked over to Sam, handing him a replacement for his empty glass. They exchanged a few words that Jackie couldn't hear, then laughed together. Frankie leaned down to say something more intimate to him, and then they both laughed again.

Jackie arrived at the table and chose the chair opposite Nick, pulled it out, and sat. "Hi," she said to him. "I'm Jackie Li. I'm leading the workshop this weekend." She held out her hand to him.

Nick had to pry his eyes from his phone, but once he had, his smile was genuine, and he shook her hand with enthusiasm, getting partially up out of his seat as he did so. "A pleasure, lady doctor," he said with charming affectation. "I am Nicholas Maddox, and that delightful creature over there, admiring herself, is my wife, Natalie Pasternack. If history repeats, she'll join us eventually."

"Welcome to the Gray Fox," said Jackie. "I'm looking forward to spending the next few days with you." And for a moment, she believed she was telling the truth.

"Ahem." Jackie stood and cleared her throat. She tapped her spoon on the edge of her wine glass.

Everyone had arrived and was seated at the table, including Bonnie and Jim, who were also afforded places there. Sam remained distant, in his armchair, while Frankie, Lu, and Card had disappeared into the kitchen, presumably to finish dinner.

The piano man brought the song he'd been playing to a gentle halt when Jackie clinked.

Then all eyes were on her.

"Hello, everyone," Jackie began and then promptly forgot everything she'd been planning to say. She looked around the table, her smile frozen on her face. "Welcome."

The pause stretched long, until Jackie reached into her pocket and pulled out her notes for the introductory speech. She looked them over, then said, "I'm Jackie Li."

Most of the people at the table applauded—all but Art who sat back in his chair with disdainful nonchalance to observe the goings on.

Jackie felt the heat rise into her cheeks for the third time that day, her heart responding to the renewed rush of adrenaline into her system. She waved the applause away and said, "Please, call me Jackie." She looked again at her notes and read a blurb she'd taken directly from the brochure. "The Gray Fox Inn welcomes you to the first annual Holiday Happy Marriage workshop. We have activities planned for daytime, and in the evenings you'll have homework." She took a deep breath. "Tonight is our welcome dinner, prepared for us by Lula and Card Miller, the inn's owners."

"No homework for the kiddies tonight?" said Art, derision and a touch of drunken slur in his voice.

Jackie looked at him, her smile still in place. "No. Tonight is all about getting settled in and relaxing. If you have any questions about the workshop, I'll be available."

Art said, "I have a question."

"All right. Go ahead." Jackie folded her hands together in front of her. Her exchange with Art was already resembling a tennis match, with everyone else—the spectators—turning their heads right and left as each of them spoke.

"I wanna know," said Art, definitely slurring his words, "what makes you qualified to tell me how to improve my marriage. How long have you been married? Is he here? 'Cause I got some questions for him too."

Jackie's mouth dried up.

Everyone was looking at her.

"I..." Jackie stuttered. "I... I'm not married."

Art gave a guffaw. "You've got to be kidding me. I told you this was going to be a joke, Ada." He looked around the table, seeking others who agreed with him. No one else rose to the occasion, but Art didn't look any less smug.

Jackie opened her mouth again to say something, but nothing came out. She'd had the same doubt from the beginning, and in five minutes or less, Art had called her out.

"Dinner is served," said Card with extra boom in his voice. He, Lu, and Frankie arrived like the cavalry to save her, trays holding platters and bowls in hand.

Slowly, Jackie sank into her chair, as deflated as a leaky balloon. She couldn't help glancing at Sam, to see if he'd heard, to see what he was thinking.

Sam was gazing into his glass.

A heavy hand landed on Jackie's shoulder and gave it a squeeze. Jackie didn't even bother to look up, but she knew it was Card, giving her moral support. She wanted to crawl up to her room and never come out again.

From the middle of the table, Bonnie's exuberant conversation was drawing others in as well, and Jackie gratefully let her extroverted friend take the reins. Though dinner looked and smelled wonderful—honeyed ham, mashed sweet potatoes, baked beans, vegetable pot pies, steamed broccoli, and a fresh salad—Jackie found she wasn't hungry.

At her earliest opportunity, Jackie excused herself and went to the public restroom at the back of the dining area. She locked herself in a stall and buried her face in her hands. Taking several deep breaths, she tried to blow out the tightness in her muscles and ease the headache that was building at the back of her head.

The sound of someone else entering brought her head up, and Jackie quickly set about doing her business. She didn't want anyone to see her feet under the door and know she wasn't there to pee.

"Jackie?" came Bonnie's voice.

"Yeah." Jackie's gratitude that it was Bonnie was palpable.

Bonnie stayed out by the sink. "That guy's a jackass. Don't let him get to you."

"I know."

"What does it matter if you've been married or not?" Bonnie said, building up to a rant. "I mean, would he not go to an oncologist who hasn't had cancer? A butcher who is vegetarian? Or a gynecologist who doesn't have a vagina?"

"Good points all." Jackie emerged from the stall and stepped up to wash her hands. "I don't blame him. He's right. I don't know what I'm doing."

Bonnie frowned at Jackie in the mirror, meeting her gaze

there and wagging a finger at her. "Stop saying that. You're smart and compassionate. And if they didn't think you'd make a great cupid, you wouldn't have been guilted into being here. Seriously. That Amore guy thinks you can do it, and so do I."

"I'm not so sure. Have you seen those couples?"

"Yeah," said Bonnie, pulling a face. "The only ones who look like they're in love are the lesbians, and I'm suspicious of them. Why would they come for a couples' workshop if they're so in love? Anyway... You're doing great. Don't worry." Bonnie stepped forward and wrapped her arms around Jackie from behind, putting her chin on the other woman's shoulder and smiling at her in the mirror. "Tonight is just about getting to know each other, right? And now we know who the biggest asshole in the group is." Bonnie's smile tipped crooked and her eyes glittered with amusement.

Jackie laughed. She put her hand on Bonnie's arm, holding it. "You saved me back there. Thanks, Bon."

"Hubs and I aren't going anywhere. If we have to spend our entire Christmas being a buffer between you and Art the Fart, then we're happy to do it. We've got your back." Bonnie gave Jackie a squeeze, then let her go. Together, the ladies walked out of the restroom and returned to the table.

Jackie felt refreshed, lighter, and even managed a smile as she sat back down. From there, the evening progressed much more smoothly, especially after Art had moved back to the end of the bar and took up texting with focused concentration. No one complained, not even his wife. She was having a great time, if her bright laughter and easy conversation were any indication.

Through the course of dinner, dessert, and aperitifs, Jackie began to get a feel for her couples.

"So, Nicholas," Jackie said. "What exactly do you do?"

Nicholas looked at Jackie through the fall of his long hair, only one eye showing. Slowly, he sat back, tenting his fingers in contemplation before replying. "My job is community building," he said. "My fans are loyal, and many of them look, dress, and think like I do. My taking all of this—" He indicated himself with a sweep of both hands. "—Public, gives my fans validation and permission to be themselves, to congregate with others like themselves, and to evangelize their lifestyles to the world. In many ways, I'm a modern-day priest, but my religion is art."

"Art? You're an artist?"

"Not the kind of art you mean," Nicholas answered Jackie. "I make art with my life, my aesthetic, and my daily rituals and choices. Life is the medium. And in that context, we are all artists." His eyes list up and he held up a finger, reaching for his phone. "Ooh. I need to record that." He fiddled with the screen, then said into the phone, "Life is the medium, and we are all artists. Lends a whole new meaning to finger paints."

Jackie turned to Natalie, who was reading something on her phone. "What about you, Natalie? What do you do?"

Natalie looked up, but didn't stop moving her thumbs right away. She said, "I'm an entrepreneur. I blog. I vlog. I podcast. But make no bones about it, I'm in it for the money. It's all part of my multimedia enterprise."

"How did you get into all this?" Jackie asked.

"The first time I went viral, I'd been out to a goth club. Same one where I met Nicholas, actually." Natalie sent a small smile toward her husband. "Ever since, I've been stuck being goth. It's not really who I am, but I'm willing to play to my fans. I have over a hundred thousand now."

"They give you money?"

Natalie shook her head. "I sell merchandise and memberships in my private club. Sometimes, they send me gifts, but that's a slippery slope. Some of those gifts come with strings. I prefer clean commerce. You pay, and I give you what you ordered, be it a t-shirt, a mug, or an absinthe spoon. I also have a channel where I give make-up tips and talk about how to be more awesome. That's where I make the most. The company that hosts my channel pays me so they can advertise to my fans. It's lucrative."

Jackie made a mental note to look them up online and see just what all the fuss was. She muttered, "I wonder if anyone would be interested in waitressing tips."

Natalie shrugged and went back to her phone.

"Dr. Li," came a quiet voice at Jackie's shoulder. Gita Gupta-Smith stood there. Jackie turned in her seat to better see her. Gita had ancestry from South Asia, her skin the particular brown shade of cinnamon bark. She had thick, shiny black hair, cut to shoulder length and layered, her natural curls turning up the ends. Dressed in a denim skirt with knee-high boots, a simple white blouse, and a tweed jacket that could have been worn by a professor at Oxford, leather patches on the elbows and all, she had a collegiate style that suited her well. From the documents Sam had given her, Jackie knew she was in her late twenties, only a year or two younger than Jackie was herself.

Ruth Gupta-Smith came up behind her wife and gave a little wave. She wore a pair of straight-legged jeans, zip-up ankle boots, and a long-sleeved gray t-shirt. Over both, she had on a long olive-green cardigan with a handkerchief hem that draped all the way to mid-calf. Though she was obviously not from the same global region as Gita, her skin was also tanned and her eyes dark. She wore her auburn hair long, parted in the middle.

"We wanted to introduce ourselves," said Gita, indicating herself and Ruth. "We are the Gupta-Smiths. This is my wife, Ruth, and I am Gita."

Ruth added, "Gita means song." She smiled until she looked at Gita. Her smile faded into a frown that matched the one on her wife's face.

"I'm sure Dr. Li does not care to know the meaning of my name," Gita said. "We mustn't trouble her with trivialities."

Jackie dove in. "It's a lovely name."

This inspired the smile to return to Ruth's face. "That's what I tell her—every time."

"Yes," said Gita, her smile tight, "every time."

Ruth took a breath and changed the subject. "Dinner was wonderful."

Gita added, "And thank you for offering this workshop. We're looking forward to spending this holiday time with you."

"Thank you," Jackie replied. "You too." She was about to extend the conversation when both women turned almost simultaneously and walked away.

Ada Kaluza filled the gap the other women had left, bending at the waist to put herself on Jackie's level. She wore a multicolored layered pantsuit that screamed Arizona bohemian. The turquoise rings on her fingers furthered the impression. Her hair was cut to just below her earlobes and highlighted with various shades of blond to camouflage the gray.

"Hello, dear," she said. "I'm Ada. Please forgive my husband, Art. I'm afraid he's here by force, and so he's rebelling in whatever way he can. He came out of the womb complaining it was too warm."

Jackie laughed. "It's okay. He doesn't want to be here?"

"Oh no," Ada threw a glance over her shoulder at her husband, who was still perched on a bar stool, enamored with his cellphone. "He'd much rather be at home with his girlfriend, who doesn't seem to mind his belligerent moods."

"His girlfriend?"

Ada nodded solemnly, "His sixth since we've been married—that I know about, at least."

Incredulous, Jackie asked, "How long have you been married?"

"Technically fourteen years." Ada leaned close enough that Jackie could smell the red wine on her breath. "Though god knows why. The only reason he's here is because of our prenup." She pulled back, much to the relief of Jackie's personal space.

"Your prenup?" Jackie didn't understand.

"We thought we'd be clever and put in a clause that we have to attend at least six marriage counseling sessions before we can divorce." She waved her hand in dramatic angst. "We were young. What can I say?"

"So," Jackie was catching on. "You're telling me that you're only here so you can fulfill your prenup requirements and then get divorced?"

"I'm dreadfully sorry." With a light touch, Ada rested her hand on Jackie's shoulder. "I wanted you to know so you didn't expend too much energy on us. We're a lost cause."

"Oh," said Jackie.

"Of course, I'm willing to give it one last shot," Ada said. "There was a time when I loved him. He's just turned into such a pill in the last dozen years or so. I can barely stand to be around him." She leaned close again. "A part of me is grateful to his bimbo for keeping him out of the house." Ada laughed, though the sound was dry and not a little bitter. "I'll see you bright and early tomorrow. I have a bubble bath calling my name."

"Have a good night." Jackie watched the woman go, then looked over at Art as he laughed at something on his smartphone. *Could this cupid challenge get any harder?*

"Hey!" announced Natalie from the window. "It's really coming down out there!"

Jackie pushed up out of her seat and joined the other woman at the window. Snow was coming down in big, fat chunks. She couldn't see more than ten feet out into it.

Card and the piano man stepped up beside Jackie, both craning their necks to see out. Up close, Jackie got a good look at the piano man. He was the same height as her, thick shoulders and chest, narrow hips. She guessed him to be in his early forties. He was handsome in a European playboy sort of way and wore strong, but not unappealing, cologne.

Card said, "They're callin' for up to twenty inches tonight." He looked over at the piano player and told him, "Looks like you're stuck here, my friend. I'll have Frankie make up a room for you."

The piano man, when he spoke, used excellent English delivered with a softly lilting accent, "I can think of worse places to spend the apocalypse. I don't need anything fancy. A couch and a blanket will do. Thank you."

Card laughed. "We can do better than that."

Natalie held up her camera and spoke up to it. "I'm in an Agatha Christie mystery, my flurry friends. We're snowed in, trapped in a mysterious inn in the mountains. I suppose if anyone were going to murder their spouse, this would be the perfect spot, the perfect night, to do it." Natalie tipped her head back and laughed a diabolical laugh, the fingers of her free hand dancing lightly at her decolletage.

Jackie swallowed loudly.

CHAPTER 18

Jackie hurried through her morning routine, mindful that her first morning session was at ten o'clock. By nine, she was in the dining room, ready for that country breakfast she'd already gotten so used to.

The only person she saw was Lu, who appeared alert and cheerful. No one else was around, not even Sam. She was glad someone had had the foresight to start the morning sessions at ten, to give people time to sleep in, if they wanted. It was Christmas break, after all.

As Jackie enjoyed her breakfast and coffee, she thought back to the dinner the night before and her disastrous welcome speech. Like Ada, there was a part of her that wished Art and his belligerent moods would be elsewhere during the day's sessions.

Three couples. Three true loves. Jackie saw hope for Gita and Ruth, as well as for Nicholas and Natalie. But Ada and Art? She couldn't even imagine them in love. It was hopeless. There had to be a third couple she could bless.

The swinging door to the kitchen flapped open and Frankie entered the dining room with a tray of homemade biscuits. She set it on a table by the wall, near the juice pitchers and coffee cistern.

Frankie. Frankie and Sam. The moment the idea occurred to her, it took up residence. They had to be the third couple. It wasn't Bonnie and Jim, and it wasn't Lu and Card. Jackie knew they'd already been blessed.

There was no one else. A mixture of triumph and disappointment churned in her stomach, though she didn't fully understand her own emotions. A glance at the old cuckoo clock by the door told her she'd better hurry if she wanted to prepare before the couples arrived at the first workshop. She took her plates and glass to the dirty dishes tray, downed the last dregs of her coffee before refilling the mug, then headed for the conference room.

Sam arrived first, hobbling in on his crutches. Frankie was right behind him.

"Mornin'," Sam said. "You need anything?"

Jackie looked up from where she was arranging chairs in pairs, facing one another.

Frankie went to check the water cooler, coffee cistern, and other supplies set out for the attendees.

All business, mind on the task at hand, Jackie said, "I'm going to need you both to help me demonstrate the first exercise. Would you mind? You can do it sitting down."

Sam said, "Sure. Frankie?"

Frankie leaned against the drink counter and crossed her arms. "What do we have to do?"

"It'll be easy," said Jackie, smiling. "I'll let you know. Come on up here." She indicated a pair of chairs near the front of the room.

"It can't take too long," Frankie said. "I'm needed in the kitchen for breakfast clean-up."

"No problem. As soon as the demonstration is done, you can go." Jackie watched them both move to their seats. She thought about how good they looked together, both attractive, with so much in common. A lump sat high in her chest, working its way into her throat.

The couples started wandering in, Gita and Ruth first. Both were dressed casually, though Gita had an exotic cut to her jacket, with its mandarin collar and cream-colored pattern reminiscent of the arches in Middle-Eastern architecture. Her pants were loose, but thick enough for a winter's day. Ruth was the epitome of business casual—chic and practical. She wore straight-legged black jeans and several layers of long-sleeved t-shirts in shades of gray and white. Both of them carried laptop bags with them.

Bonnie and Jim came in holding hands, pausing just inside the door to look around. Bonnie looked like a red-haired Christmas elf, with her hair caught up in flippy pigtails high on her head. She wore a peppermint-swirl skirt that hung to her ankles and an evergreen sweater duster with a snowman embroidered on one pocket, a snow-woman on the other. The sleeves of her white blouse had ruffles on the ends that went all the way to her knuckles. At her neck, she had on a bow tie in festive plaid.

Jim was dressed in shades of brown, from his cable-knit sweater down to his corduroy pants, and finally the argyle socks just visible in his penny loafers. The socks didn't quite match.

Bonnie scooted up to Jackie at the front of the room. "Hey! You ready?"

Jackie pulled her eyes off Sam—and Frankie—and faced her friend. "I think so. We'll find out. It can't go any worse than last night."

"Don't worry about that," Bonnie said. "That dinner was just awkward all around, and Art?" She shook her head and rolled her eyes. "Reminds me of my dad."

"Ooh, sorry," said Jackie. Bonnie never mentioned her parents, except in terms of how hard she works to never have to go visit them. For some completely obscure reason, they never liked Jim, and they never let her forget it.

"Dr. Li," called Sam, pulling Jackie's attention to where he and Frankie had seated themselves. "Maybe Bonnie and Jim could demonstrate for you?"

Jackie quickly shook her head. "No. No, I need you to do it, please. I promise it won't take long. They're needed...for something else."

Sam tightened his lips and narrowed his eyes. "All right, if you say so."

"Told ya," said Frankie in an aside that traveled to Jackie's ears.

Bonnie leaned in and said quietly enough not to be overheard, "What are you having them do?"

Jackie put her back to Sam and Frankie. With a conspiratorial dip of her head, she answered, "I think they might be in love. If so, they could be my first couple. I need to check."

"Yeah," replied Bonnie. "I was wondering about what you were going to do since Art and Ada are doomed, and that other couple cancelled."

"If it's not Sam and Frankie, I don't know what I'm gonna do. I guess I'll call Amore and see what he says."

Bonnie made a scared face.

"I know. I don't want to talk to him again, ever, but..."

A minute before ten, Nicholas and Natalie made their entrances separately, each filming themselves with their smart phones as they walked into the conference room.

"I went out into the snow this morning, and all I can say is 'Thank the goddess I brought my thigh-high boots with me this weekend.'" Natalie was indeed wearing her boots with a short skirt, bustier, and ruffled blouse—all black. She'd done her make-up in a vampiric style, and her hair was caught up in little clips that made it look strategically chaotic.

Nicholas spoke to the phone as he entered as well. "It's cold as death here, though I have a notion to make snow angels later. Drop me a message if you think I should." Nicholas was wearing a bolero jacket with beaded embroidery on it, over plain black pants. His dark hair still draped down over one eye, and he appeared to have freshly shaved the other side that morning. His dark eyeliner and merlot-colored lipstick emphasized the drama of his demeanor.

Once in the room, they both put their cellphones away.

"Take a seat facing one another, if you would," Jackie instructed them. "We'll be starting in just a minute. Has anyone seen Art and Ada this—"

At just that moment, Ada entered the room, with Art following close behind. "Good morning!" Ada called to the gathering.

Everyone replied. Art went straight to the drink buffet and started pouring himself a cup of coffee.

"Over here, Ada," Jackie said, indicating a pair of chairs. "Art. When you have your coffee, you'll be here."

Though Art glanced over his shoulder, his only reply was a grunt.

Under her breath, Jackie uttered, "Not a morning person. Good to know."

Bonnie, still standing beside her, whispered, "Not an anytime person, I suspect."

Aloud, Jackie said, "Let's get started, yes?" She closed her eyes for the length of one deep and bolstering breath, then opened them to look at each couple in turn. "I'd like you all to face your partners, please, and hold each other's hands. Both hands, please."

Everyone easily followed the instructions, except Art. He settled into his chair, coffee in one hand, cellphone in the other. Ada offered her hands, but he made a production of having to turn off the screen on his cell, then put both it and his coffee down on the conference table. He paused for one last sip of the coffee.

Everyone else waited.

Jackie moved to stand beside Sam and Frankie. "I'd like everyone to close their eyes, please." She put a hand each on Sam and Frankie's shoulders. "Now, think about a time when you were happy with your partner, a special celebration maybe, or a date night?" While the couples did this, presumably, Jackie watched them closely for any sign of a glow, any sign of the true love spark.

"Think about where you were," she guided them, feeling like

she was thirteen again, holding a seance with her friends during a sleepover. "What were you doing?"

Ever vigilant for even the smallest spark, Jackie waited. She watched, a hawk waiting for its prey to pop its head out of its hole.

"C'mon, c'mon, c'mon," she breathed to herself.

Nothing was happening—except Art's breaking his hold on one of Ada's hands to adjust himself. Jackie wished she'd had her eyes closed too.

"Think about how you felt," she said. "In today's world, it's so easy to forget the things that make us happy, to get carried away with our troubles and trivialities. Right now, I just want you to remember a time when all that mattered was that you were together and in love."

Jackie looked down at Sam. He and Frankie were performing the exercise along with everyone else. A lock of his hair had toppled down onto his forehead, and Jackie had the instinctual urge to brush it back into place. She remembered the day they'd spent ninety minutes in the car together, driving to the airport. It had been easy. So easy, just being with him. In that moment, she realized she'd never been so instantly at ease with anyone as she was with him. Instant friends, almost. She hadn't been on her guard or pretending to be anyone else. And since she was thinking about it, she realized she never had been anything but her true self with him.

"That's really nice," she said to herself, a whisper she didn't intend for anyone else to hear.

Sam opened one eye and tipped his head to peer up at her. His other eye opened too when he found her looking at him. They stayed like that for a long moment, several breaths in and out. Until Art cleared his throat and broke the spell.

"Good job, everyone," she said aloud. "Nice work."

Not a single spark. Not a flicker of true love in the room. Jackie stepped back away from Frankie and Sam, removing her hands from their shoulders.

"You can open your eyes, but don't drop hands. Now, quietly, I'd like you to tell each other what you remembered and why it means something to you."

Jackie faded into the background, watching the couples. She stepped backwards until she was in the doorway, then abruptly turned and hid out in the hallway. She pressed her forehead against the wall, palms too, and closed her eyes.

"Dammit," she said, because she knew what she had to do. She balked, wishing she could do anything else. Unfortunately, it was the only option she could see. Reaching into her pocket, she pulled out her smart phone and called Amore.

As the phone was ringing, Amore entered the hallway and walked slowly toward Jackie. He said nothing, not even once he was standing right in front of her.

Jackie hung up. She had plenty to say. "Something's not right," she told him, her voice low, but edged with a hint of panic. "One of the couples didn't show up, and the others are... broken. How am I supposed to bless three by Christmas when this..." she waved her hand toward the conference room, "...is what I have to work with?"

Amore folded his hands over his stomach but didn't bother to interrupt her.

Jackie continued, voice a quiet and intense hiss, "Have you seen these people? I thought I could maybe get two, but nobody is glowing, not like before. None of them. If it's true love, shouldn't they just light up like a Christmas tree? If they are, I can't see it. Maybe my cupidness is broken?"

With a dry expression, Amore closed his eyes and shook his head.

"Well?" Jackie demanded.

"Did you read the manual?" Amore asked.

"Yes!" Jackie insisted, then lowered her voice again. "I read it. I know what to do when I find true love, but that's the problem. I don't see any love in that room—at all. Some of them aren't even pretending anymore."

They stood together in silence for a moment. Then Jackie had an inspired thought. She reached for Amore's arm. "Can't you just tell me who the three couples are?"

Amore stepped nimbly out of reach and raised an index finger to keep her at bay. "Jacquelyn," he said in as condescending a tone as he'd ever used with her. "Love requires work, sacrifice, and compromise. It requires compassion. For that, your couples must be able to see one another. True love doesn't just happen, and even when it does, it's easily undone." Amore leaned away from her, narrowing his eyes to examine her face. "Did you read the whole book?"

Jackie opened her mouth to say she had, but then she remembered the chapter on troubleshooting. She had skipped that one. She closed her mouth again.

"As I suspected," Amore said. "I suggest you try again. Everything you need is in the cupid manual." The tall, silver-haired man strode back the way he'd come. "Don't bother me until you have properly consumed the entire text."

"But wait!" Jackie called. "Can't you give me a hint?"

Without turning to look at her, Amore wagged an *uh-uh* finger over his shoulder just before turning out of sight at the end of the hallway.

"Dammit," Jackie said for a second time, and she meant it even more.

Stepping into the doorway to the conference room, she found everyone looking at her. They'd dropped hands and turned in various directions, destroying the neatly organized ambiance the room had had before she left. It was chaos, and all eyes were on her.

"The next exercise," she said, "is a trust exercise. One of you will fall backward into the others' arms, and the other will catch you."

CHAPTER 19

After everyone filed out for lunch, Jackie sat alone in the conference room, her face in her hands. She thanked her lucky stars that no one had dropped their spouse in the trust exercise, though there had been one or two close calls. Asking Jim to "spot" people had been her best idea all week.

Love, she thought. *True love.* She'd never been in love. Not really. Not true love. She'd had plenty of infatuations that started with wishful thinking and ended with heartbreak. With Mitch, she'd fallen for a fantasy. He'd never been more than a stranger to her. If he'd been the man she'd thought he was, he never would have broken up with her like he did—on her birthday, by text message.

It's so easy, she thought, *to delude yourself about love. How do you ever know the real thing?*

A knock came at the threshold to the room, and Jackie looked up to find Lu with a tray in her hands. "Hungry?" she asked with a smile.

"As a Texan in a vegan restaurant," Jackie replied, though she didn't move from her seat.

"Well," said Lu, "Good thing I brought you a sandwich." She came in and set down the tray. It held more than just a sandwich. There were barbecue potato chips, a fat pickle, a half-dozen cherry tomatoes, and a large peanut-butter cookie.

"Looks great," Jackie said. "Thanks." She sat up straight.

"You looked like you were deep in thought," Lu said. "I'll leave you to it." She headed for the door.

"Lu?" Jackie said.

Lu stopped and looked back. "Yeah, hon?"

"How did you know you were in love with Card? Like for sure in love?" Jackie looked up at Lu and felt how desperately she wanted Lu to have the secret and share it.

Lu's eyebrows went up, and she studied Jackie for several seconds. "Now that," she said, "is not an easy question to answer. Maybe I should sit with you for a minute?" She returned to the table and put her hand on a chair.

"Please." Jackie gestured toward the chair.

Lu settled in and put her elbows on the table, entwining her fingers as if praying. "How'd I know I was in love with Card?" She pondered. "I reckon I knew for sure about a year after we'd been dating on and off. We were in high school, and I remember going to the county fair in my senior year. We both had entries in the 4-H Horse Showing competition." Lu smiled with warm nostalgia. "Oh, I wanted to win that so badly. I'd been beat for three years straight, and I saw that year as my last chance at the blue ribbon."

Jackie asked, "Did you win?"

Lu laughed softly and nodded. "Well, in a manner of speaking, yes. See, Card was showing a stallion named Buckwheat Chaff. That horse was gorgeous, and Card had spent four years training him. My horse, a beauty named Cinnamon Spice, had only been with me for a year, but I'd worked day and night with her. She and I were of one mind."

Jackie interjected, "Wow."

Lu said, "After the first round of competition, everyone was saying how it was a toss-up between my horse and Card's. That one of us was bound to win."

Jackie leaned forward, intent.

"I just kept remembering how it'd been Card who gave me the best life advice I've ever had. He said, 'Lu, you walk straight up to Cinnamon and look her right in the eyes. Then you tell her what you want from her. Tell her straight. She'll hear you, and you'll take the blue, no problem.' I'd been using that technique with her, and it was working."

Jackie's heart was melting. "Is that how you knew?"

Lu shook her head. "No. See, standin' in Cinnamon's stall with her, I realized I wanted something more than to win the blue. I wanted to see Card win it. So, I told everyone Cinn had an injury and withdrew from the competition."

"Oh my god, Lu!" Jackie whispered. "That's when you knew?"

Lu shook her head again. "No. I knew when I climbed up into the stands to watch the next round and realized that Card had also withdrawn. He was there, seated with his family. Our eyes met, and we both understood what we'd done. My heart filled like it never had before, and that's when I knew beyond a shadow of a doubt that I Loved him with a capital L."

Jackie saw it then: the glow. It emanated from Lu's heart, warm and soft. Her breath caught for a moment, then she exhaled on a sigh.

Lu continued. "That man gave up his last chance at a 4-H blue ribbon so that I could have it. Since neither of us were in the runnin' anymore, the blue went to a two-year-old named Cupboard Love. Next time I saw Card, I walked straight up to him and looked him right in the eyes, and I told him straight that I wanted to marry him. And he heard me. We got hitched the followin' spring."

Surprised, Jackie's eyes opened wide, and she laughed. "You proposed to him?"

"I did. Broke all tradition, but I knew with all my heart that he was the one for me." Lu laughed and leaned in close to Jackie to say with more than a little sass, "No way I was gonna let that stallion get away from me."

Jackie's head lifted with her laughter. "What a great story."

"It's my favorite one," Lu replied. She sat back.

Jackie wanted to clarify just one thing. "So, you fell in love because he'd sacrificed everything for you?"

Lu seemed surprised. "No, honey," she said. "Because we both had." She reached out to rest a hand on Jackie's arm. "That's the secret. If only one of us had, I or he would've been a martyr. And true love doesn't make martyrs. It makes partners who—by putting each other first—find just the right recipe for happiness. It's all about compassion and empathy. Card had listened to my dreams, and I'd listened to his. We both thought we were steppin' aside for the other. He and I wouldn't be together, if *both* of us hadn't taken that step. Do you understand?"

Jackie thought for a minute, then replied, "I think so." Truth was she'd never experienced that kind of love, not since her parents had been alive. And even then, their sacrifices for her had been mostly one-sided. She tried to emulate their parenting with Jazz.

"My parents had that with each other," Jackie said, realizing it was true.

"Had? Are they…"

"Passed away. Years ago."

"I'm sorry to hear that. Must've been hard on you."

Jackie just nodded. After a moment of silence, she said, "It was hard on both me and my brother. I've been sort of his parent ever since. He and I don't have that kind of love. With him, I'm the one who does all the sacrificing."

Much to Jackie's surprise, Lu laughed. "Oh, sweetie. Don't let that bother ya. It's different with kids. With them, the parents are always the ones sacrificing so the child can have everythin' they need. That's the way of the world. Don't go thinkin' he doesn't love you for it, 'cause I guarantee he does." She patted Jackie's arm again and pushed back her chair. "I better go see how lunch is goin'." With that and a warm, knowing smile, Lu stood. "Don't go lookin' for love. It'll find you. And when it does, it'll smack you in the face like a lemon meringue pie: sweet and sour all at the same time." She chuckled at her own analogy and left the room before Jackie could find anything else to add.

The afternoon session dragged at first. Neither Sam nor Frankie showed up, and like her attendees, Jackie was suffering from low energy in the wake of too many carbohydrates at lunch. She caught herself starting to yawn and stifled it. Standing at the front of the conference room, Jackie took inventory of all the couples sitting in their chairs, again facing one another. The body language on them was telling. Art and Ada sat at cross-purposes, perpendicular to one another. Gita and Ruth both faced Jackie, waiting for their cues. Nicholas and Natalie were inverted images of each other, each engrossed with his or her own cellphone.

"All right, everyone," Jackie said, raising her volume a little to capture everyone's attention, even though no one else was talking. "On the table beside you, you'll find notecards and pens."

She went to the whiteboard and wrote, 'I like (blank).'

"I want you to take a notecard and write down one thing you like about the other person. Fill in the blank. Don't put your name or your partner's name on it. Then put that card back on the table, face-down."

They all did as asked.

While they were doing that, Jackie wrote on the whiteboard, 'I wish my partner would (blank) more.'

"Now," instructed Jackie, "I'd like you to take a fresh card and write down one thing you wish your spouse would do more of. Then place the card face down on the first one."

The couples had the hang of the exercise, and they all quickly wrote something down.

Jackie wrote up, 'I could be better at (blank).' She then strolled around the room, hands clasped behind her back. "Lastly, please take a new card and write down one thing you could do better in your relationship."

When they'd all finished, Jackie picked up all the cards and shuffled them. She pulled one at random. "Who would like to go first?" Gita glanced at Ruth, received a nod of approval, then raised her hand.

Jackie moved to stand beside them. "Thanks. We're going to

do some roleplaying. I'd like you to look at the card, Gita, and pretend that you are the one who feels like this. I want you to express it to Ruth. Ruth, you can respond, if you want. Then, we'll talk about strategies for better communication."

Jackie looked at the card she'd chosen. It said, "I want more sex." She debated pulling a new one but decided to let Fate have its way. She handed it over.

Gita read the card and, to her credit, didn't even flinch. She set the card face-down in her lap and looked at Ruth. "Sweetheart," she began. "You know I love and respect you."

Ruth nodded.

Gita spoke with matter-of-fact frankness. "I just want you to know that I need to have sex more often."

Art guffawed.

Everyone turned to look at him except Ada—who was too busy rolling her eyes.

"Please," Jackie said, holding up a hand. "Go on, Gita."

Gita shrugged. "That's all. I just want more sex. Because I love and respect you, Ruth."

Jackie smiled, pleased that Gita had understood.

Ruth took Gita's hands. "I hear you, my love, and because I love and respect you, I will...have sex with you any night you want, except when I have a migraine."

"Excellent!" cried Jackie. "Now, I want to point a few things out to everyone. I suspect that Gita and Ruth have had some training in better communication because they did everything right. They looked each other in the eyes and paid attention to the conversation. They listened. Gita started by reminding Ruth that she loved her, and when she expressed her need, she used the personal pronoun 'I.' She didn't accuse. She didn't say, '*You* don't give me enough sex.'"

Jackie looked around at everyone.

Art leaned toward Ada and said in a whisper that everyone else heard too. "You don't give me enough sex."

"Wonder why?" Ada said under her breath, also audible to everyone else.

Jackie cleared her throat, ignoring Art and Ada. To Gita and Ruth, she said, "Well done. Natalie, how about you go next?"

When Natalie slid her phone into her pocket, Jackie took that as agreement. She shuffled the cards, then pulled one out.

With a glance, she saw that it said, 'I wish my partner were happier.' She handed it to Natalie.

"Remember," Jackie said, "your job is to express that to Nicholas."

Natalie read the card, straightened her spine, and faced Nicholas. Their eyes met as if for the first time that day, and for a long minute, there was silence as they looked into each other's eyes. A slow smile spread on Nicholas's merlot-colored lips.

Natalie said, "Nick, my love, my light. My greatest wish is for your happiness. As a matter of fact, I wish you were happier more often."

Nicholas nodded sagely, considering with a slight crease wrinkling his brow. "I see," he replied. "I believe I'm happy—as happy as I can be, considering the dark vagaries of life." The dramatic lilt to his voice gained momentum. "As a matter of fact, I can prove it to you. To all of you lovely people. We are all happy underneath the sorrows we show to the world." He stood, waving his arms in a grand gesture. "To love is happiness itself." He took Natalie's hand in his and guided her to her feet.

Jackie cleared her throat.

Nicholas said, "Tell me, beautiful lady, what it is that makes you happy, and we will be off in search of it, for it will make me happy too."

Art grumbled, "You've got to be kidding me." Elbow propped on his leg, he had his forehead in his hand.

Natalie looked around the room then said with equal drama, "Snow! Snow is what makes me happy."

"Then let us tarry no more," Nicholas replied. "To the snow! Come one, come all! Let us frolic until our fingers are frozen, our toes are blue, and our noses are red." He led Natalie toward the door.

"Wait!" said Jackie, but everyone was getting to their feet and following the Pied Piper, chattering rather...happily. Jackie made no further effort to stop them.

She called, "Don't forget tonight is date night!"

No one responded.

Jackie stayed in the same spot until they were all out then went to the whiteboard and erased what she had written.

◆♥◆

CHAPTER 20

After the mass exodus from the workshop, everyone—except Jackie—spent several hours playing in the snow, making a huge snow fort on the lawn, and recording it all for social media.

Jackie had watched them through the large windows in the lobby, keeping a keen eye out for any sign of true love.

She didn't spot a spark from anyone except Jim and Bonnie. Those two were her compass. Their glow let her know that she wasn't a lost cause in the love detecting arena.

Eventually the couples trickled back inside with red cheeks, stomping boots, and smiles. They chatted as if they were all old friends, though none of them were chatting with their own spouses. Then, they scattered to the four winds, some returning to their rooms, others relaxing by the fireplace, and some even heading to the hot tub and sauna.

That night was date night. Jackie had been planning it for days. She'd explained what would happen to the couples and had encouraged them to take advantage of the evening's ambiance to woo each other. As dinnertime approached, Jackie went to the dining room to decorate the tables with flower petals and candles.

The piano player was there, practicing. He looked up as Jackie entered. "Afternoon," he said, standing. He had a velvety accent reminiscent of foreign lands far to the south.

Jackie guessed him to be in his early fifties and liked how the firelight sparked off the salty strands in his salt-and-pepper hair. *Debonair* was the word she put to him in her mind. Though dressed simply in dark gray dress pants and a cinnamon-colored wool sweater, he carried himself with grace and class. Jackie gave a little wave.

"Still stuck here, I see," Jackie said.

"Yes." The pianist came forward to meet her halfway, hand outstretched. "Though I do not mind staying in such a magical place."

Magical? Jackie wondered. She slid her hand into his, but she was suddenly on high alert. There was something...different about him.

"I am Enrique Velasquez," the man said, his teeth white in his open smile. Up close, he was even more handsome in that cavalier, Zorro sort of way.

"Jackie. Li. Nice to meet you." Putting her hands on her hips, she surveyed the room. "Tonight is date night for the couples, Enrique, so we need the music to be romantic. Got any ideas?"

Enrique's smile tipped into a crooked grin, and he said, "I have many ideas when it comes to romance. By the time I am done with them, these couples will be transported back to when they first fell in love."

"Really?" Jackie said, suspicion creeping in.

"Oh yes. Trust me." Enrique narrowed his eyes in thought. "We will start with some sweet country love songs and work our way up to the tango."

"I like the sound of that," Jackie said. "You know how to tango?"

Enrique looked offended, though a teasing twinkle remained in his dark eyes. "How can you ask that? I am an Argentinian. We learn to tango in our mothers' wombs."

Jackie laughed.

"See what you think," said Enrique. He returned to the piano and began playing a sexy, sensual tango.

With her hands to her cheeks, Jackie gave him an impressed look.

He continued to play various love songs as Jackie finished decorating for date night. With those she knew, she sang along under her breath, and the afternoon passed quickly.

Date night was semi-formal, and when the couples started arriving in the dining room, Jackie was pleased to see that they'd taken the event seriously. She herself had returned to her room to shower and was dressed in the cream-colored sweater dress she'd worn on her birthday.

Bonnie had—with her usual foresight—decided to bring it along when they came from Alexandria. To keep her legs warm, she put on thick black tights and wore the simple black shoes she'd purchased for her "work" outfits. No one was going to confuse her with Cinderella, for sure, but then this ball wasn't about her. *Besides,* she told herself, *you'll be too busy catering to true love to worry about how you look in comfortable shoes.*

Although Jackie took extra time getting what little make-up she had just right, she was still only the second person to arrive in the dining room. Enrique was the first, and he was already playing a beautiful, salsa-flavored version of "White Christmas."

Gita and Ruth entered first. They came in holding hands and took the table closest to the fireplace. Gita had worn a saree of the same blood red as her lipstick. The flowing fabric was embroidered with black vines. Underneath it, she wore a long-sleeved black shirt. On her wrists and at her neck, spectacular gems sparkled in the firelight. Ruth wore a jacquard pantsuit covered with a subtle flower pattern in shades of silver, gold, and rust. Her white blouse was unbuttoned to just below her breasts with casual insouciance that nicely balanced the posh tailoring of the pantsuit.

Jackie picked up the wicker basket that Lu had found for her and approached their table. "Good evening, Gita. Ruth." Jackie held out the basket. "I'm confiscating phones this evening, if you have yours on you."

"Ooh," said Gita. "An evening without the leash. How lovely." She took hers out of the little purse she had set on the table by her plate. Ruth also produced hers, and the two phones went into the basket.

"Thank you," said Jackie. "Enjoy your date."

Nicholas and Natalie had entered with their usual pomp. Nicholas was helping Natalie with her chair as Jackie approached. Natalie needed help to avoid damaging the long train of her skirt. She resembled Morticia Addams. Her form-fitting dress was made of midnight blue velvet, and the ruffles at the sleeves and hem seemed to take on a life of their own. Her makeup—including the lipstick—had a blue tinge that complemented the dress. Her four-inch-heeled shoes further explained why she needed help getting seated.

"Good evening," Jackie said. "You both look wonderful."

"Thank you," they said, feigning a blush in tandem.

Jackie waited until Nicholas was in his chair as well, then

she held out the basket. "May I have your cellphones, please?"

They looked up at Jackie with surprise—nay, horror—on their faces.

"Why do you want our phones?" Nicholas asked, clutching at his as if it were the only thing standing between him and death.

"So you can focus on each other this evening," Jackie replied. She'd expected some push-back and had planned her rebuttal. "It's only for a couple hours, and you can recap the evening for your followers once the date is over."

Nicholas's gaze met Natalie's, and they both looked terrified.

"Trust me," Jackie said. "No harm will come to them, and you'll get them back after dinner."

It took another moment of eye contact between Nicholas and Natalie, but then they nodded. The silent communication that passed between them had the feeling of a pact, one made with determination despite the sacrifice. They both put their phones in the basket.

Art and Ada were settling down at a table near the windows. Art wore a typical business suit in dark gray, and Ada was dressed in a chocolate-colored floor-length gown that showed off her curves. It had a boat-neck, long sleeves, and fitted bodice. The skirt was full and rippled around her legs as she walked. Wrapped around her shoulders, she wore a paisley pashmina in forest green and various other earthy colors. Jackie hoped she looked that good when she was in her fifties.

By the time Jackie arrived at the table, Art was already seated and looking down at his phone.

"Good evening, Ada, Art," Jackie said. "I hope you had a good afternoon."

"Oh yes," said Ada. "I found the hot tub. What a wonderful hotel this is!"

"It's an inn," corrected Art under his breath.

"Well," said Jackie, "I am asking people to turn over their cellphones for the evening." She held out the basket.

Art's eyes rolled up to look at Jackie's face, though his head didn't move. "You're kidding, right?"

Jackie shook the basket. "I'm not. I'd like you to focus on one another. This *is* date night, after all."

Ada was already pulling hers out of her clutch. She dropped it in the basket.

Art scowled. "I'm not doing that."

"C'mon, Art," Jackie said, trying to be polite. "It's just for a couple of hours. Humor me."

Jackie felt the resistance as if it were a physical thing.

Art said, "Fuck that. I'm not—"

Ada interrupted him. "He's expecting a text from his girlfriend who doesn't know the meaning of patience. He's afraid that if he misses it, she'll replace him with someone younger."

"I am not," Art denied.

Jackie tried again, "It's just a couple of hours, Art." She leaned toward him so she could lower her voice. "You came here for a reason. Don't you think you owe it to yourself and to Ada to give it your best shot?"

To Jackie's surprise, Art snorted and barked a short, sharp laugh. "Hell no," he said, pushing back his chair. "The only reason I'm here is because of that stupid clause in the pre-nup. So you can stop trying, Doc. I'm going to the bar." He moved away from Jackie and around the other side of the table. There, he paused beside Ada, put his hand on her shoulder, and asked with snide venom, "Can I get you anything, my love?"

Ada leaned away from him and pushed his hand off her.

Jackie watched the man stride to the bar. With a heavy sigh, she sat down across from Ada. "Are you okay?"

Ada gazed across the table at her, and Jackie was surprised to see there was no hurt in her eyes. "Of course, my dear," Ada replied. "I've been with that man for fourteen years. Believe me when I say that my skin has grown thick. Let him keep his phone. His girlfriend can have him. She's young enough that she doesn't know any better—yet." The corners of Ada's eyes crinkled with her smile, an expression of satisfaction. "Don't you worry. I'm looking forward to this dinner as a single woman with a mind of her own. It may well turn out to be the best date I've ever had." She laughed.

Jackie offered Ada her phone back, but the woman put her hand up. "I will persist in solidarity with the others."

Bonnie and Jim entered the dining room, looking happy, arm in arm. Bonnie was wearing suede ankle boots, a houndstooth miniskirt with black cable-knit leggings, a long-sleeved black sweater, and a fringed scarf with burgundy roses. Jim matched her style. He wore a retro-40s double-breasted jacket in black pinstripe with matching wide-legged trousers and wing-tip oxfords.

Jackie couldn't help but smile when she saw them. She stepped forward to greet them.

"Hi, guys," she said. "You're adorable."

Bonnie gave a little bow. "Thanks, babe." She reached out to tug on the sleeve of Jackie's sweater dress. "Glad you got to wear this again. The best revenge is being gorgeous, am I right?"

Jackie put her hand to her heart in gratitude. She had felt queasy when she'd seen herself in the mirror upstairs. Bad memories had risen up of a spoiled birthday. "Right. Mitch has no idea what he missed out on."

"Amen, sister!" Bonnie always knew the right thing to say.

Jim scanned the room. "When's eats? I'm starving."

"Soon. You're just in time." Jackie gestered to them to follow her toward the one remaining date table.

Bonnie and Jim handed over their phones without complaint. They held hands and gazed into each other's eyes. *If only,* Jackie thought, *the other true lovers were as easy to spot as those two.*

Lu, Card, and Frankie started serving drinks and appetizers, so Jackie retreated to that quiet little couch by the second fireplace where she'd eaten chicken soup with Sam. To her surprise, she found Sam there, reading a book, foot propped up on the couch with him.

"Sorry," she muttered and turned to go.

"Join me," Sam said. He closed his book. "Lu's bringin' my dinner over here, so you may as well eat with me."

As if on cue, the smell of food reached Jackie's nose in full force, and her stomach growled.

"How's your..." Jackie waved a hand at his foot.

"Better," he replied, waving his own hand at an empty armchair. "How are things goin'?"

Jackie heaved a sigh, then sat as directed. "Fine," she lied. Leaning out to where she could see the dining room beyond the edge of the fireplace, she took inventory of the couples.

One. Gita and Ruth were talking to one another. *Good sign,* Jackie thought. *Maybe there's a chance they'll spark soon.* She squinted at them, looking for any sign of a glow. Nothing.

Two. Nicholas and Natalie toasted with their champagne

glasses. For once, they were looking at each other instead of at their cameras. Jackie breathed out a sigh of relief, feeling hopeful for them. *Still no glow,* she thought, *but maybe soon.*

Three. Ada and Art were in different worlds. Art hadn't left the bar where he had his martini at hand, and Ada was up out of her seat, strolling around the room like a tourist in a museum. She paused at the tall windows and looked out into the snowy landscape.

Every last hope that Jackie had had for Ada and Art finding true love was dead. There had to be another couple at the inn that were falling in love.

Jackie sat back and watched Sam from under her lashes. *God, he was handsome.* Sitting there, reading a book, dressed in jeans and a blue-plaid flannel shirt, his hair just a little too long, his hands so big and strong... Jackie cleared her throat and sat up straighter.

Sam and Frankie. Jackie considered the idea again. Her own burgeoning feelings shoved aside, she debated how she could get them over the hump. She needed to know how he felt.

She said, "Frankie's pretty awesome, wouldn't you say?"

Sam looked up at her. "Yeah. She's the best."

"You two would make a good couple." Jackie folded her hands in her lap. "You've got so much in common."

"I suppose we do," Sam replied, his voice gone contemplative.

Jackie hoped that meant he was considering the idea. "How long have you known each other?"

Sam closed his book and put it down. "Since high school, I reckon. Long time. She was Crystal's best friend."

"Lu's daughter, Crystal?"

"Yeah." Sam spoke quietly, almost to himself. "Frankie helped me pick out her engagement ring."

"She cares about you," Jackie told him, matching her volume to his. "A lot."

"An' I care about her. After Crystal died, I'd have been lost if it weren't for Frankie. She got me through it and kept me from doing anythin' stupid."

"I'm glad she did."

Sam leaned toward Jackie so abruptly it startled her. "Are you?"

Jackie nodded. "Yeah. I mean, we all need people in our lives who take care of us. That's what love is. You're lucky you have her." Her eyes met Sam's and stuck there. Energy buzzed from her throat down to the bottom of her belly, where it pulsed with yearning.

"What about you?" Sam asked. "Do you have someone you're lucky to have?"

Still caught by Sam's eyes, Jackie shook her head. She started, "Have you ever thought about..." but trailed off.

Sam asked, "About what?"

Jackie finished, "About maybe being more than friends with..." Electricity crackled in the air between them.

"With?" Sam swung his legs around, setting his injured foot on the floor.

"With Frankie?"

The spell broke with the huff that came out of Sam. "Not for a long time," he said, the quiet having gone out of his voice. He sat back again. "Stop psychoanalyzing me. I don't need a matchmaker, especially not a fake one." There it was, that barely concealed anger and disgust Jackie had heard when Sam had first learned her identity. "Shouldn't you be checking on your *patients?*" He put extra emphasis layered with sarcasm on that last word.

Jackie didn't blame him, though she couldn't explain to him how she'd gotten roped into misrepresenting herself. She wished she could, but she knew what he thought of her. Anymore added weirdness would just confirm what he believed.

A crash sounded in the dining room. Jackie leaned out to see what had happened.

Gita was on her feet, her chair overturned behind her. Though she was keeping her voice low enough that it didn't reach Jackie, her body language was as clear as arctic water. She wagged an index finger at Ruth, the other hand on her hip. Her face twisted in an expression of fury and her mouth moved tightly over each word she spat.

Jackie took a quick glance around the room. Frankie had returned to the bar, but Lu and Card were nowhere in sight. Nicholas and Natalie were staring at Gita with wide eyes. Art was gone, and Ada was seated at the piano beside Enrique, from where she was openly watching Gita's outburst. Enrique didn't stop playing, and the slow, sweet backdrop of "A Christmas Love Song" added to the discord of the moment.

Ruth crossed her arms but made no reply.

Gita threw her hands in the air, gathered the end of her saree to her chest, and stormed from the dining room.

Ruth got up from the table and left as well, her cheeks as red as Rudolph's nose.

Jackie said, "Crap," just as Enrique finally stopped playing. The word rang out into the silence.

Everyone turned to look at her.

Jackie slowly leaned back in her chair, moving out of their line of sight.

CHAPTER 21

"Perfect," Sam had said with a note of derision after Gita and Ruth had stormed out.

Jackie excused herself and followed in their wake, unsure of what to do. She found Ruth seated alone in the lobby, huddled in a fan-back chair by the fire.

Jackie approached the other woman with caution. "Is there anything I can do?"

Ruth shook her head. Her face was shiny with tears. "Leave me alone. This retreat was a mistake. I never should've let Gita talk me into it."

Jackie perched on the arm of a nearby couch. "You'll work this out. It was just a little fight."

"Just a little fight?" Ruth looked straight up at Jackie, her eyes flashing with anger. "You don't get it. Gita and I don't fight. Ever. This isn't a fight. This is the end." A ripple of sorrow melted the hardness of her expression, and she curled tighter upon herself. "Just leave me alone, Jackie."

"What were you arguing about? It can't be *that* bad."

"Go away!" Ruth shouted.

Suddenly, Sam was at Jackie's side, guiding her to her feet with a hand on her elbow. "C'mon, Jackie," he said. "You've done enough." He put his crutches under his arms, inclined his head, and lifted his eyebrows to indicate they should go.

Jackie followed his lead, her head and heart heavy.

When they were out of earshot of both Ruth and the dining room, Sam pulled up short and turned toward Jackie. His crutches made the move awkward.

"Maybe you should just leave," Sam hissed. "You're more trouble than you're worth."

"Excuse me?" Jackie couldn't believe what she was hearing.

"The roads have cleared up. I'll drive you to Alexandria in the morning."

Jackie stared at him. "I..." She just nodded. Maybe he was right. Maybe it was time to throw in the towel. Tears filled her eyes, blurring her vision. *I will not cry,* she told herself. Squeezing her eyes shut against the tears had the opposite effect. Two big ones rolled down her cheeks. She left them there, hoping Sam wouldn't notice them, and fled toward her room. The first sob hit her halfway up the stairs.

Head down, she barreled to her door, fumbled with the key card, and pushed inside, shutting the door soundly behind her. She leaned against it, slid down it to sit on the carpeted floor, and sobbed.

I suck, she thought. *I am going to let Lu and Card down. I'm the apocalypse.* For a long time, she assaulted herself with a cruel string of thoughts.

Finally, exhausted, she got up in a haze. She washed her face, brushed her teeth, put on her flannel pajamas, and crawled into bed. As she lay there, trying to fall asleep, she went over it all again: Kupidopoulos in the hospital, Amore and his threats, Art and Ada who never had any intention of reconciling, Ruth and Gita whose hearts were breaking, Nicholas and Natalie who were so enamored of their own images they couldn't see each other, and Frankie and...Sam.

Jackie had no illusions about the depths of her failure.

Somewhere in the midst of all that misery, Jackie had a thought. *I can't give up.*

♥

The next morning, Sam's words, "Maybe you should just leave," continued to echo in Jackie's mind. She had awoken with the resolve to tell him she wasn't leaving, that she refused to give up.

"I'm not a quitter," she told herself in the mirror as she got ready for the morning session. The theme of the workshop was "Honesty Hour," and Jackie hoped it would allow the couples to work out some of their differences. She planned to mediate as they said whatever was on their minds. Now that she was facing the prospect, she found it terrifying. She considered doing something else, but all the research she and Bonnie had done said that communication was key to any strong relationship. She put on her most professional clothes (gray pantsuit with a peach blouse and argyle sweater vest, comfortable shoes) and headed out to get coffee before the workshop began.

As she left her room, another door in the hallway also opened, and Ada stepped out.

Jackie immediately noticed that she was still wearing the gown from the previous evening. Ada's hair was a nest of tangles at the back of her head, and she hadn't removed her make-up.

Ada turned back toward the threshold and leaned in for a kiss...from Enrique.

Jackie gasped aloud, but neither Ada nor Enrique noticed. Their kiss was passionate, but brief. They exchanged a couple whispered words that Jackie couldn't hear, then Ada turned to go. Her expression was one of sleepy satisfaction.

Ada came toward Jackie. She said with relaxed cheerfulness. "I won't be coming to any more workshops." She didn't stop walking but spoke as she passed.

"Okay," Jackie replied, watching the woman sashay by and stop at the door to the room she shared with Art. She laughed quietly to herself, then swiped her card and disappeared inside.

Ada and Enrique, Jackie thought. *Never would have predicted that.* And yet, it made so much sense. She did the math. *Lost one true love (Ada and Art), maybe gained one (Ada and Enrique)? Maybe lost Gita and Ruth? Maybe Sam and Frankie will replace them?*

Jackie shook her head to clear the numbers. She needed coffee.

When Jackie arrived in the lobby, she found Art at the front desk, paying with his credit card, checking out. His suitcase sat at his feet like a faithful dog. He had his phone to his ear and was carrying on two conversations simultaneously.

"I'm coming home, baby," he said into the phone. "This bullshit is finally over. Hold on. I have to check out." He set the phone on the counter.

"Sam will drive you to the car rental office," Lu said, voice all business.

Art grumbled his response to her, "About time they got the roads cleared." He stowed his card and receipt in his wallet, put the cellphone back to his ear, "I'm back," then picked up his suitcase.

"Of course," he said. "I'll bring you here. You'd love this place."

He turned around and caught Jackie's eyes. As he passed her, he grunted, "My girlfriend's going to love this place." The words and the eye contact were a direct attack on Jackie, as if to rub her nose in the fact that he had won.

"Good-bye, Art," Jackie said to his back as he headed straight for the front door.

Jackie found Lu watching her. The other woman said, "Well, I'll be damned if he ain't a turd wrapped in gold foil."

"I failed with him and Ada." Jackie sighed.

"No, you didn't," Lu said. "You never had a chance with them. Some couples are doomed from the start. And that isn't on you. There's no forcin' love." She nodded a couple times to underscore the gem of wisdom.

No forcing love, Jackie thought. *Like me and Mitch.* Mitch felt years and continents away, though it had only been a few days since he'd broken up with her, broken her heart. *No,* she realized, *he hadn't broken her heart. He'd disappointed her, yes. He'd cut off any chance that they could find love together. But it had only been a chance, a wish, a hope, not true love.*

Jackie continued her quest for coffee and, once she'd acquired it, she slogged back toward the conference room. Passing through the lobby, she saw Sam balancing on his crutches as he put Art's suitcase in the trunk of his car. She hurried her steps to avoid being seen, hustling to turn the corner and get out of sight before he noticed her.

The large conference felt uncomfortably empty with only two couples in attendance. Nicholas and Natalie were there, tired and hungover. Gita and Ruth had come as well, though the distance between them gaped like the fissure to Hell.

Jackie assumed Bonnie and Jim had opted to sleep in. *Great,* she thought, a touch of irritation at its edge. She really could have used the moral support.

Frankie buzzed in and out, making sure the drink buffet was fully stocked.

Once everyone had settled in, Jackie closed the door and moved to the front of the table.

"This morning," Jackie said, "we're going to work some more on communication. Before we begin, I want to make this room our safe space. You can say anything you want, and it will not leave this room. Does everyone agree to that?"

The four of them all nodded.

"Good," Jackie said. "Now, I'd like to hear how you thought your date went. Nicholas, why don't we start with you?"

Nicholas smiled directly at Natalie, who returned his smile. He opened his mouth to reply but was interrupted.

"Jackie?" asked Gita, gentle and polite. "Is this truly a safe space? We can say anything we want?"

All eyes turned to Gita.

"Yes," Jackie replied, encouraged that Gita wanted to share. "Go on."

Gita waved a hand toward Ruth as she said, "We're not happy with how the sessions are being run."

Jackie's neck tensed. "I know you and Ruth had a—"

"No," Gita interrupted her. "Everyone. A few of us were talking yesterday."

Jackie asked, "Everyone?" She looked to Nicholas and Natalie to find them nodding along.

"Everyone."

"Oh."

"We're not satisfied. We expected a different approach."

Jackie made a conscious effort to hear what Gita was saying without reacting, though the tickle in her nose warned that tears might be just below the surface. *Safe space,* she reminded herself. Then, aloud, she asked, "What kind of approach were you expecting?"

Gita shrugged and looked over at Ruth before answering, "More focus on specific problems, I suppose."

Jackie parroted, "More focus?"

"Yes. Mediation, maybe. So we can work out the problems." Gita leaned forward, her rant gaining momentum. "We aren't like Art and Ada. We *want* to find solutions. We're not here to play in the snow..."

Jackie shook her head. "That wasn't—"

Gita interrupted her. "We don't want date nights. We're here to work on our relationship, to get to the bottom of our troubles. You're supposed to be a counselor, but..."

"All right," Jackie said. "Let's talk about your troubles."

Suddenly, the room went dead silent. Gita hung her head. Ruth crossed her arms and legs. Like Jackie, Nicholas and Natalie waited with bated breath for Gita to spill it.

Finally, in a voice so quiet as to almost be inaudible, Gita said, "I want a baby, and Ruth doesn't."

Ruth leaned forward, mouth opening to retort, but Jackie stopped her with a hand.

"Go on, Gita," Jackie said.

Gita continued, "I try to be understanding, but one of us has to give. Why does it always have to be me? She doesn't want a baby, so she gets to decide for both of us? It's not right."

This time, Ruth spoke despite Jackie's gesture. "You don't get to decide for both of us either." She looked around at everyone but Gita, as if seeking allies, "Who wants to spend years changing diapers and wiping snot? I love our life. We have fun. We're free. We make enough money between us to live more than comfortably, but if we bring a baby into the mix, then all that goes away." Ruth groaned in frustration. "Why can't you see that, Gita? I don't understand why you want a baby!" She turned to the side in her seat, away from her wife.

"I want a baby *because* we are so rich. We have so much love to give, and we could provide a child with the best kind of life. You're being selfish, Ruth. You want to keep me all to yourself. But I want more than that." She appealed to the others in the room as well. "I would have a half-dozen babies if I could. I have four brothers and sisters, and we had so much love in our house. Something was always happening, and—"

Ruth interrupted, "And your parents were run ragged trying

to feed, clothe, and care for you all. Is that what you want, Gita? Your dad worked himself into an early grave, and your mother can't even stand up straight anymore."

Gita's voice reached a pitch and volume that belied the red rushing up her neck. "My mother and father had to work hard because we didn't have anything."

Ruth gave Gita a know-it-all look. "My point exactly."

"Let's—" Jackie tried to intervene but failed miserably when Gita suddenly got to her feet, tears shimmering in her eyes. Through gritted teeth, she said, "You are not the woman I married. I don't know who you are. This... this... marriage... is over." With that, she rushed to the door, jerked it open, and left.

Everyone stared after her in silence.

Slowly, Ruth got to her feet. "About that safe space, Doc," she said. "Maybe not so safe." She followed in Gita's wake.

No one spoke until the door had closed again behind Ruth.

Nicholas said, "We had a magical date night. I just wish we could have gotten it on camera."

Jackie looked at first one then the other as they smiled at each other. This lasted for two seconds, maybe three, then the couple took out their cellphones in tandem.

Jackie looked down at her bare wrist and said, "Look at the time. It's almost lunch. How about we take a break." She pushed out of her chair and walked out of the conference room in such a thick post-drama daze that she almost didn't see Sam there, leaning against the wall.

CHAPTER 22

Sam's expression was dark. He stood leaning on his crutches, watching Jackie.

"You're back," Jackie said.

"Yeah. Dropped Art off at the car rental place. You ready to go?"

"I'm not leaving." Jackie planted her feet and lifted her chin.

"I can't. I have a job to do."

Sam chuckled, though the sound held little mirth. "You surely don't think you're going to get paid for this, do you?"

Jackie tried to walk by him, but he leaned into her, blocking her path.

Voice low and serious, Sam said, "You're a fraud. And you're not getting a penny from Lu and Card. You hear me?"

Jackie avoided looking him in the eyes. "I don't care about the money." Truth was, she hadn't even known there was payment involved. "I'm not here for that. I made a promise, and I intend to do my best to keep it." As she talked, her resolve grew stronger. She met his gaze. "I'm on a mission, and I'm not going to give up just because the going gets a little tough." She squeezed her lips together and nodded with determination.

Sam gave a dry chuckle. "A little tough? Lady, you're trying to put out an inferno with a water gun. This whole event is a disaster." His tone shifted slightly, and Jackie heard the undertones of fear and worry in it. "This fiasco isn't going to save the inn. Maybe nothing can." He turned on his heel and limped away on his crutches, his back a solid barrier to any retort Jackie may have given. He spoke to himself as he left, quiet and angry, "If the inn goes under, it'll kill Card."

Jackie waited, letting him get well ahead of her before moving toward the dining room. Her nerves jangled with every step she took, even after she lost sight of Sam.

The dining room wasn't empty, but the two people she'd been looking for weren't there. She wanted to talk to Bonnie. She needed someone to be on her side.

Ada and Enrique sat together at the piano. Enrique played while Ada sang. She had a rich, alto voice that managed to soothe Jackie's nerves a bit.

For a moment, Jackie was stopped in her tracks by the happiness on their faces. It was the most beautiful picture she'd seen since she'd arrived. There was an ease between them that was both romantic and comforting, like the best chocolate truffles.

Frankie was behind the bar, and Jackie made her way there, taking a stool from which she could watch Ada and Enrique.

"I need a drink," she said aloud.

"What's your poison?" Frankie asked.

Jackie considered it. "Do you have hot chocolate?"

"Yeah. You want peppermint schnapps in it?"

Jackie couldn't remember the last time she'd had hot cocoa with peppermint schnapps. It brought back memories of college football games, the chill of autumn, and a thermos passed among her friends. "Why not?" she replied.

Life had been so different before her parents had died. That one event had changed everything for Jackie. *Derailed* was the word that came to mind. If she'd stayed in college, she would have had the knowledge she needed to help these couples. She'd have had a degree, maybe even a doctorate. *Dr. Jacquelyn Li* would have made sense. She'd been on track to graduate with honors.

"I was happy once," Jackie said aloud to herself. She couldn't remember ever having been so carefree and happy as she'd been in college, certainly not since she'd made the decision to drop out to take care of Jazz.

Frankie set a steaming mug that smelled like heaven on the bar.

"Thanks," said Jackie with a small smile. She pulled the mug to herself and wrapped her hands around it. "So...you seeing anyone, Frankie?"

Frankie leaned against the bar. "You hitting on me, Dr. Li?"

Jackie chuckled. "No. But I can't help but notice the spark between you and Sam."

"Spark?" Frankie laughed. "You really are terrible at matchmaking. I'm not Sam's type."

"Oh, I don't know," Jackie said with sly intention. "The more I watch him, the more clear it becomes that he really cares about you."

"So you said." Frankie rolled her eyes then grabbed a bar towel and started washing dishes.

"How about those two?" Jackie's gaze returned to Ada and Enrique. Her hot chocolate had cooled enough to drink, and she held it to her mouth, taking small sips. It was creamy, minty, and delicious. The steam rose to fill her head with intoxicating aromas.

"Didn't see that one coming," Frankie replied, looking across the dining room.

"Me either."

Before Jackie knew it, the hot chocolate was gone. She slid

the mug toward Frankie. "Hit me again, bartender."

Frankie picked up the mug. "I guess it'll be okay, since you're not driving." She smirked.

Lu started making trips out of the kitchen with trays of sandwiches and salad makings. She set it all out on the buffet table, studying the layout like an artiste as she wiped her hands on her apron.

"Lu and Card are so nice," Jackie said, affection and schnapps warming the words. Then, before she even knew what she was saying, she added, "I wish they were my parents." The sentiment stuck in her chest, making her throat tighten up. The truth was she didn't wish Lu and Card were her parents so much as she wished her parents were there at the inn with her. It was so easy to imagine her own parents in a place like that, living long happy lives together, snowed in, decorating for Christmas, cooking feasts for the guests. The ache spiked, and Jackie turned to her hot chocolate for solace.

"Hey, you," said Bonnie, sneaking up on Jackie and resting a hand on her shoulder. "How's it going?" She sounded so chipper, so detached from reality.

"Terrible," Jackie said with a deep frown. "Oh, Bonnie. Everything is all screwed up. Art left, Gita and Ruth are breaking up, and...and...it's all my fault. I'm useless."

"What are you talking about?" Bonnie took the stool beside Jackie.

"I can't do anything right. This is a nightmare."

Frankie cleared her throat.

Bonnie looked up and said, "Coffee?"

"And another one of these for me," Jackie announced, indicating her mug.

"Coming right up." Frankie moved away.

With a big sigh, Bonnie tilted her head at Jackie. "Girl, are you kidding me?"

"What?" Jackie didn't notice the alcohol-induced thickness of her tongue. Her misery was gaining momentum. With more accusation than she intended, Jackie added, "Where were you this morning? I needed someone to be on my side for once."

"For once?" Bonnie's eyebrows went up.

"Yeah! They all hate me. Even Sam." Jackie leaned toward Bonnie and whispered far more loudly than she intended, "He called me a fraud." She poked a finger at Bonnie's knee. "And he's right."

"I think you've had enough hot chocolate," Bonnie said. "Have you eaten?"

"Not hungry." Jackie nabbed her mug before Bonnie could take it away, holding it to her chest in both hands. "This mug is the only happiness I've had in... years."

"What are you talking about?" Bonnie asked, irritation leaking into her voice.

"Where were you this morning?" Jackie asked, changing the subject.

"Me and Hubs slept in." A soft smile played across Bonnie's lips. "Though there wasn't much sleeping involved."

"Oh sure," said Jackie. "While I'm getting chewed out by everyone and their lover, you're in bed, doing god knows what."

Bonnie chuckled. "We're married. We're allowed."

"Not when I need you," Jackie said, voice rising. She completely missed the humor in Bonnie's retort. Continuing, she said, "I brought you up here to help me, not for vacation. I needed you, and you weren't there."

Bonnie's eyes narrowed, but Jackie didn't notice. She just kept talking. "True love, blah, blah, blah. I get so sick of you rubbing that in my face. It's so unfair. I'll never have that, but do you care? No. You're too busy playing kissy face, holding hands, and *sleeeeping* in. Can't you see I'm having a crisis, Bonnie? Why am I always the one taking care of everybody else?"

Bonnie held up a hand. "Stop being such a martyr, Jackie." Her tone was alien to Jackie, one she'd never heard before. It had a no-nonsense, hard edge to it, and Jackie realized that Bonnie was angry. Jackie had never seen Bonnie angry before. "Jim and I dropped everything and drove three hours to get here, so you would have clothes. We helped you plan this stupid seminar."

Jackie set her mug on the bar but didn't pull her hands off it. Snarky, she said, "Yeah, and got a free stay at a fancy inn."

"You think that's why we came?"

In that moment, Jackie did think that. The peppermint schnapps had zapped away all her reason, leaving only raw misery behind, and she wanted to snap at someone. Bonnie was convenient. "I'm stuck here, and Jazz is in Alexandria. I didn't ask for this, but I can't say no. I give and give and give, and what do I get for it? Trouble, that's all. If you were really my friend—"

"Fine," Bonnie hissed, sliding off the stool. "How about we get out of your way. I wouldn't want to *take advantage of your friendship*." She headed for the dining room doors.

"Fine!" called Jackie, nearly tipping off her stool. "I don't need you anyway!" She threw back the last of her hot chocolate and stood, wobbling a moment until she steadied.

Frankie watched her without comment.

Jackie gave the bartender a salute then followed in Bonnie's wake. She got as far as the lobby. A glance out the big windows told her it was snowing again, coming down in fat, fluffy chunks. She turned toward the front doors, anger in her steps, and pushed right through them.

The cold air outside hit her lungs and cooled the heat in her cheeks. Jackie walked along the front patio, still ranting at Bonnie in her mind. Her pantsuit jacket wasn't thick, but she buttoned it all the way and wrapped her arms around herself. She liked how the cold made her feel, how it cleared the peppermint fog.

There, at the edge of the forest, stood the stag, the same one Jackie had seen on her first morning at the inn. It was watching her. Jackie stopped in place. *Magical*, she thought. As she watched it back, she became aware of the darkness inside her, of the resentment and anger that she'd carried since her parents had died. It occurred to her that she'd been right. It had all been her fault, but not the way she'd meant it before.

The stag blinked its dark eyes at Jackie then lifted its head to eat a few dangling, dried leaves from a tree. It was Christmas personified, snowflakes sticking to its back and antlers. So calm and unafraid of her.

Jackie breathed in the chill air, pulling it deep into her lungs and feeling clarification spread through her body. Her shoulders relaxed for the first time in days.

The sound of a car starting caught Jackie's attention, and she looked up just in time to see Jim and Bonnie driving away. Instantly, she regretted everything she had said, and tears gathered in her eyes. "What have I done?" she said aloud, perhaps to the stag. It turned its head to look at her. "I'm an idiot. What is wrong with me?" Her misery reached a new low, and Jackie sat down on a wrought-iron bench on the patio.

Before long, she noticed she was shivering. "So, I'm cold," she told the stag. "So what? I deserve to suffer. I brought all this on myself." Even to herself, she sounded whiny and pitiful, but she couldn't stop. She said, "Everyone would be better off if I were gone."

The stag jerked its head up as if in surprise.

Jackie said, "You know I'm right."

"Right about what?" said a quiet, almost gentle voice. "About freezing to death?"

Jackie looked up into Sam's brown eyes. "Tell him." She gestured toward the stag. "Tell him what a fraud I am."

Sam looked at the stag, then again at Jackie. "Don't bother. I already know." He adjusted his crutches and held a hand out to Jackie. "C'mon. Let's go back inside. You're shivering."

Jackie wasn't just shivering. She was quaking. Her butt was wet where she'd sat in snow, and her muscles were getting tired. "I'll come in soon," she said. "As long as I'm shivering, I'm not likely to die of hypothermia."

Sam shook his head, a little smile of amusement on his face. "As long as I'm here, you're even less likely. Come on now. Let's go." He waggled his fingers to coax her up.

Jackie stood. "All right. You know, you really should go out with Frankie. You'd make such a good couple."

Sam's scowl returned in an instant. "Is that so?"

Jackie nodded. "Yuppers." She took a step toward Sam, and her legs gave out. She tipped forward and would have fallen if Sam hadn't been there to catch her against his chest. He took a steadying step backward, using his crutches to stabilize both himself and her. His arm went around her, and he hugged her to him.

"Oooh," Jackie said after a moment. "You're warm." She buried her face against his chest. "Oooh. You smell good."

Sam was shivering too. Jackie put her arms around him.

"What..." Sam started to say but didn't finish his thought. Nor did he pull away. Instead, he leaned in. His free hand took Jackie's chin and lifted her face.

"You're a nut," he said to her, but the usual derision was missing.

Jackie heard only warm affection. It surprised her. He was

so close that she could see the color variations in his irises and feel the warmth of his breath on her cheek. Her eyes locked on his lips, and suddenly the one thing she wanted more than anything was to kiss him. Pushing up on tiptoe, she did just that—a soft kiss right on his mouth. No mistletoe this time.

Sam's hand slid back into her hair, and he kissed her back. It was slow and sweet. His lips and nose were cold.

"Mmm," Jackie intoned when the kiss ended. Her face still so close to his, she added, "You smell like peppermint."

"No," Sam replied, voice intimate, "*you* smell like peppermint."

Jackie lifted upward again, wanting more, feeling a new kind of need stirring in her belly and chest.

Sam did not object immediately, his mouth firm and responsive in the first seconds of the kiss—until he did object. Then, he pushed her back. "You're drunk," he said.

Jackie felt the rejection as fully as she'd felt the warmth of the kiss, all the way to her toes. Though he had accused her of being drunk with a gentle matter-of-factness, she couldn't help but feel chastised. "So what?" she replied. "I'm an adult. I'm a strong woman, and I can take care of myself. I don't need…anybody."

"Uh huh," Sam said. He gently maneuvered her into position to begin walking toward the inn's front entrance. "Let's go, Wonder Woman. I'm getting frostbite."

"No, you're not," Jackie said with a giggle as she started making her way back inside. She waved over her shoulder, without looking back. "Bye, Mr. Deer. Stay warm."

She stumbled, feet slipping on the icy patio, and latched onto Sam's arm.

Sam did his level best to keep her from falling while juggling his crutches. They halted for a moment while they both steadied themselves.

"Easy there, cowgirl," Sam said. "One step at a time."

"I'm fine," Jackie insisted. She put a hand on the wood-paneled exterior of the inn, her head spinning. "Ooh, forget that. I don't feel so good."

Sam laughed quietly. "I suspected."

Jackie made it inside and then all the way up the stairs to her room.

Sam followed her the whole way, directing and supporting her where necessary. He watched as she collapsed across her bed, then—when she didn't move again—he removed her shoes and jacket, ignoring her mumbles of protest and feeble attempts to help that only hindered the process. He encouraged her in under the blankets and covered her to her chin.

For a long moment, he stood over her, watching her sleep. He gently brushed a strand of hair behind her ear and heaved a mighty sigh. Before leaving, he stoked up the fire and closed the drapes against the afternoon sunlight. On his way out, he glanced back into the firelit room one more time then shut the door extra gently so as not to wake her.

CHAPTER 23

Jackie lifted her head off the pillow to look around. It took her a moment to take in her surroundings. The air in the room held a chill, and Jackie pulled the covers up to her chin. The lights were all off, and the closed drapes cut off any light that may have been left outside. The darkness made the room feel empty and lonely. It muted the room's jewel tones and curbed the velvety flow of the curtains. It dampened the glowing embers in the fireplace.

Desolate was the word Jackie thought to describe her surroundings. *Desolate. Like my soul,* she mused.

The memories of her peppermint-fueled foolishness returned to haunt her in reverse order, and she moaned aloud.

"Oh my god," she said. "I really am an idiot. I have to make this right—somehow." She sat up, realizing for the first time that she'd been sleeping in her clothes and that she had the ghost of a headache stirring at the back of her head. A glance at the alarm clock told her it was nearly dinner time. She'd slept for hours.

Lying beside the clock was the Cupid Manual.

Jackie pushed up to sit with her back against the headboard

and reached over to turn on the lamp. A golden glow spread out into the room, embracing Jackie with its faux warmth. She picked up the book. It felt small in her hands, unreal and fragile. When she opened it, the shuffle of the pages was especially loud in the room's silence.

Jackie didn't know what she was looking for as she turned page after page, until she came to the *Troubleshooting* section. A light went on in her brain, and she began to read, consuming every word, every tip and trick, and every piece of encouragement.

Love will reveal itself, but only in its own time.

True love does not tolerate doubt.

The cupid's job is to recognize and acknowledge it, not to create it.

Love grows best in a state of compassion.

The chapter's conclusion listed three things to do if her mission didn't seem to be working out. 1) Be patient. 2) Be compassionate. 3) Be relaxed.

Jackie didn't understand everything she read nor why it would work, but the words stuck with her. When she'd read the entire *Troubleshooting* chapter, she set the manual aside and got out of bed. Her stomach growled as she opened the drapes, and she realized she hadn't eaten all day. No wonder the schnapps had hit her so hard.

Her clothes were wrinkled, and her hair made her look like a two-year-old boy who just got up from his nap. Jackie did her best to smooth herself but didn't bother to change clothes. More than anything, she wanted to eat, to get on with the business of cupiding, and to apologize to Bonnie—*oh, and to Sam.*

Because she'd earned a little comfort, Jackie put on her fuzzy ho-ho-ho boots instead of shoes. They fit her mood, which had nothing to do with professionalism and everything to do with humility.

Out in the hallway, she knocked on Bonnie and Jim's door. Only silence responded.

The maid came down the hall, pushing her supply cart.

"Mary?" Jackie called. "Have you seen my assistant, Bonnie, and her husband?"

Mary's eyebrows rose, and she tipped her head in surprise. "They checked out this morning," she replied. "I've already cleaned their room. You didn't know?"

Then, Jackie remembered them driving away. She remembered the fight. She remembered the horrible things she'd said to Bonnie, and her headache suddenly became more than just a ghost. It materialized at the nape of her neck and clutched at her temples.

Mumbling her thanks, Jackie hurried past Mary, heading for the stairs. She pulled out her phone and paused on the top stair to call Bonnie. Fear and worry made her hand shake. As the connection began to ring, Jackie put the phone to her ear.

"C'mon, c'mon, c'mon," she said, listening to each ring as it came and went.

"Looks like you'll have to leave a message," Bonnie's recorded message said. "Bonnie is probably too busy enjoying the sun in Italy or skiing the Alps or consuming beer and brats in a Munich café. She'll call you back."

"Bonnie," said Jackie after the beep. "It's me. Look, I'm ridiculous. I didn't mean those things I said. I just had a meltdown, and...you got caught in an avalanche of my self-loathing. I'm really sorry. I am so grateful to you and Jim for coming up here. Please call me back. Please?"

Jackie felt no better after leaving the message. She stood there for a minute longer, hoping Bonnie would call back right away. When that didn't happen, she pocketed her phone and descended the stairs to the lobby.

Twilight had turned to early evening outside, and the Christmas lights in the lobby were at their most twinkly. Combined with the crackle and flicker of the fireplace, they made a festive picture that contrasted sharply with how completely un-festive Jackie was feeling inside.

The aroma of food—warm and savory—drifted out from the dining room to tantalize Jackie forward.

Everyone else had already arrived, making noise, moving chairs, filling plates, and talking. They all sat around one big table like a family. Gita and Ruth were both there, though they weren't seated next to one another. Nicholas and Natalie were at the table, phones close at hand. Even Enrique was with them, seated beside Ada, and fitting in with ease. Lu and Card had taken up places at the table, as had Sam. They were all talking with an energy that frightened Jackie. She balked at joining them, feeling unworthy and not wanting her dark cloud to spoil their evening. Instead, she headed for the bar where Frankie was putting together a tray of drinks.

"Well," said Frankie, "if it isn't Peppermint Patty."

With a huff, Jackie hoisted herself up onto a stool. "You poisoned me."

Frankie laughed, a smirk lingering on her lips.

After a moment, Jackie said, "Just admit it."

"Is there something I can get you?" Frankie asked, still not denying it.

"Coffee," Jackie said.

"With schnapps?"

"No schnapps. Aspirin. You have any back there?"

Frankie studied Jackie for a few seconds while pouring a beer from the tap. "Comin' right up," she finally said. With her usual efficiency, she poured a quick mug of coffee and set it, along with a sugar bowl and creamer, on the bar in front of Jackie. She pulled a bottle of water from the refrigerator and a jar of generic aspirin from a cabinet, adding them both to the collection of remedies. Without another word, Frankie picked up the tray of drinks and left.

Sam appeared at her side. "Feeling better?"

Jackie looked up at him, knowing she looked like hell. "In some ways, yes. In other ways, no." She lifted a finger to indicate he should hold on, then shook out two aspirins and swallowed them with a long drink from the water bottle.

While she did that, Sam leaned his crutches against the bar and sat on the stool beside her. He watched with a look of bemusement on his face. "I think," he said, "that peppermint schnapps is your nemesis."

Jackie could not argue with that. She hoped the aspirin would kick in quickly. Turning on her stool to face Sam, she studied his face. The amused gleam in his eyes, the strength of his jaw, the crutches leaning against the bar, and his lips... The memory of their kiss in the snow returned, and Jackie was captured for far too long. When the corners of his mouth turned up, Jackie was staring at it.

Blinking, Jackie looked away.

Sam said nothing.

"I think," Jackie said finally, " I owe you an explanation."

"Several."

Sparing a glance, Jackie saw that the smile was still firmly in place on his lips. This gave her courage. "It wasn't my idea to come here. I got roped into it."

"Really," Sam said, tone flat.

"Yes. I put a guy in a coma, the guy who was supposed to be here. So, I owed it to him..." She stopped, realizing how lame it all sounded. She shook her head and slumped over her steaming coffee mug. "Never mind. I just took on more than I could handle. Love is so complicated."

Sam snorted. "You can say that again."

"I've been going about this all wrong, trying to make people fall back in love with each other." Her dawning realization solidified as she spoke. "I don't have that kind of power. My power—if I have any at all—is in recognizing love when I see it." Her hands gestured of their own accord as her confidence in what she was saying grew. "And love—true love—doesn't need anyone to make it happen. Certainly not me."

"Who are you?" Sam asked. "Really."

Jackie met his gaze, considering the question. With as much sincerity as she could muster, she said, "I'm Jackie, a waitress from Alexandria, just trying to make ends meet and keep her little brother out of trouble. I'm not a doctor, and I'm no expert on love." She gave a wry chuckle. "I'm sorry, Sam. This week has been one long nightmare."

Sam frowned. "Has it? You haven't enjoyed any of it?"

The question brought memories and images to mind, of seeing the lobby for the first time from the top of the stairs, of mistletoe, of a majestic stag, of amazing meals, and of Christmas music. She remembered how it had felt to be pressed against Sam's chest, to have his arms around her. She couldn't deny that, along with all the suffering, she had experienced some of the most memorable moments of her life.

"Some of it," she said with a smile. "But not the kisses. No, sir. I did not enjoy those."

Sam was taken aback for a moment until he realized she was joking. Then, he tipped his head back and laughed aloud, as spontaneously as he ever had. Several eyes in the room looked their way.

Jackie laughed too, though more subdued.

Sam's cellphone rang. He pulled it out of his pocket and looked at the screen. "Sorry," he said, answering it. "This is Sam."

Jackie turned her attention back to her coffee. It was warming her from the inside out. She loved it with all her heart.

"That's horrible," Sam said. "Yeah, yeah. Hold on." He put a hand on Jackie's forearm to get her attention. "It's the children's home. They've had a fire, and they want to know if they can shelter here."

Jackie gasped.

Sam looked over at the seated couples. "They have a place for tonight, but not for tomorrow." Using only one of his crutches, phone in the other hand, he slid off his stool and approached the dinner table.

Jackie followed him.

"Card? Lu?" Sam told them what he'd heard. The concern on everyone's faces was immediate.

Lu started to speak, but Card halted her with a hand on her shoulder. He looked at Jackie and said, "You okay with this? What with your seminar and all?"

Jackie looked around at everyone. They were waiting for her reaction. Her mind was already churning out the implications of having an inn full of children at Christmas time, and with a spark of genius, she knew it was exactly what everyone needed. "Tell them to come," she said with a grin. "I have a plan."

The mood in the room brightened by several degrees.

CHAPTER 24

Jackie hit her stride.
We'll need places for them to sleep.
We'll need activities to keep them busy.
We'll need presents for them for Christmas morning.
We'll need cookies. Lots of cookies.

Stepping up to stand beside Lu and Card, Jackie spoke to the gathering. "I know the last couple days haven't been what you all wanted them to be, and that's my fault. But now we have the opportunity to make the next couple of days very special for a group of children kicked out of their group home by a fire. Kids who don't have families. They need us. We can make this one of their most memorable Christmases, if we pull together. Will you help?"

The response was unanimous as evidenced by the twinkles in everyone's eyes and the smiles on their faces.

"Yes!" said Natalie, and all the others cheered. "What do you want us to do?"

Jackie looked to Lu.

The other woman grinned. "Card can show you where the Christmas closet is." She waggled a finger at her husband, "But you know the rules, Cardinal Miller."

"Yes, ma'am." Card saluted her.

"Rules?" Jackie asked.

Lu ignored or didn't hear the question. "You'll be needing what's in there. And we can open the third floor for the children. We've got a whole lot of mouths to feed, so I'll be in the kitchen with Frankie. You're in charge out here, Doc."

"I'm on it," said Jackie. "All right, everyone. Take ten to put on working clothes, and we'll meet back here to set things in motion." A wave of people headed back to their rooms, and Jackie brought up the rear.

All down the hall, people stopped in tandem at their doors, flashed their keycards, and stepped into their rooms. It was a beautiful choreography, and Jackie felt a sense of excitement and urgency as she bustled around, changing clothes and gathering the items she would need to coordinate such an effort.

In four minutes and thirty-five seconds, she was back in the dining room, setting up her laptop on the bar and getting down to business. The others trickled back in over the next couple minutes, and Jackie was ready for them.

Sam had called back the director of the children's home to get a list of the children's names and ages. It turned out there were six of them, all girls, between the ages of seven and sixteen, and all nice, not a single naughty one among them.

Jackie assigned Ada and Enrique to help Mary prepare

bedrooms on the third floor. She asked Nicholas and Natalie to make a stocking for each of the children. Sam had the most experience with children, being an uncle to four rowdy ones. Since he couldn't move around as easily, Jackie tasked him with planning games and activities for them. Lastly, she turned to Gita, Ruth, and Card.

"You two," she said to Gita and Ruth, "are with us. Card, can you show us this famous Christmas closet?"

Card clapped his large hands once, loudly, and grinned. "Follow me, ladies. You're about to enter Santa's wonderful world of wrapping paper and tinsel."

As it turned out, he wasn't kidding. The walk-in closet had stacks of boxes, all filled with decorations, wrapping paper, and a Santa suit on a hanger, covered with dry cleaner's plastic.

The general response was, "Wow."

Card held the Santa suit up for inspection. "Not too moth-eaten. I wear this every year when the children come to carol for us."

It wasn't hard for Jackie to see Card as Santa. He had the beard, belly, and dimples for it. "That's wonderful," she said. "Do they get to sit on your lap and tell you what they want?"

Card leaned down and put a heavy hand on Jackie's shoulder. "Not usually. Puts too much pressure on 'em. When you have so little, it's sometimes hard to ask for things you know you'll never get. But we always do have presents for them. I did the Christmas shopping early. The presents are in this box here. Maybe our elves wouldn't mind wrappin' them?"

"Not at all!" said Gita. Ruth nodded enthusiastically.

Card patted the box. "I got some guidance from the home's director, so some of them are labeled with names. Those are intended for specific kids. You can divvy the others up as you think best."

"So, Card," Jackie said, standing with her hands on her hips, looking at a lifetime's collection of Christmas paraphernalia. "What are the rules of the closet?"

Card laughed. "The rules don't apply to the closet. Jus' to me. I'm not allowed to lift heavy things or over-exert myself, whatever that means. But you don't need to worry about that. Lu worries enough for all of us." He gave a dismissive wave of his hand and stepped out. "I'll leave you kids to it."

Jackie watched him go, thoughts clouded for a moment.

Gita pulled Jackie from it. "We're ready to dive in," she said.

"Great! You and Ruth oversee the present-wrapping station. You can set it up in the conference room. I suggest you start by going through these boxes. Find tape and scissors—"

Gita interrupted, "Ribbons and bows. Yes. We're on it." She looked at her partner with excitement. "Right, Ruth?"

Ruth's smile reached her eyes. "Right! Consider us your present-wrapping elves, Jackie."

Gita and Ruth started carrying boxes to the conference room and scavenging for whatever else they'd need.

Jackie, feeling accomplished, returned to the dining room. Sam was seated at the table, making notes on a piece of paper. He looked up as Jackie entered and smiled.

Jackie finally felt like things were going her way. She took her laptop to the table and settled in beside Sam to fine-tune her plan and to listen to his game ideas.

"What about a Santa's Elf Scavenger Hunt?" he suggests. "Maybe we can ask Natalie to draw some elves on index cards, and we can hide them around the inn." The more he talked, the more excited he became. "We can tell them that the elves have been captured in the cards, and that in order to be saved, the children need to find them all and then tear the cards in the light of the Christmas tree. We can give a candy prize for each elf saved. What do you think?"

When he faced Jackie, seeking her approval with that smile of his, Jackie's heart swelled. Her grin spread and, without hesitation, she said, "I think you're... I mean, I think that's wonderful."

The team worked until midnight when Jackie went around to check on their progress and to send them to bed.

The next morning, Jackie got up early, alert and ready for action. She went through her shower routine, then dressed in jeans and an oversized navy sweater. Applying make-up with a light touch, she looked at herself in the mirror. Something was different.

The woman gazing back at her had an energy she hadn't

had in a long time. She wanted to get out and face the day. She was eager for the adventure ahead. Jackie couldn't remember the last time she'd felt that way, but she smiled at herself and watched as her shoulders relaxed a bit more.

"I've got this," she told herself, and she actually believed it.

A glance at the clock told her she still had a few hours before the children would arrive. "Right!" she affirmed, clapping her hands once and turning away from the mirror. "Next stop: coffee and breakfast."

She left her laptop behind in her room. The plan was in place now. She wouldn't need it anymore.

When she entered the dining room, she found Card and Lu there, seated at a table and eating breakfast.

"Merry Christmas Eve!" Lu called, waving her over. "Grab you a plate from over there and come eat with us."

Jackie did, sitting down with them. "I can't believe it's Christmas Eve already. This week has gone by so fast." She realized that she was a bit sad about it being over soon—especially that morning when everything was going so well.

"I reckon you're anxious to get back to Alexandria, aren't ya?" asked Card. "You've probably got plenty of patients there who need you."

Jackie served herself some fried hash from the big bowl. Her immediate instinct was to reply as she would have when she first arrived. *Yes, I have so much to do, and I need to get back to work.* But then a new voice rose inside her, and she said, "Alexandria seems so far away." The truth of that one sentence hit her, followed by a stab of guilt. She added, "I miss my brother, and I really shouldn't leave him alone for much longer, but...if I could, I'd move in here with you and never leave."

A tinkling arpeggio came from the piano, as if on cue, and everyone looked to find Enrique had stealthed in and was seated there, flexing his fingers.

"Good morning, Enrique," called Lu.

He gave her a smile and a wave, then his attention shifted to the doorway, and his smile spread even wider.

Ada was entering, dressed with her usual class, though the curls of her hair were less polished, left to their natural exuberance. She greeted them all, but her steps took her straight to Enrique, and she joined him at the piano with a kiss to his lips.

A soft spotlight shone down upon them, warm and golden in color. It gave them a glow similar to the one Jackie had seen with Bonnie and Jim. It caressed them, and when Ada scooted a tiny bit closer to Enrique, it warmed even more.

"Oh my god," breathed Jackie.

"Yes, ma'am," laughed Card. Quietly, to the table, he said, "If I didn't know better, I'd say they were a match made in Heaven."

"You see it too?"

Card chuckled deep in his chest. "You'd have to be a blind man to miss that." Shaking his head, grinning, he returned to his bowl of oatmeal.

Suddenly, Jackie felt nervous. She knew what the book told her to do, but a whole slew of What-Ifs traipsed across her mind. *What if I'm wrong? What if it's too soon? What if? What if? What if?*

Lu said, "Bless their hearts."

"Excuse me?" Jackie heard a call to action, though she didn't think Lu could have meant it like that.

"Love can surprise you sometimes. When it's real, it comes when you least expect it." Lu spread a healthy helping of blackberry jam on her toast.

Jackie watched the couple at the piano for a moment longer. The glow didn't fade. It was as if it were calling her. She felt the pull deep in her belly.

"I'll be right back," she said, standing.

Neither Card nor Lu paid more than passing attention to where she was going, as if what she was about to do was perfectly normal.

It didn't feel normal to Jackie. It felt monumental. The closer she got to the couple, the stronger the pull, and she began to feel the warmth emanating from the glow. Quietly, she stepped up beside them and put her hands on their shoulders.

Ada and Enrique smiled at her, but not for long. Their gazes were magnetized to each other, and as they connected again, Jackie said, "Blessed be thy love."

There was no angelic host singing hallelujah, no flash of brilliant white light, no spark of magic at Jackie's fingertips.

However, Ada and Enrique both broke out in spontaneous laughter, a sound so filled with delight and happiness that it drew the attention of everyone in the room.

"Thanks, Jackie," said Ada. "You're sweet."

Jackie returned to her seat at the table, basking in her own inner glow. She's found one. She'd blessed her first couple.

"I did it," she told Lu, Card, and Sam—who had seated himself with them while she was up.

"Did what?" asked Sam.

Jackie just shook her head and returned to her breakfast. Corned beef hash and scrambled eggs had never tasted so good.

The pile of presents under the tree had tripled in size, all wrapped and labeled with the names of the children. Some had the scruffy appearance of unskilled wrapping, and Jackie knew Sam had done those. Others had extravagant wrappings, and Jackie learned that Natalie had done those. She found them all endearing, both the polished and the unpolished.

The artist was currently stationed in the dining room near the windows, bringing elves to life on index cards. Her husband, Nicholas, sat beside her, filming her and giving a running commentary on their mission, the children, and how he felt about it all. He relayed the suggestions they received from fans watching them for the elves' identities. Natalie responded with enthusiasm, holding up each finished elf for the camera's inspection before moving on to the next one.

One hour to go before the kids arrived. Jackie was getting excited. She knew in her heart that this was going to be a magical Christmas for them, and she was dedicated to making it so.

"Help!!" The call came from the kitchen. It was Frankie. "Lu! Lu! Come quick!"

Lu was at the fireplace in the lobby, filling stockings hung there with candy and trinkets. Jackie's gaze shot to her as she broke into a run. Jackie followed on her heels.

"Call 9-1-1!" Frankie shouted.

Lu rushed through the swinging door to the kitchen.

Jackie slowed to avoid getting hit in the face by the door.

"Card!" Lu cried from inside the kitchen, her voice filled with anguish.

CHAPTER 25

Jackie stood frozen by the sight that greeted her in the kitchen.

Card was on the floor, leaning against one of the stainless-steel cabinets, his face as white as snow. He wore a grimace of pain and was clutching his chest, trying to breathe.

"Call 9-1-1!" Frankie repeated, looking up at Jackie.

A familiar voice at Jackie's shoulder said, "I've got it." It was Sam. He put a hand on Jackie's shoulder, more to steady himself than to comfort her. "This is Sam Campbell at the Gray Fox Inn, out on Gray Fox Road." He paused a beat, then said, "Oh, hey, Tina. We need help. I think Card's havin' a heart attack. Can you get someone out here, quick as possible?' Another pause, then he said, "Okay, thanks."

Sam hurried away but returned a minute later with the lap blanket off the couch. He pushed past Jackie and went to Card. "Here, buddy," he said. "Let's keep you warm." He covered the man with the blanket.

Lu was keeping it together, petting Card's head and softly encouraging him. "It's gonna be okay, baby," she repeated over and over, punctuated by, "I love you," and "I love you so much."

Jackie had first-aid training, but her mind had skipped a beat. Once her shock cleared, she said, "I'll go meet the ambulance and show them where to come."

No one responded, so she just left.

The others were all standing around in the dining room, huddling with their partners, weak and tense with worry. They had questions, but Jackie didn't have time for that.

As she hurried toward the lobby, she said, "Card's not well. Sam called an ambulance." She knew it wouldn't soothe anyone, but knowing what was happening was half the battle. She didn't stop, but half-ran to the front doors of the inn and stationed herself there, watching the spot where the driveway disappeared beyond the trees. A movement at the corner of her eye drew her attention. The stag stood here, watching her.

A cold draft came in through the windows, chilling Jackie, and she wrapped her arms around herself. She realized that her heart was beating in her throat, and her nose was starting to run.

Someone draped a heavy leather coat over her shoulders, and she found Nicholas and Natalie standing on either side of her. For once, neither of them was recording the moment.

"He'll be okay," said Natalie, draping an arm around Jackie's waist and pulling her close.

Jackie held the coat tightly around herself. It was big, and it smelled of Nicholas's cologne.

Nicholas said, "It's a good thing the kids haven't arrived yet."

Jackie awoke to the other problem they faced. She said, "We're going to all have to pull together once they show up."

"Don't worry," said Natalie. "We can do this. Everybody's plugged in and pumped." She gave Jackie a squeeze.

It felt like forever for the ambulance to arrive, but finally, it turned the bend and came into view.

Immediately, Jackie pushed out the door and went to stand on the front patio, waving.

A cop car followed behind the ambulance as they made their way up the snowy drive.

Jackie watched them approach and park at the entrance. A man and a woman emerged from the rescue vehicle and opened doors on the side to pull out cases with equipment. It seemed to take forever.

"He's in here," Jackie told them when they were finally coming toward her. Nicholas and Natalie held the double doors open for them all to pass inside.

The next minutes went by in a blur.

Card held Lu's hand as they rolled him out to the ambulance.

Jackie watched them go, arms hanging limp at her sides.

Sam came to stand beside her. "We never should have done this retreat. What a fiasco."

Jackie felt a wave of guilt wash over her. She watched in shock as Sam turned abruptly away and went back inside.

Natalie said, "Don't mind him. He's just upset."

Jackie shook her head. "No. He's right. Maybe if I'd handled all this better…"

No one spoke up to correct her.

With all her heart, Jackie wanted to go after Sam, to assure him that Card would be fine, but she didn't know if that was true. She didn't know if Sam would ever even speak to her again.

As the ambulance pulled away, Nicholas said, "We're about to be overrun by a gaggle of girls."

Jackie considered that, what it would mean if the children arrived to see the adults so upset. She shouted, "To the dining room, everyone! Team meeting!" She shifted into quick motion to get there before everyone else did.

Jackie waited until the others were all there, including Mary, who looked like she'd been crying. Seeing that, Jackie herself felt tears threatening again, but she fought them back.

Sam was in an armchair at the back of the room, huddled there with Frankie. She had her cheek resting on the top of his head, arms around him, and they were talking quietly.

Jackie couldn't take her eyes off them. A low, thrumming sadness filled her as she watched. It occurred to her that maybe her efforts at bringing them together had worked. Were they the next ones she would have to bless? In an instant, Jackie knew that she would take no joy in doing so.

I want him to be happy, she thought. *Even if it means he's with Frankie...and not me.* Those last three words came as a revelation. Jackie understood that she had come to care for Sam. More than that, she was falling for him. Had fallen for him.

Jackie took a deep, stabilizing breath, then turned to the group gathered around her. "I know this is hard," she said. "We all love Card and Lu. We're all worried, but we also have a mission. The children will be here any minute," Jackie said. "We can't let them see how upset we are. It's on us to make this the best Christmas they've ever had. Even if it means hiding our feelings. Do you guys think we can do that?"

Everyone nodded, and a couple mumbled affirmation, but their expressions didn't lighten.

Jackie sucked in another deep breath, licked her lips, and stood taller. She put a smile on her face. "When Card comes home, we can tell him we were the best Santa's elves he could ever hope for. *When* he comes home, he won't want everyone to have spent Christmas worrying about him. He'll want Christmas cookies and torn wrapping paper and smiles. Lots of smiles on all our faces. I know it'll be hard, but we can do this! Am I right?"

The response was stronger—smiles spreading—and produced more replies.

"Right."

"Yes."

"We can."

Jackie said, "We need to do this *for* Card and for the children." She looked over at Frankie and Sam. "Even if...it means hiding our feelings."

"Who's going to play Santa?" Mary asked, voice forlorn.

Jackie got stuck without an answer to the question. She considered Sam, but he was still on crutches.

"What about you, Nicholas?" Jackie asked.

Nicholas shook his head. "Me? Play Santa? They'll see right through me."

Jackie could see his anxiety building. "It's okay," she said. "We may have to do without Santa. Or maybe I could be Santa?"

Ada perked up. "Wait. I have an idea. Instead of Santa, Jackie, you could be one of Santa's elves. We can explain that the big man is busy getting presents ready, and he sent you to be his representative."

"Ooh!" cried Natalie. "Nick and I can do your hair and make-up. Turn you into a proper elf."

Mary offered, "Lu has a sewing machine. I can take in that Santa suit for you."

"Thanks, everybody," Jackie said. "You guys are the best." And she meant it.

Frankie moved to the windows and stood there, looking out toward the driveway.

Just then, the front doors of the inn opened, and the cacophony of many bootsteps came inside.

"They're here!" Enrique announced.

Sam put his crutches in motion, heading for the lobby.

"Okay," Jackie said. "I guess I'll be Santa's elf."

After all, she thought, *it can't be any harder than being a cupid, can it?*

◆♥◆

CHAPTER 26

Nicholas and Natalie put on a show for the children, entertaining them with sock puppets they'd put together with nothing but glue, felt, socks, and imagination.

All six girls were seated on the floor, on a pile of rugs, pillows, and blankets that had been set out for them. Paisley was the youngest, at seven years old, and Chloe was the eldest, at sixteen. Three of the girls—Brie, Denisha, and Precious—were closer in age, and it was difficult to tell whether they were eight or nine. Matina was thirteen. They were all dressed in jeans, t-shirts, and pink hoodies with the Daybreak Children's Home logo on the back.

"And so," said Natalie from behind a set of drapes hung on a rolling luggage cart, "the Christmas fairy flew all the way to the North Pole to find her best friend. Her little wings were so tired by the time she got there that she collapsed and couldn't talk!"

The children all gasped as the sock representing the fairy fell with a thump to the surface of the luggage cart and trembled there.

"Wake up, Christmas fairy!" said the other puppet in Nicholas's voice—his interpretation of a fairy voice. Nicholas spread his fingers and released a sprinkle of glitter on his downed friend. "I know you're not really a sock," he said. "Just like me. We've been cursed, and we need to find the magic that will save us."

"A kiss," said the Christmas fairy. "A kiss with true love." She twitched some more, still on the ground.

"Hurry!" cried Denisha.

"Kiss her!" Paisley begged.

"Should I kiss her?" asked Nicholas's sock fairy. "Do I love her with true love?"

"Yes!" cried all the girls together.

Nicholas's fairy nodded at the audience, then bent over the Christmas fairy. But, before kissing her, he said, "Oh Christmas fairy, may I kiss you?"

The Christmas fairy lifted up a bit and turned her eyes to the audience.

"Yes!" the children all cried together.

"Yes!" said Natalie's sock puppet. "Please kiss me."

And so, Nicholas's puppet planted a kiss on the Christmas fairy. The sound of exaggerated smooching came from behind the curtain, causing several of the girls to giggle.

Then, a light shower of tiny plastic snowflakes arced out and rained down upon the girls, during which Nicholas and Natalie made a quick transition, hiding the socks and emerging from behind the curtains themselves, in each other's arms.

"Oh, Nicholas," said Natalie with just a touch more drama than was necessary. "Our love is true! We're saved!"

"I'm not a stinky ol' sock anymore," cried Nicholas. "I am so happy!" He looked out at the children. "We never would have made it without your help. Thank you, children, for telling me and the Christmas fairy to kiss."

"Kiss again!" Denisha cried. The others all quickly joined in.

Nicholas pulled Natalie closer and pressed his mouth to hers. Bending her into a dip, he pulled the curtain around them, hiding the rest of the kiss and putting the final touch on the show. They both emerged from behind the curtains with a dramatic jump and took deep bows.

"Did you like that?" asked Natalie.

The children were already cheering, and it only got louder at her question.

"It's time for lunch," said Robert, appearing next to Jackie. "C'mon, guys. Let's wash our hands before we eat."

Excited, the girls took off at a quick trot. Robert reminded them not to run, and they slowed into exaggerated speed-walking.

It did Jackie's heart good to see them so happy and engaged. She walked over to Nicholas and Natalie in time to hear one straggler, a tiny girl of about seven, say, "Thank you," before hustling off to catch up with the others, walking quickly, not running.

"That was so much fun," Natalie cried. "You were amazing, Nick."

"No, you were amazing," her husband replied.

"Jackie!" Natalie's eyes shone. "Shall we tell her, Nick? Make it official?" She held out her hand to Nicholas, and he stepped up beside her, taking it.

They both beamed. "We," said Nicholas, "have decided to start a new vlog."

Jackie started to frown a bit, but then he explained. "Both of us, together. We're going to call it 'Nick and Nat,' and it'll be all about married life as hyper-creative individuals."

Natalie said, "You inspired us, Jackie, and we realized how many couples out there might need a little magic in their lives."

"Or at least," Nick added, "permission to have a magical marriage. Nat and I are great at this. We can inspire others. It's going to be a huge hit."

By the time they'd finished explaining, Jackie was grinning. "You two are amazing," she told them.

Nick and Nat turned to look at one another. Their eyes met, and a golden glow blossomed out of their hearts.

Jackie's breath hitched.

"I'm your number-one fan," Nicholas told Natalie.

She replied, "Yes. You are."

Jackie placed a hand on each of their shoulders. They didn't appear to notice her there. She said clearly, "Blessed be thy love." A tingle warmed her palms. With a full heart, Jackie slipped away, heading for the dining room and lunch. *Two down,* she thought. *One to go.*

As the children finished their lunch, Sam stood.

"Girls," he said, "Santa called. He needs your help."

Jackie watched the girls wiggle in their seats. Even the oldest girl, Chloe, came to attention.

Sam continued, "Some of the elves have gone missing, and Santa thinks they're being held captive here at the inn. It's going to be up to you to find them. Can you do that?"

"Yes!" cried the children.

"There are rules," Sam told them. "You can't go outside. It's too cold out there for elves anyway. And you can't go into any of the bedrooms upstairs. Those are all locked. Also, there are no elves in the kitchen. We already checked there, so stay out of the kitchen. The kidnapped elves could be anywhere else, though."

The children started looking around before they'd even left their seats.

"Once you find them," said Sam, "bring them to the Christmas tree in the lobby, and we'll set them free."

They didn't need encouragement. Off they went, in search of elves trapped on index cards.

Sam followed the troops into the lobby so he'd be ready when they found their elves.

Jackie cleared tables using a plastic bin to carry the dirty dishes to the kitchen. The simple task gave her something to think about besides Card. She didn't know what would happen if he never came home. *Would Lu be able to run the inn by herself?*

Laughter and girlish squeals pealed from the lobby. They must have found one of the elves. The sound offset Jackie's worry and, once she'd loaded and started the dishwasher, she went to stand in the dining room doorway from where she could watch Sam "free" each elf presented to him and give the finder a bag of candy as a reward.

It was just starting to get dark when a car drove slowly up the long driveway, headlights in the lead.

Sam was still receiving found elves, so Jackie went to greet whoever was arriving.

Much to her surprise, Eloise from the department store got out of the car. Jackie almost didn't recognize her at first, as the woman was bundled up in a heavy down coat, a wool cap, and a thick scarf, but when Eloise's eyes landed on her, there was no mistaking the scowl and the intensity of that gaze.

Jackie forced a smile.

Eloise opened the trunk and pulled out a few shopping bags bulging with stuff.

Jackie hurried out to help her. "Oh my gosh. Hi."

"I brought some things for the kids," Eloise said, matter of fact. "We done heard about the fire."

"That is so kind of you, Eloise." Jackie took a pair of heavy bags from the other woman.

"It's clothes and toys. Books. We didn't know if they had presents or not." Eloise shut the car door with a bump of her hip. "Where you want them?"

"C'mon inside," said Jackie, heading to the front door. "We can take them to the present-wrapping room." She led the way.

Gita and Ruth were in the conference room, boxing up the wrapping supplies.

"More presents?" cried Gita, hurrying forward to meet them. "That's wonderful! We'll get them wrapped."

Once the presents were spread out on the table for sorting, Jackie and Eloise stepped back out of the way. Eloise removed her hat and coat, hugging them to her. "So," she said to Jackie. "You and Sam a thing?"

"What?" That was the last thing Jackie had expected to hear come out of Eloise's mouth.

Eloise spoke sagely. "I saw how ya were the other day. I'm glad. It's long overdue for him to find somebody."

"Sam and I aren't—" Jackie started, but Eloise interrupted her.

"That boy was broke in half when Crystal died. He loved her like a cloud loves the sky. I ain't never seen no one hurt so bad for so long. It does my heart good to know he won't be alone anymore."

Jackie didn't have the heart to correct her. Instead, she said, "Eloise, would you consider staying for supper with us? We have a ton of food, and you're more than welcome. Afterward, we're going to do cookie-decorating with the kids. We could use your help."

Eloise considered then replied, "I can do that. I've got a couple of my homemade pecan pies in the car. I'll go get 'em."

Before Jackie could blink, Eloise was off like a shot, each footfall heavy and loud as she hurried down the hall, slinging her coat back on as she went.

Jackie followed at her own pace, arriving in the lobby just as another car pulled up behind Eloise's. Jackie watched it, mildly curious, and then sucked in a sharp breath as the doors opened and Bonnie and Jim emerged. A moment later, the back door opened, and Jackie saw another familiar face: Jazz.

With his name on her lips, perhaps a bit louder than she'd intended, Jackie ran to the front door.

"No running," said a little girl's voice, but Jackie was already pushing out the entrance and crossing the patio.

"You're here!"

"Hey, Jacks," said Jazz. "These two nutcases kidnapped me."

"We did not," insisted Bonnie, grinning. "Much."

Jackie didn't know whom to hug first. She went for the first person she came to, which was Bonnie. All the words she'd been wanting to say spilled out in a rush. "I'm so sorry. I didn't mean what I said. I was horrible. I'm sorry."

Bonnie hugged her back. "Apology accepted," she said. "I knew you didn't mean it. I also knew you were really worried about Jazz, so we figured we'd surprise you."

When they broke apart, Bonnie waved her hand elegantly toward Jazz. "So you like your Christmas present?"

Jackie laughed. "It's a little scruffy, but yeah. I love it." She hugged her brother, who begrudgingly returned it.

"I'm starving," he said.

"Merry Christmas to you too," Jackie said, laughing. "C'mon. It's freezing out here."

Jim got a hug too, then they all headed inside.

Sam was there, in the lobby, surrounded by a circle of young ladies who were all waving index cards with drawings of quirky elves at him. His attention, however, was on Jackie and her entourage.

By the time Bonnie, Jim, and Jazz were settled into their rooms, it was time for dinner. The tables had all been pushed together to make two long dining tables, one for grown-ups and one for the kids. Jazz couldn't have been happier. Jackie seated him on one side of her and Bonnie on the other. Conversation flew all around her, and it felt like one big happy family.

For Jackie, the only dark spots were not knowing how Card was and seeing Sam with an arm slung along the back of Frankie's chair, talking and laughing with her at the other end of the table. Jackie put both out of her mind the best she could, instead grilling Jazz on school and his time at the Rasmussens.

The rest of the evening went well. Jackie and Jazz helped the little girls decorate sugar cookies along with Gita and Ruth. They made three dozen of them, two of which would be set out for Santa. The girls voted on which ones they would be. They chose one decorated by little Paisley and one by Chloe, the eldest, who turned out to be quite the cookie artiste.

◆♥◆

CHAPTER 27

Christmas Day dawned early. Jackie awoke to a quiet knocking on her door. Her room held a chill that had snuck in when the fire burned down to embers in the fireplace. She heard the girls going down for breakfast, their high-pitched voices carrying through the inn.

Jackie rolled out of bed and went to the door.

Natalie stood there with a smile and a black dress bag in her arms. "You ready, Miss Elf? Those girls will tear through breakfast to get to the presents Santa left for them."

Jackie laughed and stepped back to invite Natalie in.

The next hour was spent getting Jackie ready. She showered while Natalie was setting up her make-up and hair station.

The elf suit fit her surprisingly well. Marie had turned the dark red velvet coat into a dress that hung to mid-calf. A thick black belt cinched it in at the waist. The coat had faux fur at the ends of the sleeves and around the edge of the built-in short cape that draped over her shoulders. Golden swirls embellished the front, giving it a magical feel. Jackie paired it with white tights and her black shoes.

Natalie invited Nicholas in, once Jackie was decent. He did her hair while Natalie applied her make-up. By the time they were done with her, Jackie had her hair up in high pigtails, with explosions of curly ribbons coming off them, and her gold and glitter make-up made her sparkle.

Jackie studied herself in the mirror, grinning. "Magical," she said, not quite recognizing herself.

Natalie and Nicholas went ahead so they could give her the signal when the children were ready. She made her entrance to the cheers of all who were there, including the adults.

The night before, while the kids were sleeping, Gita and Ruth had moved the presents from their hiding place to under the tree. Jackie had already gone to bed, so she was as wide-eyed with surprise as the children when she saw how big the pile was.

"Merry Christmas!" she called out and received a rowdy response.

"Where's Santa?" asked Paisley with bright eyes.

Jackie put her hands on her knees, playing the part of a coquettish elf, and said, "He's at the North Pole. He was up all-night delivering presents, and now he's exhausted. He sent a message for you all."

"What? What?" the girls asked.

"Santa said to tell you that he's very proud of how good you've been this year. He sees how you take care of each other, and how hard you work in school. He wanted you to know that even though he doesn't get to see you this year, he loves you all and sent some very special presents that he thinks you'll love."

"Yay!" A general cheer went up among the girls.

Jackie went to the tree and made a production of searching for just the right present. From smallest to biggest, she handed out the first ones. Each girl had a handful of presents, some practical, some just for fun.

Wrappings were removed, and packaging discarded. When Jackie looked around, she saw only smiles. Her heart sang.

Once all the children's presents had been distributed, Jazz came up to Jackie and handed her an envelope.

"This is for you, Jacks. Merry Christmas."

Jackie thought how grown up he sounded, his voice resonant. She looked at him. Really looked at him and saw her parents in his face. She saw the young man he was becoming.

She said, "My present for you is at home."

Jazz shook his head. "Nope. We brought them." He pointed to the small pile of presents Jackie had bought for her brother and wrapped weeks earlier.

With her arm looped through his, Jackie pulled Jazz over to them. "You thought of everything!" she said. "Open them!"

Jazz shook his head. "No. You need to open yours first." He indicated the envelope. It was probably a Christmas card, but it was thicker than normal. In previous years, he'd given her coupons for work around the apartment. That was probably it, but she played along with a wink. "I wonder what it is."

Inside, she found one of the cards she'd bought the previous year to send out to friends and family. He'd signed his name under the "Merry Christmas." The mysterious nugget was a folded piece of paper tucked there. Jackie handed the card to Jazz and unfolded the paper.

As she read it, her nose buzzed, and her eyes filled with tears. Her hands started to shake.

Two words stood out starkly among all the others: full scholarship. Jackie looked up at her brother and asked, "Is this real?"

Jazz was grinning from ear to ear. "It's real. I start in the fall, and you don't have to spend a penny."

"Oh my god!" Jackie cried and pulled Jazz into her arms. She hugged and hugged and hugged him, crying, until he gently extricated himself.

"Jacks. People are staring."

Jackie didn't care. She took Jazz's face in her hands and kissed him on the forehead. "I am so proud of you," she said.

"Now," said Jazz, "you can take the money we saved and use it to finish your Psychology degree, like you wanted."

That hadn't even occurred to her, but as her brother said it, the full implications blazed into her brain. She looked at him, in shock.

"Jackie?" Jazz looked amused. "You hear me?"

"Yeah," she said, then repeated it several times. "Yeah, yeah. Yeah." She looked down at the paper in her hands.

"Can I open my presents now?" Jazz asked.

"Yeah." A stampede of thoughts stormed through Jackie's mind. *I can go back to school. My life can begin. Jazz is going to college. Mom and Dad would be so proud.*

Bonnie came to stand beside her. "He's a good kid."

"I know."

"You did a good job with him."

Once again, tears swelled into Jackie's eyes. She turned and gave Bonnie a hug.

"You big softie," Bonnie said, holding her best friend tightly. After a moment, she asked, "So, did you get all three true loves?"

Jackie stood back. "I found two of the three. I think Sam and Frankie might be the third, but they just won't spark."

"What about Gita and Ruth?"

"I've been watching them all week, and it's just not there. I've given up on them."

Bonnie thought about that then asked, "Isn't today the last day?"

"Yeah," Jackie said. "I have until midnight, I guess."

"Like Cinderella. What happens if you don't get the third?"

Jackie shrugged. "I don't know. I fail."

"So, Sam and Frankie, huh?"

Sam was on one side of the room, and Frankie was on the other.

Jackie said, "There's too much going on. I need to push them together somehow. Get the romance going."

"A kiss can have magic," offered Bonnie.

Jackie remember her mistletoe kiss with Sam.

"I've got it!" Jackie said. There was mistletoe hanging in the center of the threshold to the dining room. "If we can get them over there, under the mistletoe, maybe it'll happen. What do you think?" She brushed her hands down her suit. "You get Sam. I'll get Frankie. Okay?"

"On it!" Bonnie gave a grin and a salute. "Does this make me a cupid by association?"

"Absolutely!" Jackie laughed and headed off to get Frankie. Boldly, she walked right up to the other woman and asked, "Frankie, can I talk to you? Over here?" She led Frankie to the doorway between the lobby and the dining room.

"What do you want?" Frankie asked.

"Have you heard anything from Lu?"

Frankie relaxed a little. "Not yet today. Last night, she said she was staying at the hospital with Card. The doctor's supposed to have the results of the tests today, and they wanted to keep an eye on him overnight."

Sam and Bonnie came up beside them. "Oh look," Bonnie said. "There's Frankie." She physically pushed Sam forward.

Jackie pointed up at the mistletoe.

Both Frankie and Sam looked at it, then at each other.

Holding her breath, Jackie felt a wave of anxiety pass over her. She wanted to find the third couple, but she didn't want it to be Sam and someone else. *Who am I,* she thought, *to stand in the way of true love? He deserves it.* She took a step back.

One of the children noticed them and called, "Kiss her! Kiss her!" The other children caught on and started a chant.

Frankie blushed, and Sam fidgeted. They looked into one another's eyes, and Jackie prepared herself to step in and bless them.

Together, Frankie and Sam moved toward one another, and at the last minute, they both turned their faces so they each kissed a cheek.

Jackie's shoulders fell with a combination of relief and disappointment that they had no glow. She started to leave, but felt a hand on her elbow, tugging her to one side and turning her around. Sam slid an arm around her waist and pulled her in close.

Jackie looked up at him with surprise. "Sam?"

"Kiss her!" the children chanted. "Kiss the Christmas fairy!"

The room went quiet as Sam leaned in. He said, "Oh Christmas fairy, may I kiss you?"

It felt perfect in his arms. He held her just right.

Jackie didn't have it in her to protest or pull away, not even to turn her cheek. She wanted his kiss. She barely got the word out, "Yes," before Sam's lips touched hers.

The warmth of the kiss spread down Jackie's neck, all the way to her fingertips, and down her spine, all the way to her toes. This wasn't like the others had been.

Sam wrapped his arm gently around the back of her head, hiding the kiss from the children. The press of his lips lingered then became passionate, exploratory, and thrilling in a way Jackie had never experienced. The smell of him filled her, intoxicated her.

Jackie could have gone on like that for hours, days even, wrapped up in his arms.

But, a familiar voice interrupted them, working its way into her consciousness through the fog of wanting Sam. It was Card.

Jackie pulled away. Her eyes locked with Sam's for a moment before they both turned toward the inn's entrance doors.

Card and Lu had come in from outside, and the children had abandoned the mistletoe show to go greet them. A crowd of kids and adults surrounded them, all happy beyond measure. Card looked healthy. His pallor was rosy, as usual, and he was laughing.

Sam slid away from Jackie, and they joined the welcoming party.

"Indigestion?" cried Frankie in disbelief. The lobby was filled with laughter, followed by a hug parade on Card.

The morning progressed as one long series of conversations, jokes, and games. Jackie turned into a kitchen elf, helping Frankie to prepare the big Christmas dinner. They had a turkey in the oven and many side dishes in the works. The smells that filled the kitchen intoxicated Jackie. Although Jackie's expertise in the kitchen extended to boxed mac-n-cheese and scrambled eggs, Frankie was in her element. The other woman had no trouble at all telling Jackie what to do either, and Jackie let herself be ordered about with cheer.

Dinner was served in the early afternoon—a joyous, noisy affair. For the first time ever, Jackie knew what it was like to have a large family. As she looked around at everyone, her new friends, she knew she was a part of something special. Ada and Enrique, Nick and Nat, Sam, Lu and Card, Frankie, and even Eloise. They had all found places in her heart, and Jackie couldn't imagine never seeing them again once Christmas was over. In that moment, she vowed to return, every year.

Jackie stood and clinked her glass. Everyone grew still, watching her. "I want to make a toast," she said, raising her glass. "When I first got here, I was lost. I had no idea how this week would go, and—frankly—I didn't know what I was doing here. Then, one by one, you welcomed me. None of the good that has come from this weekend is because of me. It's all because of you. Every one of you. I have learned so much from you." Jackie felt her emotion rising and had to pause a beat before continuing. "You are the meaning of Christmas magic, and I will always be grateful for the memories we created. Merry Christmas!"

As Jackie lifted her glass a notch higher, everyone else did the same, with a general cry of "Merry Christmas!" They all drank to that.

Food coma settled everyone down after dinner, and the younger children toddled off to take naps. Card napped too. The pace and noise levels came down, and Jackie helped clear away the dirty dishes and wrap up the leftovers. Bonnie was there as well, and they moved around the kitchen together in that familiar, easy way they did in the diner.

"So," said Bonnie as she came by with a half-eaten bowl of mashed potatoes. "How about that kiss, huh?"

Jackie played innocent, "What kiss?" but she felt a zing at the memory. On the move, she pushed back out into the dining room, leaving Bonnie behind. She grabbed several empty serving dishes, stacked them, and returned to the kitchen with them.

"The one that nearly had you floating to the ceiling?" Bonnie said without missing a beat. She was scraping left-over cranberry sauce into a smaller plastic container. She made a funny kissy face.

"Oh," Jackie replied. "*That* kiss." She beamed.

"You like him." Bonnie said it as a statement, not as a question.

Jackie set the dishes she'd brought in on the stainless steel. "I do." She couldn't keep a flush from rising into her cheeks.

Bonnie passed by Jackie, heading for one of the big refrigerators with the covered bowl. "So, him and Frankie?"

"Just friends." Jackie hurried back out into the dining room to gather more dishes. Bonnie came out as she was returning.

As they passed one another, Bonnie asked, "So, who's the third true love?"

Jackie didn't stop to answer. She didn't need to. She had no clue. Gita and Ruth had failed to glow. Frankie and Sam too—*thank goodness*. The inn was full of people at the moment, but none of them seemed like good candidates. She placed the stack of plates in her hands on the sink and began scraping the food off them into a bin, a portrait of waitressing efficiency.

Bonnie appeared at her side with a stack of her own. "We should set Eloise up with someone," she said.

Jackie laughed. "That would be amazing."

They were both silent for a moment, working side-by-side, scraping plates, then Bonnie asked, "Are you going to tell him?"

"Tell who? What?"

"Tell Sam you like him."

"I hadn't thought about it." Jackie considered the idea of having a conversation with Sam about her blossoming feelings for him. The thought made her uncomfortable and uncharacteristically shy.

Bonnie gently reminded her, "We leave tomorrow."

Jackie had been avoiding thinking about that. "I know," she said quietly. "We'll see how it goes. If I get the opportunity, I'll tell him tonight. If not, I'll tell him tomorrow when I say good-bye. Less pressure that way. If he doesn't feel the same, then it won't be a big deal, and neither of us will need to hang out feeling awkward."

Bonnie added, "That'll just be the end of it."

"Exactly." Jackie turned away, heading back to the dining room.

With all the Christmas dinner dishes cleared and washed, Bonnie wandered off to find Jim, and Jackie found herself standing in the dining room contemplating a nap. She didn't, however, want to sleep through a single moment of that day, so instead she opted for a cup of coffee.

Enrique and Ada were at the piano, playing and singing a beautiful rendition of "I Heard the Bells on Christmas Day."

Jackie stood at the window, drinking her coffee, and listening to the timeless song. It was snowing again, but lightly, and the view took Jackie's breath away. She realized again how much she would miss this place once she was gone. What would happen if it went under? She couldn't even imagine that happening, the closing of the doors forever, the covering of furniture, the death of the fires in the fireplaces, the final locking of the doors. A "For Sale" sign, perhaps. And Lu and Card anywhere else but there. It was unthinkable.

And yet, it occurred to Jackie that they hadn't charged anyone for that extravagant Christmas meal, nor for the rooms made up for all the guests. How could they afford it? *Is this,* she wondered, *the last hurrah before turning off the lights?*

"No," she said aloud. "That is not an option." A plan began to take form in her mind. A plan to get guests into the inn, and like the plan to make a memorable Christmas for the children, this one also involved enlisting everyone's help.

Jackie spent the rest of the afternoon talking out her plan in quiet corners, letting everyone know that the inn was in trouble and that it needed their help to thrive.

The plan came to fruition when everyone gathered in the

dining room at exactly five p.m. to sing. Jackie positioned them all around the piano, including the girls. Enrique played, and they sang. Natalie had set up her cellphone on a stand and filmed the whole thing. They all decided on "Let It Snow! Let It Snow! Let It Snow!" as the inn's theme song.

And they sang.

The energy in the room was high, the camaraderie palpable. Although the younger children didn't know the lyrics, they came in on "Let it snow!" with great enthusiasm to make up for it.

No matter what, everyone had so much fun, they sang it twice, then jumped into "Rudolph the Red-Nosed Reindeer."

And that's when Jackie saw it. The glow. It was coming off Gita and Ruth...and Matina. The three of them stood arm in arm, singing to and with one another. The women had found what had been missing.

Jackie skirted around the group, moving up behind the couple. She put a hand on each of their shoulders—one on Gita, and one on Ruth, and said, "Blessed be they love." And it was blessed. Jackie had found the third couple with true love.

Gita looked over her shoulder at Jackie, leaned in, and said over the raucous singing, "We're talking about adopting an older girl. Turns out Ruth just didn't want to deal with an infant or toddler. But I think we're falling in love with Matina. Who knows? We're going to keep talking about it. It's all thanks to you."

Jackie shook her head, but she was grinning. "Not me," she said. "This is all you." She hugged Gita then hugged Ruth for good measure. They looked so happy, and that made Jackie happy too.

When she looked up, she saw Sam watching her and gave him a smile. He nodded in return, a surprised smile coming to his lips.

Maybe this is my chance, Jackie thought. She started toward him, but before she could get there, she spotted a new arrival standing in the doorway to the lobby: Mr. Amore. He gestured her to him.

Cupid's butler/lawyer was dressed in his usual business suit and stood with perfect posture, hands clasped behind his back. He didn't meet Jackie halfway but waited for her to come to him, then when she was almost there, he turned around and walked into the lobby. Jackie followed. The lobby was much quieter than the dining room, and Amore led Jackie to the chairs beside the warmly crackling fireplace. He didn't, however, sit.

Jackie's anxiety had spiked, and now, seeing Amore standing there with his usual dour expression, she wondered if she'd done something wrong. Because she didn't know whether she should be apologizing or what for, if so, she said nothing.

Amore finally said, "I didn't think you could do it." He sniffed. "You found three true loves. Well done." He looked as if he'd just sucked on a lemon.

"What does that mean?" Jackie asked. "What happens now?"

"It means," Amore replied, "that you are free to go. When you go to sleep tonight, you will wake up at home in your own bed."

"No, no," Jackie said. "I'll find my own way home, thank you. I have a ride."

Amore nodded formally. "Very well. I will also make one last deposit into your Love, Inc., credit card. A bonus. Don't spend it all in one place."

"Is Georgio Kupidopoulos going to be all right?" Jackie realized that she had no idea how he was. He could have died, and she wouldn't have known it—because she hadn't bothered to ask. She'd been that caught up in her own drama. She couldn't believe it.

Amore looked down his nose at her, as if he could read her thoughts. "He's awake and recovering."

A sigh of relief escaped Jackie, and she rested her palm against her forehead. "Oh, thank goodness. Please tell him how sorry I am for what happened."

Amore nodded then, back to business, said, "I'll be taking back the Cupid Manual, and of course, your cupid sight. You don't need either one anymore. We will never see each other again."

Jackie felt gratitude all of a sudden, though she couldn't put her finger on why exactly. All he'd done was make her Christmas miserable. *No, she thought. That's not right.* Her Christmas hadn't been miserable. It had been the most wonderful Christmas she'd had since her parents had died. It had been a gift.

"Thank you, Mr. Amore."

Amore didn't need an explanation for the gratitude. He took

it in stride, as if he knew exactly why. He simply nodded, then said, "I believe there's someone coming to speak to you."

Jackie looked over her shoulder to find Eloise approaching. When she turned back to Amore, he was gone. Just gone.

"I see you," said Eloise with that same suspicious tone and squint of eyes that she'd used in the store. "I see you hiding out here all by yourself. C'mon back. We're about to sing 'We Wish You a Merry Christmas,' and it won't be the same without you. C'mon, girl. You belong with us." She smiled, and it transformed her face.

CHAPTER 28

On the morning of the 26th, Bonnie woke Jackie by knocking on her door.

Jackie rolled reluctantly out from under the warm blankets, lumbered to the door, unlocked and opened it, then went immediately back to bed and pulled the covers up over her head.

Bonnie came in and leapt onto the bed beside her, lying on her stomach and looking at Jackie. "Today's the day," she said.

"The day for what?" Jackie grumbled.

"The first day of the rest of your life." Bonnie snuggled up to Jackie. "You ready? Jazz is already snarfing down breakfast in the dining room. Me and Jim are packed. We're just waiting for you now." She gave Jackie a squeeze.

"I still need to pack." Jackie groaned.

"Out of bed, sleepy head." Bonnie gave Jackie a shake, then rolled away and stood, looking for the suitcase they'd brought her clothes in. "Have you thought about whether you're going to quick the diner right away or wait awhile?"

"What?" Jackie uncovered her head. She hadn't given it any thought at all. With everything that had been happening the day before, she had all but forgotten that she could go back to school.

"You going to apply to the university or go the community college route?" Bonnie swung the suitcase up on the bed and opened it.

"I don't know," Jackie admitted. She pushed the covers aside and sat up. "I wouldn't mind going back to the University of Virginia, since that's where Jazz is going too, but I don't even know if the credits I earned before still count? Or if I have to start from scratch? Or if they'll even have me."

"You," Bonnie said, tone serious, "need to do some research on it."

"I need to do some research on it," Jackie agreed. She watched Bonnie folding clothes and putting them in the suitcase, thinking about all the ways her life was about to change. It suddenly occurred to her there was so much to do.

As if sensing the rising anxiety in the room, Bonnie said, "You've got plenty of time. You don't need to fret."

Jackie acknowledged that, though she was already beginning to make plans in her mind. *So much to do.*

An hour later, Jackie stood at the top of the grand staircase and looked down into the lobby. A grouping of suitcases near the doors indicated that everyone else was also getting ready to depart. It made her suddenly sad. Goodbyes had never been her forte.

She took her time descending the stairs, suitcase in hand, taking in the beauty of the lobby one last time. The sky beyond the two-story windows was blue, and because of the brightness coming in through them, the Christmas lights seemed dimmer.

Jackie felt her old life looming, so different from her Gray Fox Inn life, and she didn't want to leave.

"Breakfast before anything else," Bonnie said, taking Jackie's suitcase from her and adding it to the grouping.

As she entered the dining room, Jackie found herself looking around at everyone there, searching for one particular face. But Sam wasn't there. *In the kitchen, maybe?* she thought.

She got waves from several people, including Jazz, and sent a smile back to them. The buffet was set up for self-serve, and Jackie helped herself to scrambled eggs, fried potatoes, bacon, and the last slice of Eloise's pecan pie. Coffee was served in carafes on the tables.

Jackie sat with Jazz, Jim, and Bonnie, feeling oddly discombobulated and out of sorts.

The children were there, being surprisingly quiet.

Ada and Enrique, Gita and Ruth, Nicholas and Natalie—all quiet. It was as if everyone were experiencing the same disconnect between their time at the inn and their real lives.

Just when everyone in the room seemed to have run out of things to say, Lu and Card came in from the kitchen. Nicholas seemed to take that as his cue and stood, announced, "Lu, Card, we have something to show you." He walked over to the bar, where Frankie joined him. They turned on the big-screen TV that hung there and fiddled around with a few things.

Lu and Card came to stand behind Jackie. Lu put a hand on her shoulder, light but warm.

Everyone turned to watch as a video began to play. It started with their rendition of "Let It Snow." Other scenes played as the song continued. Nicholas and Natalie had taken it upon themselves to cut in scenes from throughout their stay at the inn and had brilliantly edited them all together. There were so many of Jackie's memories captured for all time and about to be spread across the Internet. As the music changed, she saw the children on Christmas morning and the hug train given Card when he returned from the hospital. Jackie hadn't even been aware that Nick and Nat had been filming.

The video ended with everyone singing "We wish you a Merry Christmas," panning all the happy faces, the faces that had become so dear to Jackie. They were all there. Even Sam.

Jackie looked around the room for Sam, but he wasn't there.

In the final moments of the video, the Gray Fox logo appeared, and Natalie's voice said, "Join us at Christmas or any time of year. Bring the whole family. We'd love to see you."

Jackie's weren't the only eyes in the room that weren't dry—not by a long shot. She used her napkin to dab at them just as a cheer went up around the room.

"We've got everyone's email addresses," said Nicholas. "We'll make sure everyone gets a copy to remember us by."

More hugs happened, and more continued to happen as people said their goodbyes.

Jackie waited to be the last to leave, seeing her couples off first. By the time all that was done, she was emotionally exhausted, and she still had to say goodbye to Lu and Card.

"Jackie, you are the best thing to happen to the Gray Fox Inn in a long damn time," said Card. "You're welcome here any time. And bring that brother of yours back. I promised to teach him how to fish."

Jackie laughed through her tears and hugged the big man. "You take care of yourself, okay?"

"Oh, I don't have to," Card replied. "That's what I got Lu and Frankie for."

Jackie gave him another squeeze then turned to Lu. She was immediately captured in another hug, equally tight despite the woman's smaller size. "Thanks for everything, Lu."

"You better come back to visit. Don't be a stranger."

"I won't," Jackie promised, and she meant it. "Bonnie, Jim, and I have decided we're coming back for Christmas next year."

"We'll be here," said Lu. "Waiting for you."

With her usual dry humor, Frankie added, "With peppermint schnapps."

Jackie hugged her too, only a little surprised when Frankie hugged her back.

Jim and Jazz were already getting in the car, the luggage neatly stowed in the trunk. Jackie headed that way as well, delaying, stalling as much as she could. She looked around.

"I was hoping I could say goodbye to Sam."

"He had to go to his sister's, honey," Lu said. "He thought he'd be back by now."

Bonnie asked, "Jackie, do you want us to wait until he gets home?"

Jackie considered it, but the others were ready to go. "Lu, would you tell him something for me? Tell him I said he was high maintenance."

Lu laughed aloud in surprise. "He is that," she agreed. "I'll tell him." She and Card stood there on the front patio while Bonnie and Jackie got in the car, waving even as they drove away. Just before they drove out of sight, Jackie saw them turn around and walk back into the inn arm-in-arm.

◆ ♥ ◆

CHAPTER 29

Jackie had been dreaming she was at the inn. She stretched long under familiar covers and rubbed her bare feet together. Traffic thrummed outside, but otherwise the world was quiet. She snuggled deeper into the warmth of her bed and considered whether she had any good reason for not rolling over and going back to sleep.

She thought of one. She had to find out what she was going to do about school.

It was strange to be back in her little bedroom, in their little apartment. Jazz had already left for school, so she had the place to herself and a whole closet of her favorite comfy clothes to choose from. Ultimately, it was the thought of a hot cup of coffee that got her to throw back the covers.

Forty-five minutes later, showered, dressed, and with coffee in hand, Jackie sat down at the computer to begin her research. Or rather, she'd intended to begin her research. Instead, she opened her email. She had thank-you notes from Gita and Ada, but nothing from the one person she had hoped would write. Dead air. Jackie sighed heavily and told herself, "Long-distance relationships never work out, anyway."

Again, intending to start her research, Jackie browsed the Internet and was presented with the Gray Fox marketing video that Nick and Nat had made. She watched it, her heart aching with loss. She had loved it there. She loved the people there and missed them so much. When she hit 'replay' for the second time, the doorbell rang.

"Coming!" she shouted. When she peeked through the peephole, she expected to find one of Jazz's friends or a neighbor. Instead, a bouquet of faces waited there. Lu, Card, and Frankie, with Sam in the middle.

Jackie gasped and stepped back. *Sam.* She realized abruptly that she had no make-up on and that she hadn't even combed her hair after washing it. Quickly, she smoothed her hair and did her best to straighten her sweater.

Sam knocked again.

She unlocked and opened the door, putting on her best (not so good) imitation of casual ease. "Well, hello," she said. She wanted more than anything to throw herself into his arms. Her whole body buzzed.

"Hi," Sam replied. He met Jackie's gaze and for a second, time slowed to a crawl.

"Howdy!" said Card, giving a quick salute.

Lu grinned from ear to ear, and Frankie smirked knowingly.

Jackie tore her gaze from Sam and looked at each in turn. "What are you all doing here?"

"You left," Sam said.

Eyes wide, Jackie accused, "You left first."

Sam flattened his lips and nodded. "So I did. But I was coming back."

"We couldn't wait."

"I see," said Sam. "And I'm the one who's high maintenance?"

"Mm hm."

Sam held his hands out, palms up. "Well, I'm still your assistant. Until you fire me."

"Oh," Jackie laughed a little. "In that case, you're fired. You can stop following me."

Lu shoved Sam's shoulder. "Give them to her." Her eyes shone with excitement.

Sam took a step forward, pulling a bag from behind his back. "You forgot something at the inn."

"I did?"

"Yes. Something very important."

Jackie took the bag from him and opened it. Inside, she found the fuzzy Ho-Ho-Ho boots, the ones she had borrowed while staying there. She burst out laughing.

Sam said, "They missed you."

"They did, did they?" asked Jackie, still chuckling.

"Yes, they did. They belong to you now."

"I didn't want to assume."

She searched Sam's face for any sign he was talking about more than the boots.

Lu cleared her throat and poked Sam in the ribs. Sam cast a wide-eyed glance back at her.

"You know," Sam told Jackie. "You forgot something else, too."

"I did? What?"

Sam took another step forward and put a hand on Jackie's waist, gently guiding her to him. "You forgot to say goodbye."

Jackie leaned against him, her breath taken by his closeness. "I'd rather not," she replied, voice soft with emotion.

"Good." Sam slid his arms around her. "Because I don't want you to." His body heat radiated out from him, even through his winter coat.

Jackie thought about how well she fit with him.

Sam's face came close to hers. "Please don't leave me behind."

"I didn't want to assume," she breathed.

His mouth descended onto hers, and the kiss they shared said everything else that had been left unspoken. Jackie's heart swelled with happiness as she put her arms around his neck and clung to him.

When they finally broke the kiss, Jackie gazed into Sam's eyes—those beautiful brown eyes with the long, little-boy eyelashes. She knew then that she was home.

The entourage behind him started hugging each other.

A warm weight came to rest on her shoulder, and from somewhere magical, she heard the words, "Blessed be thy love."

A tall man with curly blond hair and a white suit walked away as Sam held Jackie even tighter and kissed her again.

"I'm starving," said Card. "Can we get lunch now?"

Lu said, "That Italian place we passed on the way here?"

"I could eat," agreed Frankie.

Card chuckled. "You can always eat."

"Yeah? And?"

Sam didn't break eye contact with Jackie as he said, "We'll meet you there. We've got some kissing to catch up on first."

The others walked away, laughing.

"Family," said Sam.

Jackie put her palm against his cheek and replied, "Family."

◆ ♥ ◆

Thanks for Reading
WW111523

That concludes *Christmas Cupid*. I have more Mission Cupid stories planned, so subscribe to my newsletter to hear when they become available. Sign up now.

If you enjoyed this story, *please* take a moment to give it a review wherever you purchased it. It's the kindest gift you can give the authors you love and who love you back (like me!).

READ MORE. A Wyrdwood novella, titled "Pipsqueak," is available as a free download at:

https://www.angelmccoy.com/wyrdwood-home/.

Know anyone you think would like this story?
Please let them know about it!
They'll be thankful you did, and so will I.

Angel Leigh McCoy

I BELIEVE IN MAGICK. Whether you believe or not is up to you. Wyrdwood is the town I wish I lived in, and its residents are the people I wish were my friends and enemies.

Life can be so dark, sad, and terrifying—for us all. Sometimes it's easy to forget the things that save us from that. I hope these books will remind you that—even in our darkest hours—there is hope, light, love, and laughter.

About me: I'm the spark of creative force behind the darkly fanciful Wyrdwood project and the epic Dire Multiverse.

I'm an award-winning video game writer who co-developed stories and characters for millions of players (CONTROL, *Guild Wars 2*, and White Wolf's *World of Darkness*).

After two decades in the big city (Seattle), I've settled down in a Gilmore-Girl-style small town not unlike Wyrdwood. Life is an adventure—every day.

Follow me on Facebook and Instagram: https://angelmccoy.com/linktree/

- Facebook: angel.mccoy
- Instagram: angelleighmccoy

Copyright

Christmas Cupid
Copyright © 2023, Angel Leigh McCoy
Cover copyright © 2023, Angel Leigh McCoy
Mission Cupid series title copyright © 2023, Angel Leigh McCoy
First digital publication: 2023
First print publication: 2023

Published in the United States by Wily Writers LLC, 2023.

EBook ISBN-13: 978-1-950427-24-6
ASIN: B0CFKDH5JP

Print ISBN-13: 978-1-950427-25-3
(mass market edition)

Library of Congress: 2023915247

Also by Angel Leigh McCoy

Paperback ◆ Ebook
From Wyrdwood, the Catsitter Mysteries series

Kitty Kats, Diana Kats, and Muse (cat) stumble across mystery after mystery in the whimsical town of Wyrdwood. Kitty is a sweet fifty-something catsitter, a job that takes her into the homes of strangers. Diana is her sassy daughter who inserts herself as an unofficial sidekick to the local private investigator. Muse—well... Muse is the king of cats in exile, and his bag of secrets is just beginning to open.

This supernatural mystery series is unlike any you've ever read. Wyrdwood is a setting that will flabbergast and enchant you. And the Kats family, though small, is a force to be reckoned with when they combine their efforts.

Join us for suspenseful stories of mystery and intrigue set in the magical town of Wyrdwood.

The Wyrdwood Welcome Trilogy

Paperback ◆ Kindle ◆ Audiobook

**Viviane is in love
with a man who remembers
nothing about himself.**

When his past catches up to him, it's stranger and more dangerous than anything Viviane could have imagined. She becomes entangled in a family feud that she's hardly prepared for. Ultimately, she must go to extreme measures to save both him and herself, and in the process, she learns more about herself—and her magickal powers—than she ever wanted to know.

Nothing in Viviane's world is as mundane as she thought it was. Especially not her fiancé. It's a long fall from the moon, and her reality will never be the same.

Contains mature themes.

Free gifts! The Wyrdwood Historical Society presents three free stories:
  "Nurse Magdaleine" — free download
  "Charlie Darwin" — free download
  "Pipsqueak" — free download

www.ingramcontent.com/pod-product-compliance
Lightning Source LLC
Chambersburg PA
CBHW010542170726
48285CB00008B/2721